Falling in Love
with
Death
S.E Dymek

ISBN: 979-8-9906015-1-2

Printed in the United States

First edition January 2025

Editor: B. Mauldin with Split in Two Editing

This book is a work of fiction.

First Printing, 2025

1

Warning: This book contains scenes of sexual content, violence, trauma, sexual assault, death, adult content, and foul language. Some scenes may be triggers for some and are not appropriate for all ages. Thank you for reading.

- S.E Dymek

Dedication

To Aaralyn, Ivy, and Caiden. My biggest inspirations for everything I do. To my husband, Aaron, who is my biggest support.

Acknowledgements

I'd like to thank my parents, close family, and all my inner, dearest friends who listened to me babble about ideas and were willing to read them. I love you all. Thank you to all my readers!

About the Author

S.E Dymek is an upcoming author who has published **The Alpha's War Series:** Including Between the Alpha's War, Breaking the Alpha Council, and The Beta's Betrayal **The Star Saga:** Including The Morning Star, The Evening Star, and The North Star available with Barnes and Noble, Amazon, Kindle, and other book selling sites. She is also published on several ebook platforms. She has a passion for writing romance including paranormal romance and fantasy. All of her works include twists and turns, keeping her readers on their toes. She is a mother of three and loving wife. When she is not writing she is working as a veterinary technician. Born and raised in Rhode Island, she has found her second home in Texas.

Follow her on social media:
Facebook: S.E Dymek
Instagram: sedymek
Tik Tok: @sedymek

Website: www.Sedymek.com

Name Pronunciation

Note: There are several old world gods, goddesses, and demons in this novel, feel free to give them nicknames (as a reader myself, this is what I do)

or if you would like below is a list of pronunciations..

Kere: K- EE- r- ess

Balor: Bay-Lor

Charon: Kare-ON

Eurynomos: Eu-ry-no-mos

Epiales: Ee-PYE-uh-lees

Acheron: Ak -uh-ruhn

Aeacus: Ee-uh-sus

Augusyon: Ow-goost-EE-nus

Hemera: eem-AIR-aa

Chapter One

*T*he tires screeching filled the air as the car desperately tried to catch traction against wet pavement. The small vehicle began to hydroplane across the black tar, spinning out of control. The car slammed into a telephone pole and crunched around it. It formed to the pole as if it was now part of the car. Glass shattered as she was flung forward into the windshield. Her mother's final scream was the last thing she heard before the world went dark.

The world around her turned gray and she was lost in an endless field. Long pampas grass swayed in the breeze as she walked through. She reached her hand out, running it over the grass as she did. Her body was drawn to a tall bare tree in the center of the field. Its branches stretched upwards like long fingers trying to catch the dark gray sky. The world around her flashed black and white as figures appeared. They were all the same. Each woman had their face hidden in long black gowns and each one was sobbing. Their cries echoing around her made her stop in her tracks.

"Take your place," one said as she stepped forward and reached her hand out.

She stared at the long, thin, fragile fingers. Even though something was telling her no, a bigger part of herself said to give in. That it would be easier. She slowly began to reach for her.

"No!" His voice shattered through their cries, silencing them.

They hissed and moved away frantically trying to escape the man. He stood between her and the crying woman with his head bowed. He towered over them. His face was hidden by a black hood. The hood dipped low and the shadow from it placed his face in darkness. His presence was intimidating and he radiated power. She wasn't afraid though. There was something about him. If anything, she wanted to be near him.

"Go. Go back the way you came," he told her, his voice was deep and warm.

Her voice caught in her throat. She couldn't find the words to speak. The overwhelming feeling of needing to be near him caused her to step into him. Her hand slowly reached out to touch him. He jumped away from her touch as if it could cause him harm.

"Ryan, go," he said through his teeth.

"No," she said firmly. Hurt ran through her as he moved away from her.

"I said go!" he bellowed as he lifted his head.

She caught a glimpse of his eyes. They were the deepest, darkest black she'd ever seen. So dark, she couldn't even see his pupils.

"Now." His eyes flickered a flash of yellow, like lightning, before he stepped to her.

He reached out his hand and touched her forehead with his index finger. As his finger touched her skin the world went black and she fell into darkness.

"Ryan. Ryan, stay with us." The voice pulled her from the void.

"Mom?" Ryan asked confusedly. The pain was starting to settle in.

She opened her deep brown eyes and looked up. There were people crowded around her. Her eyes landed on a pair of familiar ones. His blue eyes flashed relief as she came to.

"Hey, they're coming, just hold on," he said. His hands were on either side of her head as he stabilized her neck.

"Will?" Ryan whispered and then everything came flashing back as she tried to look at the car.

"Hey, hey look at me," Will said firmly. He didn't want her to see.

"Will, where's my mom?" Ryan demanded.

"She's okay… you're okay. Just hold still. I need you to stay still until the paramedics get here. You're going to be okay," Will said calmly but she saw it. No matter how hard he tried to hide it, his eyes gave him away. His eyes flickered for a second and she knew.

"Mom!" Ryan screamed. She needed to hear her mother's voice.

"Ryan," Will said. He looked at the red and blue flashing lights approaching.

Will moved his hand to flag down the paramedic running towards them. The moment he did, Ryan moved her head and saw the car. Her mother flopped over the steering wheel, blood dripping out of her mouth. Her eyes wide open staring directly at her, lifeless.

"Mom!!" she screamed.

"Ryan, don't look," Will said as he tried to cover her eyes.

"Ryan. Ryan. Hey, wake up." Will's voice came through her unconsciousness.

Ryan jolted up right in her bed. Her body was drenched in sweat. Her hands shook as she tried to catch her breath.

"Shit," Ryan mumbled as she tried to focus on breathing. She ran her hand over her face and glanced at Will.

"You were screaming," Will whispered. He knew what she was dreaming about. It was the same dream she had been having for the last year and a half.

"Sorry," Ryan mumbled, trying to see what time it was.

"It's ok. Are you ok?" Will asked quietly. He had been asking her, for over a year now, to talk to someone.

"Yeah, I'm fine. It's ok. You can go back to sleep." Ryan smiled at him as she went to get out of bed.

"You sure?" Will asked. He straightened up.

"Yeah, I'm going to go get a drink. I promise - I'm good." Ryan smiled weakly at him.

"You sure? If you change your mind, I am across the hall." Will reassured her.

"I know." She nodded, waiting for him to leave.

Will let out a small sigh before leaving her room. He frowned deeply as he crossed the hall and made his way back to bed. Ryan felt a rush of relief as he left. She hated that she bothered him. She wished she could

have nightmares more quietly. She shook her head before heading to the kitchen. She looked at the clock. It was only two a.m.. It was going to be a long night. There was no way she was going back to sleep - not after that. Her mother's last scream and her haunting eyes were forever burned into her brain. It was Ryan's fault they were even out in the first place. She had begged her mother to come look at apartments with her. If she would have gone alone, her mother would still be here.

Her hand began to shake once more as flashes of the night played through her head. She knocked the glass she was holding over and spilled water across the counter top. She let out a frustrated sigh. "Towel," her brain ordered her. She turned around quickly and grabbed the kitchen towel from the stove.

Something caught her eye in the corner of the kitchen. She swore someone was standing there watching her in the darkness. She squinted her eyes trying to make out if there was someone there or was she imagining it. She took the kitchen towel and threw it toward the figure. The towel went through it and hit the cabinet. All of a sudden, there was no one there anymore.

"Damn it, Ryan," she muttered to herself. The lack of sleep was taking a toll on her.

She looked back down the hall, debating on if she should even try to go back to sleep. She shook her head and began making her way to the front door. She grabbed her hoodie and pulled it over her head as she slipped her shoes on. A cold breeze rushed through the open hallway as she opened the door. The apartment

she settled on was above a charming bookstore. A bookstore that she now managed. She was thankful for that. It was a quiet place where she could work and not really bother with anyone. She had huge hopes and dreams like college and traveling, at one point but after the accident she was just stuck in a trance she couldn't get out of. At least the store gave her some type of peace. She shoved the key into the lock and unlocked it.

The smell of books filled her nostrils as she stepped inside and closed the door behind her. She immediately felt calmer. She walked by a row of books, running her fingers over the spines of them as she did. It was almost grounding being down here. Ryan made her way to the front desk. She debated if she wanted to do actual work or escape through reading.

"Ryan." Her name was whispered so softly she didn't even hear it.

She grabbed a book off the shelf and began making her way to the deep red couch. She hated her world she thought as she squeezed her fingers around the binding of the book. At least with reading she could get lost in another.

"Ryan." The voice was sharper this time.

Ryan jumped at the sound of her name. It sent shivers down her spine. She grabbed the book tightly and turned around.

"Hello?" she whispered, looking in the darkness of the empty aisles.

Her other hand reached for the lamp on the end table next to the couch. She clicked on it while waiting for a response. Her mind was trying to figure out if she

had really heard her name. Her body reacted like it was real. The door... She forgot to lock the door. Panic rushed through her as she began to sneak away from the couch. If she left the light on maybe whoever was there would be drawn to the couch and not her. She began moving quietly but quickly through the dark store.

"Lock the door," something whispered in her ear, causing her to jump. As she jumped, her fist swung in the air.

There was nothing there. She was now trying to get to the door as quickly as possible. Her eyes locked on the door as it came into view. She began to jog towards it. Her hand reaching out for the handle as she neared it. Her hand gripped around it as she went to pull the door open. Before she could open it, the door pushed toward her. She instinctively pushed it shut. Her eyes locked with a man. Panicking, she shoved her shoulder into the door and quickly locked the dead bolt.

"Hey, are you open?" The man smiled at her.

"No. Not open. It's two o'clock in the morning," Ryan said, still bracing the door shut even though she had locked it.

"It's cold out here. I was just looking for a place to warm up." The man smiled again, his blond hair falling out of his hood.

"Sorry. Closed," Ryan said. Her heart pounded in her chest.

"Come on, just two seconds," the man said as he inched closer to the door.

"I'm going to call the police," Ryan yelled at the door.

"Open the door, you bitch!" the man said as he began pounding on the door.

The glass on the door began to crack. Ryan stepped back. Her mind rattled with each blow of the man's fist.

"Block the door," the disembodied voice snapped at her.

Ryan didn't even question it. She locked eyes on a freestanding shelf and rushed to it. She shoved her shoulder into the bookshelf and pushed it in front of the door. The man yelled and began kicking the door. Ryan backed away and turned to the front desk. She rushed over and grabbed the cordless phone. She began moving to the back of the store.

"911, what's your address?" The operator came across the phone.

"1224 East Washington. It's The Lost in Time bookstore," Ryan spit out quickly as she rushed by the red couch and clicked off the light.

"What's going on?" the operator asked.

"There's a man at the front door trying to break in. He's pounding on the door, breaking the glass," Ryan whispered.

"Are you there alone? What's your name?" the operator asked.

"Yes, I'm alone. It's Ryan. I am the manager. I put a bookshelf in front of the door but I don't think it's going to hold." Ryan spoke in a hush tone.

A loud crash was heard and Ryan instantly knew the man had kicked through the door and knocked over the bookshelf.

"He's in the store," Ryan said. Her hand covered her mouth to hide her voice as she sunk further back into the darkness.

"Do you see him?" the operator asked quietly.

"No," Ryan whispered, now going silent. She couldn't risk talking and the man finding her.

"Come on, pretty little thing. I saw you walk in here from the road. Looking so lonely. You know you want attention," he called into the aisles as he walked.

"No one would be out this late that didn't want some." He snickered.

His voice floated back to her. By the sound of it she could tell he was walking just outside the first row of books. There was nothing in the store she could even use as a weapon. She was still holding the book in one hand. If anything, she was going to hit him in the face with.

"That's fine, darling. I love me some hide-n-seek." He laughed.

He was getting closer to her. She could hear his heavy footsteps on the wooden floor. His shoes came into sight as she squeezed closer to the ground.

"Ryan, are you still with me?" the operator spoke and broke the silence.

She heard the man click his tongue and then both his feet pointed in her direction. Her heart sank when the man let out a chilling giggle as he spotted her.

"Oh, come out, come out, wherever you are." He laughed again.

"I just want to talk to you," he said as he stepped toward her.

Ryan put the phone down, leaving the operator on the line and stood up. She took a deep breath, holding the book firmly in her hand.

"The police are on their way. You should go before they get here," Ryan said. She kept her voice steady even though she could feel her body shaking.

"Oh, don't worry sweetheart. I'll be long gone before they even get here." He grinned. His hood fell back.

He had dirty blond hair and pale green eyes. He grinned widely, showing off his chipped front teeth as he flipped a knife out from his pocket. The blade clicking into place echoed around her.

"Now, if you hold still and cooperate, I won't hurt you…much." He chuckled as he stepped toward her.

Ryan waited for him to come close enough to her and swung. The book smashed into his face. He stumbled backward, seeing stars. Ryan took off running. The only way out of the aisle was to push by him. She ran by him, throwing her shoulder into him, hoping to knock him over. The man stumbled to the side but instead of falling over, it spun him towards her. He fell forward. As he went down, he caught her ankle and pulled her back.

She hit the ground hard. Her ribs felt like they crunched as she began kicking, trying to get her ankle free from him. He grabbed hold of her with both hands and pulled hard. She clung to the hardwood floor trying to stop herself from being pulled back. Long scratch marks appeared on the hard wood as her fingernails dug into it.

"You fucking bitch." He growled and continued to drag her towards him as he got to his knees.

He grabbed hold of her pajama pants and tried to yank them down. She threw her hand back, making contact with his face. But as she did, he grabbed her forearm and jerked her back. Her arm bent backward as she let out a yell. A sharp, burning pain washed over her causing her to go still. He captured her shoulders. His fingers dug into them as he forced her to turn over. He climbed on top of her and pinned her to the ground with his knees. She felt the pressure of his knees pressing into her as panic set in. Ryan dug her fingernails into him, trying to get free. Blood began to ooze from the marks her fingernails left on his forearms. He let out a yell and grabbed her by her hair. She let go of his forearms and went to stop him from pulling her hair. Her scalp stung as he yanked on it. He pulled her head forward, hitting her in the face with his fist. Before she could process what just happened her head was whipped backwards and then brought forward. She felt another sharp pain as his fist impacted her face again. Her mind screamed for her to fight back. Her hands reached for him blindly, trying to strike him. She couldn't let this happen. She tried kicking her legs but nothing was working. The man was too strong.

Suddenly, there was silence. The weight of him straddling her was gone. A low painful groan broke the silence followed by a loud crash. A scream echoed through the bookstore. She didn't know what was happening but she began trying to crawl away. Her only thought was trying to make it to the exit. She dragged

17

herself down the endless book aisle trying to get to the front door. The bookshelves rocked as she tried to use the bottom shelf to make herself move faster. As she made her way to the end of the aisle she felt her body give out.

"Police!" A voice shouted into the dark bookstore.

Relief rushed through her as she tried to make noise so she could be found. She began banging her hand on the hardwood floor. She could see a light flashing; he was just out of reach. If he only looked at the first aisle he would see her.

"Someone there?" The policeman shouted.

"Here! Here!" Ryan yelled. Her head was spinning and her stomach felt nauseous.

"God," she heard him whisper as he found her.

"Dispatch, I need an ambulance," was the last thing she heard before the world went black.

Chapter Two

*H*is screams echoed through the field as he was grabbed by the throat and dragged through the long grass field. He was screaming and kicking but it didn't stop or phase the man who continued to pull him. The noise from his screams were irritating the man who held him, though.

"Shut up," the man dragging him grumbled.

"Who are you? Where are we?" the man from the bookstore asked.

"Shut up!" he growled as he continued to move him to the clearing.

"No. Who are you?!" the man screamed, still trying to fight.

"Death," he answered, giving in.

The sky opened up and they reached an endless river. It was so dark that the river looked black. There was a dock that led out to an old ferry waiting for them. Death was tall and cloaked in black. His face was hidden by the shadow cast from the hood of his cloak. He was strong and the man couldn't get away from Death's grip.

"What are we doing?" the man yelled as he pulled at Death's hand.

"You're dead. You're meeting the ferryman." Death mumbled as he picked the man up and threw him onto the dock.

"Dead. I can't be dead," the man yelled as he began scampering away from the tall dark figure.

"You are and you need to pay your toll," Death said, pointing to the boat.

A man on the boat shifted as he looked at the scene. He dropped the gray hood hiding his face and titled his head. His sandy blond hair shifted slightly as he moved his head. The man in the boat looked out onto the dock.

"That's not the right soul," he said as he frowned at the man.

"A soul is a soul, Charon," Death answered.

"You saved her again," Charon mumbled with frustration coming out in his voice.

"That's not the point. You need a soul from that moment, here it is. Dead is dead. What does it matter?" Death asked. He shoved the man forward.

"It matters, Silas!" Charon bellowed at him.

"I am Death! I chose who to take," Silas yelled back. He bowed up at Charon.

"How long do you think she will last? This death was supposed to be more violent than the car accident. The car accident was going to be quick and simple, no pain. This time she was going to be beaten to death. It will just get worse the more you interfere. How long do you think you can protect her? How long until…others take notice," Charon said frustratedly. He shook his head as he shifted in the ferry.

"Take him," Silas said as he kicked the man into the boat.

"It's been a year and half. They are still waiting for her," Charon grumbled. He nodded out into the tall grass.

The sounds of wailing cries began to echo about the river. The screams of sorrow were haunting as Silas turned to look at them.

"I am Death! I decided! To hell with them!" Silas yelled and lighting cracked behind him.

"My old friend you are playing with things that are not meant to be played with," Charon whispered as he leaned forward to the man on the boat.

"Payment" he muttered while holding out his hand.

"Payment? You just said it wasn't supposed to be me," the man said frantically.

"Death says it's you," Charon said. He reached forward and pulled a coin from the man's shirt pocket.

Charon chucked the coin into the chest on the floor of the ferry and took his oar. He pushed the boat from the dock and looked back once more to Silas.

She took a deep breath in as she struggled to sit up. Her head felt like it was being crushed. It was throbbing and her stomach twisted inside of her. She was clenching her jaw from the pain and her body rebelled against it as it felt shaky. It was too bright and she groaned as she turned in the bed slightly.

"Ryan. It's ok," a soft voice said to her and the light shifted.

"Where am I?" she asked, still struggling to open her eyes.

"You're at the hospital. You have a concussion and lots of bruising," the voice said to her. Ryan felt a warm touch on her arm.

"I am your nurse, Shelby. Do you have anyone we can call?" Shelby asked. She still rested her hand on Ryan's arm.

"Will," Ryan said quietly.

"Ryan!" His voice came sounding down the hall.

"Will?" Ryan asked. She was still struggling to open her eyes.

"Is he family? We've been keeping him out," Shelby stated, She frowned at the guard who let Will pass by again.

"Yes. He's all I have," Ryan said. She wanted to nod her head but it hurt to move.

The nurse went to tell the guard to let him through but Ryan caught her hand.

"Wait. Before he comes in…the man... Did he…um, did he" Ryan stopped because she couldn't bring herself to say the words.

"You were fully clothed when the officer got to you. You didn't have any injuries to your private regions upon assessment when you were brought in," Shelby said quietly.

"Ok," Ryan said quietly as relief came over her.

"You can let him come in," Shelby told the guard.

Will rushed into the room and was at Ryan's side in no time. He pulled her hand into his and squeezed it gently. His eyes scanned her face. He wanted to ask her if she was ok but they were in a hospital, so clearly she was not.

"Hey," Will said to her quietly.

"Hi." Ryan smiled weakly at him.

"When can I leave?" Ryan asked Shelby.

"Doctors want to keep you for a day. Concussions can be pretty serious," Shelby said as she watched Ryan frown.

"No. I want to go home," Ryan said and pinched Will's hand knowing he was going to object.

"You can leave against medical advice but we need to let you know the seriousness of leaving," Shelby began.

"Will's a paramedic. He can watch me," Ryan said dismissively.

"Ok then, we can't make you stay, although we strongly suggest you do," Shelby persisted, really trying to make Ryan listen. She looked to Will for help.

"No. I need to be home. Will…don't," Ryan said firmly. She closed her eyes quickly as a wave of pain rushed through her.

"Like I said, we can't force you. We will give you some paperwork to sign saying you're leaving against medical advice and also some aftercare instructions," Shelby said as she locked eyes with Will.

"Ry, don't you think- Ouch!" Will said. He tried to convince her but Ryan pinched him again.

"All right, I will go get that started. An officer wanted to come in and talk to you. If you're feeling up to it, I will let him in," Shelby said, pausing in the doorway.

"Yeah, that's ok. I have questions, too," Ryan said softly. Her head throbbed.

"Ry, are you sure?" Will asked quickly.

"Yeah, it's fine." Ryan said. Her eyes went to the doorway as a man, not in uniform, walked in.

"Morning," he said quietly. His voice was warm and deep.

His voice triggered something in Ryan's core. Her chest tightened and her heart sped up. Ryan turned her head to him quickly. His voice felt familiar. Did she know him? Ryan watched him walk over to her. She felt her stomach turn from nauseated to excited. Her body reacted like she knew him - like she needed him.

He straightened his broad shoulders as he walked to her. Ryan couldn't help but look him over. He was tall and with hair as dark as onyx. The light in the room hit silver streaks that were speckled throughout his hair that reminded her of stars against a night sky. He wore it brushed back, long on top and short on the sides. His eyes were like black pools that pulled you in. She got lost staring at him.

"I'm Detective Carter, Silas Carter," he said quietly as he reached the hospital bed.

"Ryan, Ryan Morgan," Ryan replied back, still in a trance looking at him.

"Noles, William Noles." Will interjected as he looked at Silas suspiciously.

"Why aren't you in uniform?" Will asked him. He looked at Ryan quickly and wondered what was wrong with her.

"Got called in," Silas said dismissively.

"Ms. Morgan, did you-"

"Ryan," Ryan interrupted him.

"Ok Ryan, did you know the man that attacked you?" Silas asked her.

"No, I don't think so. It was dark but from what I could tell, I have never seen him before," Ryan said as she thought back to the moment she was standing in front of the bookstore's door, staring her attacker in the face.

"Never seen him around anywhere?" Silas asked as he began to frown.

"No, not that I could tell. I'm sorry. Did he get away?" Ryan asked. The detective's questions concerned her.

"No. He's dead," Silas said. The tone of his voice was flat as he stated it like it meant nothing.

"Dead," Ryan said out loud.

"So, if he's dead, why all the questions?" Will asked. He was becoming more suspicious.

"Trying to make sure this was an isolated event. Plus I have to write a report," Silas said. It was technically the truth.

Everything had been quiet for so long he needed to do some research. Did fate finally decide that Ryan did not need to be here any longer? Was it trying to correct itself? He traded a soul for a soul. Fate should have not noticed. Had someone else noticed? He had done it again; trading a soul for a soul. This time, that soul needed to be dismissed from the world. He could feel everything that man had done in his life. The attack on Ryan wasn't his first. He needed to be gone. Silas did the world a favor by taking him.

"He's dead?" Ryan asked one more time.

"Yes, dead. He deserved it," Silas said dismissively, like it didn't matter.

"How?" Ryan asked. She looked from Will back to Silas.

"Bookshelf fell on him," Silas said. He tried not to smirk since he may have had something to do with the shelf falling.

"Bookshelf?" Ryan repeated. Her eyes searched his deep ones.

"Yeah, books are heavy," Silas said as his frown deepened.

"This will go a lot quicker if you could answer the questions. So, you have never seen him before. Have you pissed anyone off lately? Bad blood?" Silas asked. He was getting frustrated and time was running out.

"No. I'm pretty quiet. I work at the bookstore and I live above it. Pretty boring," Ryan said and a rush of nausea swept through her.

Ryan could feel her body go clammy. Cold sweat started beading across her forehead. "Oh no," her mind screamed. Ryan leaned forward as she thought she was going to vomit. Her head felt like her skull was cracking. There was so much pressure. Silas looked her over and grabbed a pink container off the nightstand. He handed it to Ryan as she leaned forward with a dry heave escaping her mouth.

"Go get a nurse," Silas ordered Will. He caught Ryan's hair as she bent forward to vomit into the bucket.

Silas held the bucket and braced her. Ryan vomited up bile and began to shake. He moved closer to her. His arm slipped around her to help hold her. The

wave began to pass and she leaned into him. She could feel her body relaxing. She felt cold and leaned into his warmth.

"You're going to be ok," Silas whispered as he let her lean against his chest.

She tried to focus on the sound of his voice. She blew air out of her mouth in an attempt to calm her stomach. She shut her eyes and she began to feel better.

"I am so sorry," Ryan whispered but she didn't move away.

There was something warm and familiar about him. He wrapped his around her tighter, letting her know she could stay there as long as she wanted.

"It's ok," Silas murmured quietly.

He was having trouble finding words as his body became more and more aware of how close she was to him. He had been envisioning what it would be like to actually touch her for the last year. The way her warm body felt against his chest. The way she fit perfectly in his arms. It was like she was made for him. She was his. She sent small tingles through his skin. He had never felt anything like it. There was something about her. He wasn't going to let anything happen to her.

Images of the night of the car accident flashed into his mind. She had been thrown from the vehicle and was laying on the cold concrete. Pieces of shattered glass around her. She was supposed to be dead on impact. As he stood over her body, ready to reap her soul, he got lost in her. He noticed how small her nose was, the way her eyebrow had the smallest scar though

it. The way her mouth was shaped in a perfect pout as if her lips were waiting to be kissed. The small speckles of freckles under the corners of her eyes.

"Ryan! Please don't take her! No!" The scream came from the car.

His eyes shot up and locked on the woman in the car. She was alive and trapped. She was struggling to get out.

"Please don't take my baby!" she screamed again.

She could see him? It took him back a second. He had taken thousands of souls. Souls he didn't want to. Little souls. Souls that didn't deserve death. Souls that welcomed him. But this…this was something different. He couldn't take her. He stepped over Ryan and walked to the car. He leaned in looking at the woman inside of it. He knew instantly that it was her mother.

"You see me?" Silas asked her.

"Yes. You're Death, aren't you? Please don't take her. She has her whole life. Don't. Don't do it," she begged.

"I need a soul," Silas thought out loud.

"Take me," she whispered.

He struggled with himself. He never bent the rules before. He always took the right soul - the one that was supposed to go. He looked at Ryan and walked back to her. He snapped his fingers and his hand began to glow.

"Please don't! Take me! Don't!" the woman screamed from the car.

"Come with me. Your soul to save hers," Silas said and held his hand out to her.

"Yes," the woman said and reached for his hand.

"Detective Carter." Ryan's voice broke him from the memory. She was looking up at him.

"Silas," he said as he chased the vision away.

"Silas, I'm feeling much better now," Ryan said, going to sit up.

"Ok," Silas said, as he reluctantly moved away from her.

Will came in with a nurse. He eyed Silas as he moved to Ryan. The nurse began to check her over.

"I'm ok, I just got nauseous," Ryan reassured both Will and the nurse.

"You need to make small movements. Don't overdo it," the nurse said sternly to her.

"Yes, ma'am." Ryan smiled weakly.

"All right, I'm going to get you something for nausea. Shelby will be in with your discharge information if you're still wanting to go," the nurse said in a reprimanding tone.

"Yes, please," Ryan said. She ignored Will's grunt of disapproval.

The nurse nodded and excused herself from the room. Will went to protest and Ryan held her hand up, not wanting to hear it. Will frowned and shook his head.

"Ryan, if you think of anything here's my card. My number's on the back. If you need anything, no matter the time, give me a call," Silas said as he handed her a business card.

"Detective Carter, is that your work phone?" Will said while watching the exchange. A twinge of jealousy ran through him.

"My cell," Silas said with a small smirk on his lips.

"Your cell-"

"Thank you, Silas. I'm sure everything will be ok though," Ryan cut Will off.

"Alright. Well I will be on my way." Silas smiled at her.

"Have a good day, Silas," Will said, narrowing his eyes at Silas.

"Detective Carter," Silas corrected Will as he went to leave.

"Well, he's a little bit of an ass," Will muttered as Silas walked out.

"You're just on edge." Ryan smirked a little.

"Let's get you home," Will said. He raised his lip and wrinkled his nose at her.

"I'm sorry to always be a pain in your ass. You really are my best friend. I'm really lucky to have you," Ryan said to him.

"Yeah, I know." Will said teasingly. He kissed the top of her head.

Ryan watched Silas leave. Her eyes on his back as he walked. Her gaze wandered over his shoulders. She wondered what it would be like to wrap her arms around him. She felt a feeling of loss as he disappeared from sight. She didn't want him to leave. She shut her eyes and told herself she was crazy and it must be the head injury.

"All right. You're all set. Take these two pills for your stomach and sign here saying you're leaving against medical advice and you're good to go," The nurse handed Will the discharge paperwork. Ryan signed the one paper the nurse needed back.

Ryan swallowed the pills and nodded to Will.

"Keep an eye on her and watch for the signs on that paper. Head injuries can be very serious. Oh and don't forget your flower," the nurse instructed them.

"Flower?" Ryan asked. She looked to the bedside table where a single white tulip laid.

Chapter Three

"So you're a detective now?" Charon snapped at him. He had been leaning up against the outside wall of the hospital waiting for Silas.

"What are you doing out of your boat?" Silas snarled at him.

"Well, why not? If you can pick and choose what you get to do, why can't I?" Charon shrugged.

"Because you ferry the souls to the afterlife. No ferry, no after life," Silas said as he stepped towards Charon with anger.

"Well, you bring the souls. Sooo…No Death, no souls, no afterlife. See how that works?" Charon snapped back, matching Silas's anger.

"Go back, Charon. You know not all souls go through me," Silas said while starting to walk away from him.

"No," Charon said firmly.

"No?" Silas stopped and turned to him. His eyes locked with Charon's.

"No. You know, like nope, don't think so, not going to?" Charon said with a grin across his face.

"Don't think you have that option," Silas threatened as his eyes flashed yellow.

"You don't scare me, Death…I'm not really living." Charon smirked.

Silas growled and crossed the distance between them. He grabbed Charon by the throat and snapped his fingers. The world faded out and in an instant they were

standing in the long grass. The sounds of cries surrounded him.

"Well, shit. I forgot you could do that," Charon said. He shoved Silas away from him.

"It's still bullshit," Charon said as he watched Silas walk away.

"What's so special about this one? Why her?" Charon yelled at his back.

Silas stopped and his head dropped a little bit. Charon could see his shoulders move slightly. Charon watched Silas struggle for words. He was surprised. He had never in all these years seen his friend act like this. Business was business and Silas was always about business.

"I don't know," Silas said quietly.

"Well, I hope 'I don't know' is a good enough answer for all this mess." Charon said, pointing out in the field.

"They should just move on," Silas groaned.

"It's getting worse. The crying is overwhelming" Charon groaned as he walked to Silas.

"You don't have some family to follow around crying after? Isn't that what they are supposed to do? Be gone!" Charon yelled while walking by Silas.

"You know, this all started a year and half ago. Do you think it's connected to your girl?" Charon wondered out loud.

"They aren't my concern and I doubt it," Silas grumbled.

"Another I don't know," Charon muttered under his breath.

"I don't know. They are banshees. They are meant to be able to pass between realms. They are not alive, they are not dead. Maybe they are vacationing? Maybe there's no families left from the line they're supposed to follow? Maybe they run on belief and no one believes… Like Santa," Silas rambled on with anger in his voice as he waved his hand at them.

He turned abruptly and began to follow Charon out of the field and towards the docks. They walked quietly down to his abandoned ferry rocking in the water.

"Santa." Charon laughed, replaying what Silas said in his head. He said the last part out loud and shook his head.

"Shut up," Silas grumbled.

As they got to the ferry a small gust of wind kicked up and Silas immediately rolled his eyes. He instantly knew. He let out a long sigh. Charon squinted. He was not sure what was going on.

"So you both abandon your post?" Her words rang out from behind them.

"It's not like the dead are going anywhere," Silas snapped back.

"You should be careful what you do, brother," she said, quietly coming out of the shadows.

"Else what Kere?" he snapped back.

"You never know who's watching." Kere smiled. Her dark hair fell over her shoulder as she stepped out onto the dock.

"I am not worried. Death fears no one," Silas answered cockily.

"You should. Just because you are Death does not mean you cannot be touched," Kere warned.

"Are you threatening me, dear sister?" Silas asked. He narrowed his eyes at her and stepped towards her.

"No…No. Just warning you is all. I have to look out for my only brother." Kere smiled.

"Worry about yourself," Silas said as his eyes flickered gold.

"It would be lonely without you." Kere chuckled before she batted her eyes at Silas. Then she was gone as quickly as she came.

"Can never tell with her," Charon said quietly.

"What?" Silas asked and his eyebrows furrowed.

"Like, was that a threat or a warning?" Charon asked with a shrug.

"It's both. She is chaos and that's what chaos does," Silas said softly. He looked out over the river of souls.

"We should go back to work." Silas nodded to the river.

"See you soon." Charon groaned as he got back into the boat.

She watched them walk across the field and out to the dock. She walked among the black veiled woman and hid within. She narrowed her eyes at Death as he walked out of the grass. He was a menace. She was unsure of

35

why, all of a sudden, he cared about anything else other than doing his job but it was messing with her plans.

"What's the next move?" His voice came from behind her.

"Balor. Well, your idea of a man breaking in and killing her didn't work. The car accident didn't work," she growled.

"House fire?" Balor grinned. His eyes glowed in excitement.

"We need to figure out why Death keeps avoiding this one. We need to have someone above us step in…Maybe get them to add another Death if this one won't cooperate," She thought out loud.

"Nyx, that might be hard. He's been the best Death since he took over the role," Balor said quietly before pausing to think.

"I've never heard of having two Deaths," Balor continued.

"Well, something needs to be done. That girl is living on borrowed time and I need her here. With her here and the power she will bring, I will be able to take over all this and more," Nyx grumbled.

"Getting another Death might interfere with all that or we could make Death sticks to the rules. Force him to reap her soul." Balor smiled as an idea popped into his head.

"Stop toying with me and say what you mean," Nyx snapped.

"You need her to die. He needs to take her soul. He won't. So… We force his hand," Balor said. He drug his

explanation out. He enjoyed how angry Nyx was becoming.

She pulled her hand back to strike him and he grinned. He caught her hand as he stepped up to her.

"She needs to have something happen where she can't come back to her body. Something that destroys it. No body, no vessel to keep her soul in. He would have to take her then," Balor whispered to her.

"Hmm," she whispered. Her eyes grew big with excitement as she placed her hand on his cheek.

"You're actually pretty brilliant when you use that empty skull of yours." Nyx grinned and her green eyes seemed to shimmer.

"Only for you," he said sarcastically.

The small space between them disappeared, as Nyx's eyes darkened. The look on her face confused Balor and he pulled away. She grabbed hold of him. Her lips met his in a quick and fierce kiss. As she wrapped her hand around the back of his neck she pressed into him. He broke the kiss abruptly and pulled back. He ignored the kiss like it never happened.

"We need him to be busy, that way he can't intervene," Balor continued as the wheels in his head started to turn.

"Hmm…a large number of deaths, souls to take would keep him busy." Nyx's red lips turned into a wide smile.

"Well, it sounds like I got some work cut out for me." Balor chuckled before phasing out of the In-Between.

"Mhmm. You should go," Nyx said. She waved him off.

"See you soon." Balor chuckled, his voice fading out as he did.

The wailing women turned to her as if searching for answers. Nyx groaned as she looked at them. They were frustrating her. She waved her hands at them to swat them away.

"Charon, that idiot did have one thing right. You are all overwhelming." Nyx growled and they began to shift away from her.

"You better prove to be worth it, once all is said and done," Nyx said as she stormed off through the long grass.

Will held on to her arm as she headed to the stairway leading up to their apartment. She paused for a moment to look at the yellow tape that had closed off the bookstore to everyone. She wanted to see it. Will tugged on her arm lightly as a way to tell her it was a bad idea.

"It's a mess. We will get it cleaned up once the investigation is over. Ed called asking about you, didn't even bring up the bookstore. He just wants you to be ok." Will led her to the stairs.

"That was nice of him to call…I am so tired," Ryan muttered as she began climbing the steps.

She wanted to say something to Will about bracing her the whole way up but she didn't have the energy. Will fumbled with the lock. He jiggled it a few times before it clicked over and the door opened. Ryan let out a small breath and then walked inside. Her eyes locked on the

couch. She was so excited to see it. She moved away from Will and walked over to their leather couch and melted into it.

"Sleeping on the couch?" Will asked. A little part of himself was relieved because he could keep an eye on her better out here.

"I'm just gonna rest my eyes," Ryan said as she curled into herself.

Will grabbed the throw blanket from the back of the couch and covered her up. She let out a small hum of contentment as she snuggled with the blanket. Her eyes immediately felt heavy. Will let out a small sigh and watched her fall asleep. Her words chiming in his head, "you're my best friend." He had been friendzoned forever now and could not seem to find a way out of it. After everything that happened a year and a half ago, he was afraid he had lost her forever. No one understood how someone could survive a crash like that.

He had moved her into his two bedroom apartment, picked up the broken pieces, and was still just a friend. He shook his head as he walked to the recliner across the way. He flicked on the TV and every so often looked over at her to make sure she was ok.

Chapter Four

  She was back in the tall grass again. The sun's golden rays trickled down over the tops of the grass, highlighting them as they swayed in the soft breeze. She wandered through the grass trying to find a way out of it. The farther she walked into the grass the farther everything else looked. Despite the breeze moving the grass there was no noise. It was strange to her. She could feel the crunch her feet were making as she stepped down on the tall grass, yet no sound came from it. Then the softest sound began. She couldn't make out what it was. It was so quiet she couldn't describe it but it was loud enough that her mind recognized there was a noise. She squinted to try and see what it could be.

  "Shh. Get down." The warm voice said with urgency as her hand was tugged downward.

  "Don't let them find you," he said as he crouched down with her.

  She looked at him in confusion. He was still holding her hand. His touch made her skin come alive beneath his fingertips. He was covered in black and a hood was hiding his face…but she knew him.

  "Who-" she started to ask but nothing came out. Her mouth just formed the word silently.

  He tilted his head up just enough that his lips were exposed. He put his finger to them, telling her to be quiet. The noise became increasingly louder and then turned into a howling scream. A cry that was so guttural that it made your stomach turn and your blood run cold. Something bad

caused that sound - something life altering. Something you can't come back from. She knew that sound. She felt it in her bones. She winced from the pain and went to stand up to see who was hurting. He grabbed her wrist firmly and pulled her down. She shook her hand. She needed to see them. She needed to know them. She wanted to help. Something in her was making her go towards the cry. It was summoning her. She yanked her hand back and looked at the hooded figure with anger as she went to stand up. The screaming was deafening now.

Her back hit the ground as she was pinned to it. He pressed her shoulders down into the ground, straddling her. She was angry. Rage flew through her as she began to wiggle beneath him. How dare he stop her. She needed to go to them. She tried to sit up and push him off of her. As she fought him his hood fell back and she was struck by his deep coal colored eyes.

She knew him. She stopped fighting. Her eyes wandered over his chiseled jaw and up to his slicked back black hair. There was pain on his face and as she looked at his hair she saw each silver streak. She couldn't help but wonder if each streak in his hair was something that happened. Something painful, something he couldn't live with. His eyes studied hers as if he was looking for answers he didn't have. His hand let go of her shoulder and moved to the side of her face. He touched her like he was surprised he could at all. She leaned into his touch. The warmth felt good on her cheek.

She was lost for a moment and then the buzzing started. The buzzing in her brain caused her to want to fight. It summoned her to their cries. Her eyebrows came

41

together in a frown as she started to fight him again. He
saw it coming and was ready for the struggle. He was
inches from her face. His eyes found her lips and before he
could stop himself he leaned forward and pressed his to
hers. His lips were soft and gentle against hers but her
heart still began racing in her chest. The world went
completely soundless and all she could hear now was the
steady breaths he took as he began to pull back.

She panicked slightly, not wanting his lips to leave
hers. Her stomach was doing somersaults inside of her.
She moved her head forward to push her lips back to his.
Lust, mixed with a little disbelief, flashed in his eyes. Then,
as if he couldn't take the restraint any more he let go of her
shoulder and his hand moved to the back of her neck. His
lips moved against hers and she let his lips part hers. His
tongue entered her mouth and rubbed against hers which
sent chills through her body. She moved her tongue back
against his as their tongues danced in their mouths. His
other hand moved from her shoulder down to her waist. He
grasped her hip as the kiss heated. She arched up into him
and one hand wrapped around the back of his neck as her
other one touched his cheek. Shivers rushed through her
as she touched his skin which made her crave him more
and more.

A high pitched scream pierced through the ecstasy
of the moment causing them both to wince. Then as if it
never happened, the world was back to being silent. The
soft hopeless cries faded in the background. He looked
down at her. He was breathing heavily as his hand caught
hers when she started to move it from his cheek. He
pressed her hand into his cheek as he leaned into her

touch and let out a small breath; like the breath he released was the only thing keeping him together. She watched him closely. He was savoring every detail of this moment.

"Silas?" she whispered, his name finally coming to her.

He smiled. It was the first time she had seen him smile and it made her melt. She wanted to make him smile over and over. He let her hand go and reached behind his back. He winked as he flopped the hood back over his head. He was still straddling her.

"You weren't supposed to see me, little dove," he said. His face was concealed as he went to stand up.

She reached out grabbing a hold of his thigh to keep him in place. She shook her head slightly as if to say don't go.

"You're about to wake up anyway," he said and by his tone she could tell there was a smile.

"Wake up?" she asked as she let him go.

"Mhmm." He stood putting his hand out to her.

"What...I'm dreaming?" she asked again. She was confused because everything felt so real.

"You know, they say dreaming is the place between life and death. It's an In-Between," Silas said quietly. The deepest parts of himself wanted to tell her everything. He wanted her to know him. He needed her to. He held his hand out to her to help her up.

"Inbetween?" Ryan asked. She started to look around.

"Stay away from the crying. Do not help them. Do not go to them. Stay away from them," Silas ordered. His tone became very harsh as he spoke.

"Who are they?" she asked. Everything was so strange.

"Banshees. Hopeless, lost souls looking for more souls to steal. Cursed. They are dangerous. Stay away," he ordered again as he turned her towards him.

She looked at him as she tried to process all the information he had just given her. Something told her to hold on to it even if this was just a dream. He grabbed her hand as he pressed his lips to her forehead and the world went black.

She opened her eyes as she breathed heavily. Pain coursed through her and she let out a small groan. She was trying to get her bearings when she realized she was home on the couch. She let out a small sigh as she tried to sit up. As she moved her hand she felt something in it. Looking down she saw a single white tulip. She smiled, twirling it.

"Again? Will?" she thought as she studied it. She looked around and Will was nowhere in sight. She adjusted herself before going to sit up more.

"Hey. Hey. Don't move too much." Will's voice came into the room before he walked in.

"I'm ok," Ryan said as she moved slightly.

"All the wincing says otherwise. Here, I made food," Will said as he moved the tray of food.

"Thank you." She smiled softly.

"Welcome." Will smiled and sat down on the couch across the room.

"You know I'm ok. You don't need to wait on me hand and foot," Ryan said, rolling her eyes at him.

"Remember that time when I got poison ivy? I swelled up so bad. Blisters everywhere," Will said as he reached for a biscuit.

"Oh yeah. It was so bad. I felt so bad for you." Ryan chuckled a little.

"You brought me lotion and special soap. When everything started swelling up, you forced me to get that shot at the doctor's. Even when I was whining like a baby about the needle, you held my hand," Will said before he took a bite out of the biscuit.

"You weren't that whiny." Ryan laughed.

"But that's the point. I had poison ivy not bruises and…you have worse. So shut up and let me take care of you." Will sighed.

"Fine," Ryan said as she pressed her lips together and placed the tulip down on the coffee table.

"Who got you the flower?" Will asked. He was a little confused.

"Hmm?" Ryan asked. She looked at him with the same confusion.

"The white tulip. Where'd it come from?" Wil asked again.

"You-" Ryan said but stopped immediately as the words came out of her mouth.

"No. I mean I would have, but I didn't have time," Will said as he watched her face.

Ryan looked down at the white tulip and image of the hooded man with his deep dark eyes flashed through her head. In her dream he squeezed her hand. She felt

something as he let go. Something soft and fragile. No…there was no way the tulip could be from a dream. She looked at Will. He didn't seem to even worry about it and continued eating. Something was wrong. Something was off. She stood up slowly. Will's eyes watched her carefully.

"Bathroom." Ryan smiled as she walked out of the living room. She didn't give him the opportunity to follow her.

She took a deep breath as she walked into the bathroom. She tried shaking the feeling off that something wasn't right but it wouldn't go away. She felt something in her back pocket. She reached inside of it and found his card.

"Silas," she thought, looking down at it. She instantly wanted to call him. She wanted to hear his voice. There was this strange pull to him and for some reason she felt like hearing his voice would make her feel better. She held her cell phone in her hand and looked down at the business card. Her finger hit the phone button and without thinking she began punching the numbers in. She barely knew him but her mind and heart were telling her she needed him. Her finger lingered over the call button. She squeezed her eyes shut as she closed it out. He was a police officer and she couldn't just call him. She had nothing to say to him. "Hello… Hi. No I don't need anything, I just wanted to hear your voice..because I am insane. He doesn't even know me…God I sound needy…That would be really great," she thought. She sighed and put the card and phone back in her pocket. She needed air, needed space.

There was a noise. She squinted as if it would help her hear it better. It was soft and high pitched. It was coming from in the bathroom. It began to sound louder. It was crying. Was someone crying in the shower? She reached out towards the shower curtain. Her hand shook as she tried to give herself the strength to pull it back. It definitely sounded like a woman sobbing.

"Ryan." Will's voice came from the bathroom door as he knocked on it.

Ryan jumped away from the shower. The sound of the crying stopped instantly as if Will's voice chased it away. Ryan rushed to the bathroom door and opened it. Her heart was pounding in her chest. Her whole body was telling her she needed to be afraid.

"You ok?" Will asked as the door opened.

"Yeah… Yeah. I just. Did you hear crying?" Ryan asked, her breathing a little hard.

"No. You had just been in there a while. I wanted to make sure you were ok… You're ok, right?" Will asked. He wanted to reach out and touch her.

"I need air. I need to do something. I can't stay in this apartment," Ryan blurted out.

"Ok, where do you wanna go?" Will asked her. He was trying to help her in any way possible.

"Let's go downstairs, start cleaning. I need to do something productive," Ryan said with a nod as if she had made up her mind.

Will began to argue but saw the look on her face and knew he couldn't. He let out a small sigh and then moved out of the way.

"I'm going to put clothes on." Ryan nodded and walked by him.

Will watched her walk away. Something had definitely scared her. He looked back into the bathroom. She said she heard crying. He walked into the room and shut his eyes, seeing if maybe he could hear something. The room was silent. He frowned as he opened his eyes and pulled out his phone. Could concussions cause hallucinations? He scrolled through his phone trying to find answers.

"Ready." Ryan's voice shouted and he knew she was already moving to the door.

He sighed again and shoved his phone back into his pocket saving that thought for later as he hurried after her.

Chapter Five

*T*he plane wobbled in the air. Balor grinned as she pushed his way past the stewardess. As he walked by her he watched her shiver. He had a presence with the ladies. He watched her suppress whatever desire his touch made her think about as he moved on. He, however, was thinking about how he was going to make his move. He scanned the plane. Who was going to be his first victim? His first thoughts were the pilot. Convince him he couldn't fly, the plane goes down, lots of dead bodies to distract Death. Lots of souls not able to move on, unfinished business and such. That was boring though. He wanted more than that. Chaos, internal struggle. His eyes stopped on a few passengers. The nervous flier, the person who clearly had a bad past, and then he saw him. He was trying to keep a low profile, squeezed back into his chair. He was twitching in his seat. Balor could smell him. He had a touch of something - a touch of darkness to him with just a sprinkle of unpredictability. This was his kind of person.

"Afternoon." Balor sat down next to him with a big grin on his face.

"That seat's empty," the man said as he fidgeted in his chair and pointed to another seat.

"Well it could be…could not be." Balor shrugged.

"What? I purposely chose a seat with no one next to me. This seat is supposed to be empty," the man said. He was getting defensive.

It was so easy. The littlest thing such as someone sitting next to him sent him already spiraling. Balor almost laughed out loud at how easy this was going to be.

"Yeah, well, you see the guy three seats up. He told me to sit here because you looked like you needed someone to sit next to you. He took my seat." Balor motioned to the man who was sitting far too straight and clearly hated flying.

"He took your seat?" the man asked, his eyes narrowing in on the man sitting too straight.

Balor could feel the rage running off of him. He watched his hands begin to tremble. He loved being this close to him. Balor enjoyed the emotional rollercoaster this man was sending him.

"John." Balor smiled.

"How do you know my name?" John asked as his head whipped to the side to look at Balor.

"He told me. He said he knows you," Balor said. He was feeding off this man's paranoia.

"He told you my name?" John said as his leg began to shake as his eyes locked on the man sitting too straight.

"He doesn't know you?" Balor asked, his face filled with fake concern.

"No. I have no clue who he is," John snapped.

"Hmm, funny. Well, sorry to bother you. I'm going to go to the bathroom. Can you hold my pen for me?" Balor asked and held out a very elegant looking pen.

"Uh?" John asked, looking at the pen.

"Take the pen," Balor ordered. His voice commanded to be listened to.

"Ok," John said as he wrapped his hand around the pen.

"They're all out to get you. They know what you did," Balor whispered just loud enough so John would hear but quiet enough for him to question if Balor had said anything.

"Excuse me?" John asked, looking at Balor's back.

Balor smiled to himself as he kept walking. He found the man sitting straight up in his seat and he leaned over to him as he walked by.

A stewardess crossed paths with him. He bumped into her. She was frazzled and already looking like her life was plummeting. He felt all of her deepest darkest secrets rush into him. It was like an automatic high for him and he had to stop himself from shivering.

"They're going to fire you, you know. Also the red head has a much better rack and ass then you. That's why the pilot's leaving you," Balor hissed.

"Excuse me?" The blonde stewardess asked. She was taken aback. Her eyes snapped to the red-headed stewardess who was always hanging too close to the pilot's quarters.

"She always laughed a little too loud at his jokes. You have been dating for over two years now and still no ring. She was the reason there's no ring," he whispered all her dark fears.

"Bathroom. I need to use the bathroom." Balor smiled.

"Oh, sorry," she said quietly but the seed was already planted.

Balor smirked as he walked towards the man sitting
way too straight. The seat next to him was empty as well.
He leaned over and made a small noise in his throat.

"The plane's going to crash. We're all going to die."
Balor smiled at him as he began making his way towards
the bathroom more.

The man's mouth hung open in confusion about
what happened but his heart was pounding in his chest. He
knew this plane was a bad idea and he didn't want to go.
He wanted to stay home. His job forced him to make the
trip. A job he didn't even like. His mind started spiraling as
his breathing became faster and faster.

John watched the interaction and knew right away
that the man was in on something. He had to stop him. He
moved to the aisle seat looking around. He squeezed the
pen in his hand tightly. Waiting. He needed to wait for the
right moment. He wasn't going back. He had made it this
far and he would die before he went back.

Balor could feel the chaos in the plane raising. He
needed just a little more. His eyes wandered over a
woman with pearls draped around her neck. She was
holding a book and a small bag of popcorn; and she
reeked of entitlement. Balor vibrated. Entitlement was one
of his favorites. He stopped by her chair and he watched
her look over him with disgust.

"You buy your ticket before getting on the plane?"
Balor asked her.

"Of course. What kind of question is that?" she
snapped, upset that he would even address her.

"You know that's how they are getting you. You're
spending hundreds more that way." Balor smirked.

"Explain," she said. Her interest was now piqued.

"Well they know all of us…better off folks will purchase ahead of time to get the better seats, better drinks etc. What they don't tell you is they pocket a large portion of that money. This seat only cost a fraction of what you paid," Balor said. He was talking nonsense but he knew exactly what to say to her.

"You're kidding me. This is inappropriate," the woman said as she sat up straight.

"I'm going to talk to someone," she announced.

"Don't talk to the stewardesses, they are in on it. The only one who is not is the pilot. You should demand to speak to the pilot," Balor said with a reassuring look on his face.

"Thank you. I will," she said. She stood up and started to place her small bag of popcorn down.

"Oh, I'll hold that for you." Balor smiled.

"Ok," she said. She was no longer paying attention to what he said but handed him her popcorn.

He laughed and sat down in the seat, popcorn in hand, ready for his show. He had done enough. The woman stormed up to the pilot's door and began pounding on it. The red-headed stewardess went to intervene but by that time the blonde had stormed up to confront her. The pilot, hearing the commotion between his two love interests, opened the cockpit. At that moment, the entitled woman began yelling at the pilot. The co-pilot stayed the course. He was unsure of what was going on. Balor laughed and tossed popcorn in his mouth. He watched the pilot trying to separate the girls, who had started fighting. The entitled woman was now on the floor, blocking the

cockpit door. Balor snapped as if he knew what was going to happen next.

John came running up the aisle screaming. He jammed the pen into the man who was terrified's neck. Blood shot out instantly. The man yelled as he tried to get the pen out of his neck.

"No, no please..don't pull it out." Balor laughed from the seat.

John snatched the pen from the man's neck and as he pulled back, a blade came out of the pen. John looked down at the blade and held it firmly in his hand.

"Get him!" the pilot yells but John had locked eyes with him.

He ran at the pilot, pushing through the women. They were trampled as he jumped on the pilot and stabbed him in the chest repeatedly. The copilot who could not let go of the yoke began yelling for help. A man from the back came running up. Balor knocked over the can of soda the woman had in her cup holder and it spilled into the aisle. The man fell on top of the ladies, who were all crying and holding different parts of their bodies. One of the blonde's fingers was broken. The red head was cradling her wrist and the entitled woman was soundless.

The copilot's screams became silent and the plane suddenly tipped downward. Balor stood up and tossed his popcorn in the air. He started clapping with a devilish smile on his face.

"And…end scene," he announced before snapping his fingers and disappearing.

He phased out into a large open field and just as his feet touched the ground the plane nosed dived into the ground. Fire erupted from the wreckage.

"Beautiful!" he exclaimed as he looked at the flames and the plane's scattered pieces.

"Something is missing," he mumbled in annoyance.

"I should have kept the popcorn! Really bummed about the popcorn," he groaned and kicked a small rock.

Chapter Six

Stepping past the yellow caution lines, Ryan ducked into the store. She sighed at the mess. The glass from the door was still shattered on the floor. It crunched under her sneakers as she stepped in. She felt her body become stiff as if she was expecting something horrible to happen. She shoved down the feeling as best she could and walked farther into the store. Besides the broken glass in the front of the store there was no real damage. She spotted the broom in the corner and went to grab it. Will's steps crunched as he followed her through. She tensed at the sound as she gripped the broom.

"Don't go to the back. I will clean that up," Will said firmly. It wasn't a suggestion.

She watched him quietly walk by. This very small part of her wanted to see it. She wanted to know what happened after she blacked out. How did the bookshelf crush him? The bookshelves were stable. They weren't meant to just fall. She wanted to go see. She began slowly walking down the dark book aisle. Images of her walking down the aisle backwards, her eyes fixated on the front door, wincing after each bang, the phone in her hand. Everything replayed in her head as if they were happening all over again. Her grip tightened on the broom as she reached the area. The bookshelf that had fallen was turned over on its side and pushed to the far side of the aisle. Books were strewn about, covered in blood. Someone had tried to clean up but left the books scattered about. A dark stain where blood seeped into the old hardwood floor

screamed at her from the ground. She looked down at her feet and realized she was standing in the spot he had pulled her to the ground. She traced the spot to the bookshelf and then the stain. How did he get over there? Her eyes wandered up the wall. The wall had cracks from where the chains holding the bookshelf were torn away. The bolt being ripped out left a gaping hole, the drywall crumbling left a small pile of white dust on the floor. Her eyes landed on the hardwood once more. She squatted down, her bruised and healing fingertips touched the scratch marks in the wood. She felt nauseated as she realized those marks were from her.

"Ryan, you shouldn't be back here." Will's voice came from around the corner.

"Did they say if anyone else was here?" Ryan stood as she asked the question. Her heart stuttered in her chest.

"No…Just you and the man who broke in. Ryan, what's wrong?" Will asked as he moved towards her.

"I..It..I don't know," Ryan said softly as Will unknowingly stepped on the man's death spot.

"The bookshelf crushed him?" Ryan asked quietly.

"Yeah," Will answered, trying to understand why she was asking. Her tone was quiet but her eyes were telling him there was something more lingering in the question.

"How? Bookshelves just don't fall over Will." Ryan asked, her eyes looking past him trying to figure out what happened.

"Ry, I don't know but we are lucky it did. Why don't you head up front? If you insist on doing something, get

the glass cleaned up. I will take care of back here." Will
spoke softly.

Ryan stepped towards the spot Will was standing.
Her body began to shake as she tried to process what
happened. There was something she was missing. Her
mind snapped back to being on the ground and the pain
rushing through her head. Her body was just trying to fight
to stay alive and prevent another blow. Then suddenly he
was thrown away from her. Someone pulled him off of her.
Her whole body was shaking now. She tried to hold on
tightly to the dust pan as her hand rattled the dustpan off
the broom handle and it crashed to the floor which caused
her to jump.

"Ry. Go up front," Will said. He walked to her and
grabbed her by the shoulders to stop her from shaking.

"Someone else was here," Ryan whispered.

"Ryan, it doesn't matter. If he got up and got away
from you and the bookshelf crashed into him or if someone
pulled him off of you. Either way he stopped hurting you
and he can't, ever again. You're alive and that's what
matters," Will reassured her.

"I guess," Ryan whispered as she shook Will's
hands off her shoulders.

"I'll go clean the glass," Ryan murmured. She
started to walk away but was having trouble taking her
eyes off the fallen bookshelf.

She took two steps backward and her eyes locked
with Will. She nodded as if she was saying she was ok and
turned to walk to the front of the store. Broom still in hand,
she focused on the broken glass and tried to push
thoughts of the fallen bookshelf out of her mind. As she

58

bent down to sweep the shards into the dustpan something crossed her vision. She looked over and a flash of black faded into the far left book aisle.

"Will?" Ryan called out, not really sure what she just saw.

"It's gonna take me a minute. I might need to call Ed to get this bookshelf off the ground," Will called back.

"Ok," Ryan said, shaking her head, trying to chase away the uneasy feeling.

She swept up the last bit of glass and walked over to the garbage can. She watched the pieces fall into the trash can. She felt lost. She felt like she couldn't process everything that had happened and nothing right now felt real. She felt a rush of coldness and the room darkened. Then she heard it. It was coming from the far left aisle where she saw the black flash. It was a soft, quiet cry as if it didn't want to be heard. She couldn't help but begin to move towards the aisle, staring into the darkness. She squinted as she leaned into the aisle. A scream erupted as the dark figure appeared. Her cries were shattering as she reached out to Ryan. Long thin fingers stretched outwards to Ryan, trying to reach her. Ryan stumbled back still trying to figure out what she was staring at. The long cloaked figure draped in darkness stepped out of the aisle and was walking slowly towards her. Her cries shook Ryan to her core. The woman needed her. She was supposed to go with her. Ryan stood in a trance as the woman walked slowly towards her.

"Stay away from the crying."

His voice broke through the crying and snapped Ryan from her trance. She stepped back just in time to

avoid the woman's reach. She backed away while her mind tried to avoid becoming trapped by the cries again.

"Run!" His voice came out of nowhere as if he was there with her.

Ryan looked at the broken door and bolted for it. The bell chimed as she raced out of it. The farther she got from the crying woman the better she felt. She felt this intense need to escape. Her eyes locked on the door as the woman seemed to keep moving towards her. Ryan reached the curb, her eyes still watching the woman. There was no way she was going to come out of the bookstore, Ryan thought as she stopped on the curb. The woman stepped through the broken door and Ryan's heart dropped. Her foot slipped off the curb and she backed into the street. Her eyes were still locked on the dark figure moving slowly towards her. The rest of the world didn't even seem to notice the eerie figure. With each step the crying woman took Ryan took two more further into the street. She couldn't break eye contact with her. Ryan's limbs felt like all the blood was leaving them and her heart began pounding in her chest.

A loud honking noise came out of nowhere from Ryan's right side. Lights beamed at her as she turned. Her stomach dropped as she saw the truck heading straight toward her. She braced herself as the sound from the brakes screeched filled her ears, the sound deafening. Her nose was flooded with the smell of the tires burning as they skid against the cement. But the truck wasn't stopping. She shut her eyes because it was the only thing she could do as she waited for the impact.

She was hit hard and pushed to the ground. She was expecting more pain. She felt a heavy weight on her. She opened her eyes and found a pair of dark ones looking down at her. His eyes searched hers. He needed to know she was ok. His breathing was rapid and she could feel him shaking slightly.

"Silas?" Ryan whispered. She was unsure of anything at this point.

"Why the hell were you in the road?" he growled with anger in his voice.

"Is she still there?" Ryan asked quickly. Her head jerked to the side as she looked across the road.

"Her?" Silas asked as he moved off of her.

"The…the woman in black," Ryan said. The world rocked a little bit as she sat up.

Silas's eyes narrowed as what she said set in. He stood and looked across the road but she was gone. They were not supposed to be sent after people. Why were they coming? Silas let out a small angry noise. His hands clenched into fists. He needed to find out why. Ryan went to stand up but her arm was caught by Silas. He helped her to her feet gently. His touch sent shivers through her and the way his eyes looked into her almost made her forget that she just almost died again.

"Thank you," Ryan said quietly.

"For?" Silas asked confusedly. His hand still not letting go as if holding on to her for a little longer made her safe.

"Saving me again." The word 'again' just fell out of her mouth. She wasn't sure why she said it.

Silas turned towards her with his other hand landing on her hip. Had she seen him? Did she know? He studied her.

"I…I don't know why I said again." Ryan smiled but her eyebrows drew together in a frown.

"Hey, is she all right?" The man from the truck had finally made it out of the truck and was staring at them.

"She's good," Silas called back though he didn't even turn to look at him.

"What the hell were you doing lady? You fucking crazy or something? Who stands in the road like that!?" the man began to yell after Silas had said she was ok.

Silas stiffened up. He turned slowly and dropped Ryan's hand. Ryan watched his whole body become tense as he stepped towards the man.

"What did you say?" Silas asked as his foot touched the pavement.

The energy that rolled off Silas was deadly. It was like the world had suddenly darkened and the air was being squeezed out of it.

"Nothing. Nothing. Look, I'm sorry. I'm glad she's ok," the man said as he fumbled backwards to his truck.

"You're sorry?" Silas bellowed. His chest vibrated as he took another step towards the man, his whole body wanting to rip him apart and take his soul.

"Hey. It's ok," Ryan said as she reached out and put her hand on Silas's arm.

He felt a rush of relief as soon her hand touched him. He looked at her in confusion. He had never felt anything like that. Once her skin touched his he felt something close to peace.

"Silas, it's ok." Ryan smiled as she squeezed his arm gently.

The guy took the opportunity and jumped into the truck. He locked himself in it. The sound of the traffic invaded Silas ears. He looked around and they were back to standing in the road. He took her by the hand and led her back to the curb. His eyes still studied hers. It had been so long since he felt anything and all she did was touch him.

"Stay away from the crying," he said to her.

"What?" Ryan whispered. Her hand dropped away from his and her heart began to speed up.

"I-" he wanted to explain but he felt the shiver pass through him. He sighed. He was being paged.

Another shiver passed through him and another. He braced himself as each one passed. Something big had happened.

"I can't explain now. I have to go. Stay by your friend. I will see you soon. Don't go near anything dangerous," Silas said quickly.

He watched her eyes fill with fear as he spoke. It killed him. He put his hand to her face. She didn't know why but she leaned into it. His hand cupped her cheek as he ran his thumb across it.

"I will make sure you are safe. Stay away from the crying," Silas reminded her.

"Silas," Ryan said as he stepped away from her. She didn't want him to go.

"I have to. I'm sorry," he said while stepping into oncoming traffic.

"Silas!" Ryan yelled as a car came inches from hitting him.

The car swerved, blocking her view of him. She winced, thinking the worst as the road cleared. He was gone. She looked around trying to see where he went but he was gone, nowhere to be found. She ran her hand over her forehead and took a breath.

"What the fuck is going on." Ryan muttered to herself. She became angry as she felt abandoned by him once more.

Chapter Seven

He hated leaving her. His gut twisted inside of him. It was like he was leaving a part of himself, the part he needed most. He phased into a field, an orange glow lighting up the sky. He narrowed his eyes at the structure and then it dawned on him. Plane. He sighed and began to make his way to the plane. As he got to the plane something felt wrong. These souls were not ready to be reaped. They were not meant to expire just yet. They were forced. The lines of fate were played with. Now he had souls to reap that were not ready. He then felt something, an energy. A dark chaotic creature was there.

"Balor," Silas said out loud before turning to him.

"Popcorn?" Balor said, holding out a bag he managed to find.

"You did this," Silas growled. His eyes narrowed as a subtle glow began coming from them.

"Did…that's a thin line. I just pointed out things that were right there." Balor shrugged, popping a handful of popcorn in his mouth.

"These souls were not meant to die yet," Silas said. Anger began to bubble in his stomach.

"So, I helped with the process. Not yet…soon to be…dying… the same thing. They're all dying," Balor said as he grabbed another handful of popcorn.

As he went to shove the popcorn into his mouth Silas's fist struck his jaw. The blow sent Balor flying backwards. Blood filled his mouth as he hit the ground.

"What the fuck." Balor laughed, spitting blood on the ground as he looked up at Silas.

"You don't decide. You don't play with fate," Silas growled. standing over him, his eyes flickering yellow.

"Don't play fate?" Balor chuckled as he rolled over to get up.

"You should remember that Silas," Balor said, spitting more blood out as he stood up.

"Meaning what, Balor?" Silas asked. His whole body was vibrating.

"Meaning that if you're so concerned with me intervening with fate, that should go for everyone." Balor grinned while looking at him.

"If you have something to say, Balor-" Silas started to say.

"I am saying just because you're Death doesn't mean the living part or dying part is up to you." Balor smirked.

"If not, then we can all play," Balor whispered.

Silas lunged for him and his fist hit smoke as Balor phased out. He could still hear his cackling laugh. What exactly did Balor know, if he knew anything? His talent was playing on what could be there. Insecurities that you didn't know you had manifested. He couldn't shake the feeling though that he meant something more. He sighed deeply and began making his way towards the plane.

"**R**yan, we don't need to do everything today. Ed wasn't even thinking about you coming back to work until next week at the earliest. How's your head?" Will asked. He was fretting over her.

"It's fine," Ryan muttered in annoyance.

"Ryan…I'm just worried," Will said quietly.

"I know and I get it. I just want…everything is a mess, nothing is right. I feel off and weird but it would be wrong if I didn't feel that way," Ryan blurted out.

"Ok, so what do you need?" Will asked as he came towards her.

"I need you to just be, Will. Just stop worrying over me and can we just…go? Let's go eat and you can complain about Jane or Harry from work. We can pretend that this didn't happen," Ryan said, catching his hand in hers and begging him to just let things go.

"Pizza? Pool?" Will smiled softly.

"Oh god, yes!" Ryan grinned as she squeezed his hand excitedly.

Will pulled her into his side looping his arm around her as they started walking to the door. He stopped in front of the door, dropping away from her.

"Let me call someone really quick about the door. See if we can get it replaced," Will said and pulled his cell phone out.

"Ok, I'll go wait outside." Ryan smiled. She pulled the broken door open and stepped out onto the curb.

She looked out into the road and tried to shake the feeling she had hours earlier. "Where did he come from?" Ryan thought as she looked at the cars passing by. She

couldn't help but want to see him. He felt safe. There was a lot going on lately and she was feeling like everything was spiraling and that she was losing something. Her place in this world seemed to be slipping a little bit more each day. She felt a chill run up her spine and she suddenly felt eyes on her. Someone was watching her. She looked around trying to see where she was getting this feeling from. Her eyes looked at the people across the street. There was no one. She scanned the people walking past her and no one was looking. Her eyes landed across the road on a dark alley. It was nestled in between the two buildings and she swore she felt something from it. She could feel it pulling her, begging her to come.

"Pizza?" Will asked as he stepped beside her. She jumped at the sound of his voice.

"Yes, pizza." Ryan laughed. She tried to get rid of the feeling of being watched.

"What's your plan now?" The sound came from a broken mirror leaned up against the wall in the alley way.

"Pool halls have lots of potential and Silas is busy with tons of bodies. So the possibilities are endless." Balor snickered. He knew Nyx would be watching.

He bent down so he could talk to her reflection. He tilted his head and watched her. He knew mirrors were portals and was a little impressed Nyx had found a loophole.

"Good. Get it done. Not like the car accident, the break-in or the almost hit by car. I want it done and I want it

done tonight," Nyx said. Her hand came through the mirror and grabbed Balor by the throat.

"What happened to your lip?" Nyx asked as she studied his face.

"Anger runs in the family." Balor smirked.

"Just go," Nyx said before she dropped him.

"Yes, my queen., " Balor said in a tone bordering sarcastic as he stood up.

Nyx narrowed her eyes on him and he bowed his head apologetically. He snapped his fingers and his wounds were instantly healed.

"Ta-da." Balor smirked.

"Well, go get it done, prince charming." Nyx rolled her eyes at him as her reflection faded.

Balor chuckled as he stepped out of the alleyway. His eyes locked on her from across the street and he began following her. He measured up her friend. Her friend was strong, fit, and in shape but he was not bright in the ways of the world. Balor watched him try to get close to her. He crossed the road still watching them. He stayed far enough back but he still saw everything. The way she kept putting him in the friend zone with her moves. He would go to put his hand on her waist and she would laugh and move away. Each small rejection hurt him just a tiny bit. Balor's body tingled with excitement. This might be his way in. This might be so much simpler than he could have imagined.

Balor watched them step into the small pizza pool hall and bar. The neon sign reading "Dave's" flickered off and on as he waited long enough to keep distance between them before he stepped in. The music was

deafening as he walked past the doorway. The sound of
pool balls bouncing off each other intertwined with the
music clanging in his brain. He wasn't prepared for all the
noises to hit him all at once. He paused as he tried to focus
and then he spotted them. They made their way to the
back pool table. Ryan had stopped at the bar ordering
something while Will set up the pool table. Balor walked
over to the bar slowly.

"Can I get a pepperoni pizza with half black olives,"
Ryan requested as she leaned on the bar top.

"Sure, anything to drink?" the bartender asked as
he wrote down the pizza order.

"Umm, give me a pitcher of the house beer with two
glasses," Ryan said as her eyes scanned what was on tap.

"All right. Name?" the bartender asked.

"Ryan. We will be at pool table 15." Ryan smiled.

"Got it." The bartender nodded as he went to grab
the pitcher of beer.

"House beer? Is it any good?" Balor asked, leaning
over to her.

"Hey, um, yeah. It's better than the rest of it." Ryan
laughed a little.

"So, what you're saying is the beer sucks." Balor
smirked.

"Shh, I didn't say that." Ryan laughed again as the
bartender came over with her two glasses and pitcher.

"But you didn't not say it either." Balor chuckled.

"True. I guess you will just have to gamble." Ryan
laughed.

"Get you something?" the bartender asked Balor.

"Bourbon, top shelf, on the rocks," Balor said quietly.

"Be right back." The bartender nodded.

"Rough night or are you a professional drinker?" Ryan laughed.

"I think it's turning into a good night." Balor smiled at her.

"Ry!" Will called from the table. He threw his hands up at her as if to say come on.

"Sorry. It was nice chatting with you." Ryan smiled and began to walk away.

"Boyfriend?" Balor asked her back.

"No. Best friend." Ryan said, turning back quickly before heading back to Will.

"I know." Balor chuckled to himself.

He turned back to the bar when he could still sense her standing there. He turned slightly back around.

"Hmm?" He smiled at her.

"Are you alone?" Ryan asked. Her voice was full of concern and care.

It made Balor want to throw up but it also made him excited. She was making this easy.

"Yup," Balor said as he held up his glass of bourbon.

"You…You should come join us," Ryan said. She was still lingering.

"I should?" Balor asked, kind of surprised.

"Mhmm. You don't want to be alone," Ryan said softly.

"I don't?" Balor asked. He made a face at her like she was crazy.

"Yup. People don't drink in public to be alone, if that was the case you could buy a bottle and sit at home…alone." Ryan winked.

"I could just like being waited on. Not having to clean up after myself." Balor smirked.

"Hush. Get up, grab your glass and come play some pool. Fifty bucks says I beat you in round one." Ryan smirked.

She didn't say another word and began walking to their pool table. She had this light about her. Balor frowned but stood up. He couldn't resist the bet. He loved gambling but there was also something about this girl. He found himself intrigued by her.

"Will this is…oops, super rude. What's your name?" Ryan laughed as she set the pitcher of beer down and filled up a glass.

"Balor." Balor smiled.

"This is Balor, he was lonely-" Ryan started to say.

"Not lonely," Balor cut in, holding up a finger to her.

"He was …by himself and I invited-" Ryan attempted again to talk.

"Twisted my arm." Balor smirked.

"Shut up. You came. So obviously you're lonely and wanted company. Now let's play some pool." Ryan announced and walked away to grab a pool stick.

Balor watched her, a little dumb founded. He didn't understand her. He knew her past. Heck, he caused some of it. He had watched her walk down into the bookstore and leaned over to the drunk man who hadn't noticed her and began talking about how beautiful and alone she was. How did this girl have such a bright personality?

"Will. And yes, all the time." Will laughed, holding his hand out for Balor to shake.

"Uh?" Balor asked, taking Will's hand and shaking back just a little too hard on purpose.

"Yes, she's like that all the time," Will said as he snatched his hand back.

"Hmm..." Balor said. He watched her pick the perfect stick.

He found the way she was looking at each one intriguing but also cute. He couldn't help but smile as she picked up a stick and felt the weight in her hands.

"Where are you from?" Will asked. He watched Balor watch Ryan.

"Everywhere and nowhere," Balor answered.

"Great answer," Will said sarcastically.

"Here," Ryan said. She came over and handed a pool stick to Balor.

He smirked and raised an eyebrow at her as she thrust the pool stick in his hand. She then reached into her pocket and pulled out a two twenties and a ten. She slapped the bills on the side of the table.

"You can break." She smirked.

Balor grinned as he raised his eyebrow at her. He stood taking a long sip of his bourbon before reaching in his pocket and pulling out a fifty dollar bill. He placed it on top of hers.

"Game on." He smirked as he walked to the head of the table.

Chapter Eight

"**W**hat the hell are you doing!" Her voice snapped at him through the mirror.

He blinked at the reflection of Nyx. He sighed. It took alot of bourbon to get him drunk but he was starting to feel it.

"Gaining the girl's trust," Balor said and then almost laughed because he could hear the slightest slur.

"You are not gaining shit! Are you taking her home with you to fuck her or are we killing her?" Nyx growled and the mirror shook on the wall.

"Trust the process," Balor said quietly.

"The process looks like you're getting shit faced and making friends with the girl who was supposed to be dead for over a year and half now. Make her dead! Or so help you!" Nyx screamed and the mirror bounced off the wall and crashed to the floor.

"Hey. You alright, man?" Will's voice came through the doorway as he walked into the men's room.

"Yeah. Bumped the wall," Balor said quietly.

"It's all right. We probably should all start slowing down anyway. Ryan hasn't had this much fun in a long time, it's hard to tell her to chill." Will laughed.

"She doesn't love you," Balor said quietly.

"Excuse me?" Will asked, taken aback.

"She uses you," Balor said. His eyes settled on Will as his body began to pull on all of Will's unspoken fears.

"You're the brother she never asked for. You will be toasting her to some loser at their wedding, hate and turmoil inside of you because you know that you would be better for her but she will never see you that way." Balor spoke and his words cut like knives.

"You don't know what you're talking about," Will snapped defensively.

"I don't? You live with her, took her in when she was at her worst. Cuddled her, nursed her back to health. Got the light back in her eyes but only to be…the friend. Oh wait, wait. Best friend. Even tonight, laughing and hanging on your arm. Eating the pizza you're going to pay for, drinking the beer you're going to pay for. Invited some handsome stranger over to play pool with you both. She did it to keep the barrier," Balor said quietly as he leaned back against the wall.

"You have no fucking clue about-" Will started to snap.

"I do. I know entirely too much. She doesn't want you. She would rather have some stranger. So instead of you making love to her, she's going to be screaming my name. While you're in your room…across the hall listening to it. Hating every second of it, hating that you ever let her move in. Telling yourself she just doesn't see what she's missing. She does and she doesn't want it," Balor whispered, hitting every nerve Will had.

Balor moved to the doorway and that's when he heard him. He had been waiting for it. He turned just enough so Will's fist would graze his face. Hit his lip just a little, enough to draw blood. Balor stumbled backwards and right into Ryan.

"Will! What the hell!" Ryan said as she caught Balor.

"Woah, mate. Sorry," Balor said while acting completely confused.

"Ryan, are you ok?" Balor asked with concern as he got back on his feet.

"Me? Are you? You're bleeding," Ryan said. Her eyes narrowed at Will.

"Hey mate, I was just joking around. I really don't think you play like a girl," Balor lied. He touched his lip with his hand.

"What?" Will asked confusedly.

"You know? Trash talking..." Balor said. He made a hissing noise as he pulled his fingers away with blood on them.

"Trash talking? That was not trash talking. You didn't say anything-" Will started to say defensively.

"Will, go home," Ryan said with anger in her voice.

"What? Ry, I-" Will started to say.

"Go home. You're drunk and had way too much to drink. Go home," Ryan expressed anger in her voice as she spoke.

"You're right, things are getting out of hand. Let's go. We should leave," Will agreed, nodding as he spoke.

"Not we - you. I'll be home in a little bit," Ryan said. She turned from Will and began to look at Balor's lip.

"I'm not leaving you here alone," Will snapped.

"I'm not alone. You need to go home before the bartender who's watching us calls the cops. I am fine. Go," Ryan said sternly.

"Ryan, I can't leave you here drunk and alone," Will said firmly again.

"I'm not alone," Ryan said quietly.

"That's right. I'll take care of her. I'll make sure she's ok and gets home alright," Balor said and when Ryan wasn't looking he winked at Will.

"You motherfucker!" Will said and lunged at Balor.

Ryan caught Will by the waist and tried to pull him back but not before Will landed two more punches. Balor took them and almost wanted to laugh. This was all working out perfectly.

"Hey! You, out! Or I'm calling the cops!" the bartender yelled, pointing at Will.

"Will, go," Ryan said. She fished some ice out of her glass and put it in a napkin to hold to Balor's lip.

"All right, fine. Fucking stay but don't be calling my ass later when you find yourself in some sort of trouble. I'm fucking done," Will said. The anger in his voice masked the hurt.

"Fine," Ryan snapped back.

"Fine!" Will yelled over his shoulder as he made his way past the bartender.

"Shit. I didn't mean to cause all that," Balor said as Ryan held ice to his lip.

"It's fine," Ryan muttered. Her hand went to the side of his face to hold him still.

"Ouch." Balor smirked as she pressed the ice to his lip.

"Baby," Ryan teased. Her lips curled into a similar smirk.

Balor studied her face. He noticed the small dots of freckles that were under her eyes, the trail leading up over her nose. Although her eyes were deep brown there were hints of gold in them. He placed his hand gently over her hand. He watched her try to hide the lust that flashed in her eyes. A small smile came to his lips.

"The ice is melting," Ryan said breathlessly as she caught Balor looking at her.

She could feel the blood rushing to her face and knew that her cheeks were slowly turning red. She could feel her ears burning as her stomach twisted. She didn't know if it was from excitement or if she was scared.

"It's fine," Balor whispered. His thumb rubbed against her hand.

He shifted his stance, coming closer to her. Ryan froze. She knew that look. His eyes darkened. They were filled with hunger as he moved towards her. She could feel her lip twitch as if it knew what was going to happen. Part of her wanted to give in, wanted him to push her up against the wall and kiss her, let his hand travel over her body. But a small voice inside her was screaming, "danger!"

"I should get more ice. Your lip is gonna continue to swell," Ryan said. She moved her hand away from his lip and tried to slide out of the small corner they had backed themselves into.

"It's fine," Balor said. He caught her hand as she tried to leave.

"Hmm?" Ryan said. She stopped and looked back at him.

"Ice isn't going to help...with the swelling." Balor laughed. Mischief flashed in his eyes as he pulled her back against him.

Ryan landed against his chest and his hand moved to her hip. As she looked up at him her eyes widened with shock but there was something more in them. Balor could feel it.

"I would love to shove you up against this wall," Balor said as he quickly pushed her into the wall. His body trapped her against it.

Ryan inhaled sharply. Her knees went weak as she tried to find her mind to tell her what she should do.

"Kiss and please every part of you with just my mouth," Balor whispered into her ear.

Ryan's breath caught in her throat but her head moved slightly to the side to allow him access to her neck if he wanted to.

"Take you right here with everyone watching. Wishing they were us," Balor murmured. His lips were so close to her ear she could feel them brushing against it as he spoke.

Ryan shut her eyes. her body tingled in anticipation. Images of his mouth running over her flashed in her head and she felt herself stop breathing.

"Hey, you ok?" Balor asked. He was still holding her hand and she was no longer up against the wall.

"Uh?" Ryan asked. It was the only word she could manage to get out.

"You kind of zoned out for a second. You said something about ice and got up." Balor smiled.

"Um..Ice. Yes. Sorry," Ryan said, going to move. Did she really just make all of that up?

"Do you want to get out of here?" Balor asked.

"Yeah. Air would be great right now," Ryan said breathlessly.

"Ok, let's go. You really want to?" Balor smiled.

"Yeah. I can't really go home right now anyway. Will clearly needs to cool off," Ryan said, shaking her head.

"All right. Let's go," Balor said. He was still holding her hand as he began walking to the exit.

"Where are we going?" Ryan laughed as she let him lead her through the bar.

"Everywhere and nowhere. Wherever you want to go." Balor smirked as he walked to the door.

She looked at him for a second, the way he said everywhere and nowhere was like he was making some promise to her. She laughed a little and grabbed the door handle. Balor shook his head. He took the door and held it open.

"Ladies first." Balor smiled.

"Why, thank you." Ryan giggled. She shook her head as she walked by him.

"Where are we? Who are you?" the man asked as he followed behind Silas.

"You're dead, I'm Death, this is the In-Between," Silas said almost robotically.

He had been answering these questions for what felt like hours now. Each soul he had to escort from the plane asked the same questions. It was painful.

"Dead!" The man panicked.

"As dead as can be. Plane crashed, you didn't make it. Now, your ferry awaits," Silas said with no emotion in his voice.

"I can't be dead," the man said. He reached forward and grabbed Silas.

"Well, you are. Sorry about your bad luck," Silas said as they got to the dock.

"One more after this," Silas said, spotting Charon.

"Fix it," the man said. He yanked on Silas's arm and turned Silas to face him.

"You're dead…you can't fix dead," Silas said. He was getting annoyed now.

"I have money. I could get you nice things. Cars…girls," the man said as he tried to bargain with him.

"What? Well, why didn't you say that? Come this way," Silas said while holding his arm out.

The man smiled and walked over to Silas. Silas put his arm around his shoulder.

"Silas," Charon warned. He was not sure what Silas was doing, he was becoming unpredictable lately.

"Charon, relax. Why wouldn't I want money, cars, and girls," Silas said with his voice overly cheerful.

"Yeah, leave the man alone, Charon." The man chuckled as he walked with Silas.

In one quick motion Silas slipped his arm around the man's neck and pulled his arm across his body leaning

him towards the water. Before the man could process what happened he was dangling inches above the river.

"Hey! Hey!" the man screamed while trying not to move.

"Shhh…listen," Silas whispered to gain the man's attention.

"Silas, you can't," Charon said as he tried to get off the ferry to stop him.

A soft moan came from the river. The water was dark but seemed to have a shimmer of blue to it. The moans were getting louder.

"Shh," Silas snapped. His eyes flickered yellow as he threatened Charon.

"What, what is it?" the man whispered to match Silas's pitch.

Then the man saw them. The cries were coming from the river. Translucent people were being swept under by the current. The river didn't just shimmer blue; it was the people trapped in it.

"They are lost souls. Do you want to be a lost soul?" Silas whispered as he dipped him inches closer to the river.

One of the souls stopped floating by and opened its empty mouth to the man letting a mournful cry escape.

"No, no, no. Pull me up, pull me up," the man begged and tried to find a way to hold on to Silas.

"This is what happens when you try to fix death. Now are you dead or do you want me to fix it?" Silas snapped.

"No. I'm dead. I'm dead," the man resigned as he clung to Silas.

Silas grabbed him and pulled him back up onto the dock. The man scampered away. His breathing was heavy as he looked bug-eyed at Silas.

"Now, get in the boat," Silas growled.

The man looked like he was about to second guess it and Silas narrowed his eyes at him. They flashed like lightning, flickering from his deep cole colored eyes to yellow. He cracked a smile and around part of his mouth the skin faded away and pieces of his jaw bone and teeth began to show. His face partially turned into a skeleton.

"Boat!" Silas yelled.

The man scampered to the boat and got into it. He moved to the very back corner of it, terrified.

"Silas," Charon said with a sigh.

"What? He is in the fucking boat. Now ferry his ass away," Silas said in annoyance.

"You should go do something to take the edge off," Charon said as he pushed the boat away from the dock.

"Yeah, let me get right on that." Silas rolled his eyes but he immediately thought of Ryan.

"See you later," Charon said while shaking his head.

"Yeah because death never stops," Silas muttered. He walked back down the dock.

"Did he kill me?" Silas could hear the man asking Charon questions. He smirked. Charon might end up knocking him over board before they even made it to the other side.

Chapter Nine

Balor listened to her talk about books and watched her eyes light up as they walked. She had started talking about the bookstore she worked at and how it was under construction but he knew what she really meant. A pang of guilt settled in his stomach. What was going on with him? He thrived off of chaos, destruction, and pain. This was all of those things and yet he was feeling bad. He shook his head to chase the nagging feeling away.

"You ok?" Ryan's voice brought him out of his internal struggle.

"Yeah…I think they must have the cheaper bourbon," Balor muttered as he moved his hand to his stomach.

"Are you ok?" Ryan asked. She looked from his stomach to his face.

He looked down the alley behind her. He knew what he was supposed to do next. He was supposed to lead her down the alley to her death. His stomach twisted and he felt acid rise up in the back of his throat.

"You know, no I don't think so," Balor said as he looked behind her.

"You gonna puke?" Ryan asked and put her hand on his shoulder.

"She's supposed to be dead. She's already dead, if it's not now, it's tomorrow. You can't escape death. She is needed for the bigger picture. This has nothing to do with

you," he thought to himself, trying to get his head back on straight.

"Actually, I think so. Why don't you go on ahead? I don't want to embarrass myself. I'll catch up." Balor nodded to the alley.

"Are you sure? Honestly, I won't judge you. I could hold your hair back for you? Rub your back?" Ryan smirked a little bit.

"Nah, I'm a shy puker." Balor said and grabbed his stomach as if he was about to get sick.

"Really?" Ryan asked as she gave him a look.

"Yes go…go hurry," Balor said. He was acting dramatic and grabbed his stomach more and put his hand over his mouth.

"Go until I can't see you," Balor said as he hunched over a little bit.

"Ok…Ok, geeze," Ryan said but she hustled down the alley.

Balor sighed and stepped back from the alley. Part of him didn't want to hear or see what he knew was going to happen.

---

*T*he alley was suddenly cold, and the further she got into it, the darker the alley got. She stopped. "This should be far enough," she thought. Ryan turned back to look for Balor. What was taking him so long? Ryan rubbed her arms as goose bumps spread over them.

"Hey gorgeous, what are you doing?" A man's voice spoke softly which caused her to jump.

"Oh, sorry. You caught me off guard. My friend.
He's up there. He's coming," Ryan said as alarms suddenly
went off in her head.

She tried to take a step back but she bumped into
something behind her. She froze.

"Friend? I'll be your friend." A voice came over her
shoulder as arms wrapped around her.

"Balor!" Ryan screamed as a hand covered her
mouth and pulled her back into the darkness of the alley.

The man's laughter covered up the small scream
that Ryan got out before he covered her mouth. He
dragged her as she kicked and flailed her arms. She dug
her feet into the ground, trying to stop him. Her hands
grabbed hold of his forearm and she dug her fingernails
into his skin. The first man came up and grabbed her legs.
They carried her back. She heard more noise behind her
as she tried to twist, turn and wiggle away from them.

"Boys! I got us some fun!" the man holding her legs
yelled.

Boys... Her heart sank. There were more of them.

"Last one," Silas groaned as he walked up to
Charon.

"Well that was a long day," Charon said as he
watched the woman get in the boat.

"I need to-"

Silas stomach wrenched forward. He had not felt
pain in so long, it made his knees buckle. He let out a
groan.

86

"Silas? Woah, what the hell?" Charon asked, coming to his side.

The feeling of fear overwhelmed him. He felt utterly terrified. Something was wrong. He didn't fear anything. He was fear himself. Then it clicked. It wasn't his feelings.

"Ryan," Silas whispered as if it was a secret.

"Ryan? The girl?" Charon asked as he helped Silas to his feet.

"She's in trouble. I've got to go," Silas said. A bit of panic slipped in his voice as he spoke.

"Wait. How do you know?" Charon asked. He reached out to grab Silas's arm.

"I don't know, I just do. Stop," Silas growled and ripped his arm away.

"Silas you need to-" Charon started to say but before he could finish his sentence Silas had phased out.

"Something bad is going to happen," Charon said quietly as he helped the last soul into the boat and pushed off from the dock.

Her screams echoed back down the alley. Balor clenched his fists, fighting with himself to the point he was shaking. He gritted his teeth as he took a step into the alley. He needed to stop them. He couldn't let this happen.

"Help, please!!" Her voice sent pain through him as he began moving quicker down the alley.

He clenched his jaw as he heard them. Just when he was about to reach them, he heard a sound. It stopped him in his tracks. He knew that sound. He had heard it

before. Then the blood curdling growl erupted from the alley. He didn't need to look to know, Death had arrived.

She was laying on her back, pressed into the cold cement. She was fighting with everything she had. She was kicking, scratching, and biting. There was a man holding her shoulders down while another man straddled her. One of his hands pressed over her mouth while the other was ripping her shirt apart. His hand slipped and she bit down with everything she had. He let out a yell as blood began to fill her mouth and she moved her head back and forth ripping at his flesh.

"You fucking bitch!" he yelled as his other hand balled into a fist and slammed into her head.

She didn't let go even though her head throbbed as he delivered another blow. This time the blow was harder and rattled her brain. She saw stars as she let go of him. He grabbed his hand, still yelling, as he stared down at her in rage.

"Hit her again." The man holding her shoulders laughed.

The man who was bit, cradled his hand but seeing her teeth marks and the blood he became angry all over again. He balled his fist up and pulled back to get as much power and strength as he could into the blow. A low growl that turned into screams erupted around her. The man's fist was caught. The man blinked and in the next second he was staring at his wrist snapped in half. Then he was yanked backwards. His body hit the brick wall of the alley before the man still holding Ryan down could even blink. He glanced over at his friend's mangled body in confusion. What had just happened? He looked around and the other

men began searching for the person. The man still pinning Ryan down was grabbed by his throat and pulled backwards. Before anyone could see what happened he slumped onto the ground his throat shredded as if claws had ripped through his throat.

"What the fuck!" one of the men yelled and began scrambling to the exit.

The alley seemed to darken. Ryan scooted herself up against the wall and tried to find something to protect herself with. A broken bottle laid on the ground next to her. It wasn't a gun or a knife, but it would do. She picked the neck of the bottle up in her hand and grasped it. The alley became so dark she couldn't see. She clung to the wall as she heard the terrified screams of the remaining men. After each scream there was a loud clunking noise. Ryan could only assume it was their bodies hitting the ground. There was something bigger and badder than the six men in this alley with them. She had felt the energy shift moments before the first man was killed. It was chilling and made all of her nerves stand on end. She took a deep breath and prepared herself for whatever was in the alley, thinking she would be next.

She felt hands on her upper arms and she swung the bottle. A small groan escaped the person but the hands stayed on her. Then, as if someone turned on a light, the alley brightened.

"Hey, it's ok. I got you." His voice, she knew the voice and suddenly the hands holding her were no longer a threat.

"Silas?" Ryan whispered looking into his deep dark eyes.

"Yeah, it's me. I'm here," he said calmly.

Ryan dropped the bottle and looped her arms around his neck. Her body shook as she squeezed him tight. Silas froze for a second; he had not expected that reaction. No one hugs Death. He felt a warmness in his chest and he wrapped his arms around her. The feeling of her safe in his arms made him feel an inner peace.

"Are you ok? Did they hurt?" Silas asked as he moved his head to see her better.

He looked down at her. Her shirt was torn in half, her breasts exposed. She had scratches across her chest and abdomen from struggling. Her cheek was swollen from the punch. He gritted his teeth. He pulled back to make space between them. Ryan's face looked confused as she watched him pull his shirt up over his head. He didn't ask but pulled it down over her. She slipped her arms into it.

"Thank you... The men?" Ryan asked as she looked behind him.

"Dead. Let's get out of here," Silas said. He stood up and offered his hand to her.

Ryan looked behind him again and saw that the men were laid out on the ground. They looked like they had been sent through a meat grinder. Their bodies were bruised, bloody, and broken. Ryan looked at Silas, confused. How did one man do all that in the matter of seconds?

"Don't question it. Let's just get out of here. You don't need to spend any more time here," Silas said quietly.

She hesitated for a second. She had so many things running through her mind but when she looked into his eyes all her doubt disappeared. For some reason she

couldn't explain, she trusted him. She grabbed his hand and he led her out of the alley.

Balor watched from a distance. Anger in the pit of his stomach with a tinge of jealousy at Silas showing up and being the hero. He watched them start to come towards him and he snapped his fingers, phasing out before they could reach him.

Silas stopped as Balor phased. He felt the shift and looked around quickly. He was waiting for the next problem. He pulled Ryan behind him as he looked around.

"What is it?" Ryan asked quietly. She looked around too.

"I'm not sure. Let's just get you home," Silas said; something was going on and he could feel it.

Ryan shook her head at the statement of taking her home. She didn't want to go home. Her thoughts of Will being angry with her. She didn't want to deal with that after everything tonight. She also didn't want a lecture and him hovering over her all the while saying she should have left with him.

"I don't want to go home," Ryan said quietly.

"Ok. Well…Where do you want to go? We can't stay in this alley all night," Silas said. He put his hands on the back of his neck, trying to figure everything out.

"I…um. Ok …I don't have anywhere to go " Ryan sighed, becoming frustrated.

"Ok…I got somewhere," Silas said as he moved towards the curb.

"Ok…Where?" Ryan asked. She followed him.

Silas raised his hand to wave down a bright yellow cab. He smirked a little and shook his head at her to tell her that he wasn't saying.

"I don't know if I can handle any more surprises tonight, " Ryan said. She was hesitant as the cab pulled up to the side of the curb.

"Trust me," Silas said quietly and he opened the car door.

Ryan studied him for a second and couldn't help but give in to him. She sighed before taking his hand and he helped lower her into the car. She sat down and buckled in as she watched Silas say something to the driver. She heard him say that they were closed but Silas handed him more money. Ryan raised an eyebrow at the exchange as Silas got in next to her.

"Can I ask what that was about?" Ryan asked, her eyebrows narrowed with uncertainty as she almost glared at him.

"Nope." Silas smiled and then winked at her. The cab started off at a slow roll and then pulled out into the street.

A small voice in Ryan's mind said there was no turning back now. For some reason, she believed it. Her body knew that something was about to change.

Chapter Ten

The yellow cab came to a slow roll outside a large stone building. Ryan looked out her window, trying to see through the rain drops that speckled across it. The rain had started seconds after they got into the cab. The streets were now darker than before. She kept glancing over at him the whole car ride. Her cheeks getting flushed each time. He was sitting there shirtless. She touched the dark shirt she was wearing. He didn't think twice when he saw hers ripped and put his over her head. It smelled like him. She tried to inhale without being noticed. The warm woodsy smell with a hint of spice invaded her nose. Her body ached and she just wanted to curl up into herself and sleep.

"I told you Boss, they're closed." The taxi driver glanced in the back seat.

"And I said it's fine," Silas said. He handed the driver a roll of money before getting out of the car.

"Whatever you say," the taxi driver said to himself. He shrugged as he looked at the wad of money.

"Hey, where are we?" Ryan asked the taxi driver as her car door opened.

"Old store, something with books, that's never opened," he said quietly, counting the large tip he just got.

With the door open, rain sprinkled down inside the cab. Silas held his hand out to her. Ryan slipped her hand into his and he pulled her up out of the car. She slipped on

the wet cement and fell into him. He slipped his arms around her and pulled her safely against him.

"Got you," he said as he looked down at her.

"Thanks," Ryan said softly. Her legs felt weak but she knew it wasn't the rain, or the slip, or even what happened back in the alley. Whenever he touched her she felt weak, but it was good.

"Where are we?" Ryan asked as Silas steadied her and moved away.

"Come on, let's get out of the rain," Silas answered. He was still holding her hand and led her to the old building.

They hurried up the stone stairs to the doorway where the rain could no longer reach them. The yellow cab slowly pulled away from the sidewalk. Its red tail lights glowed as it drove away. Silas fumbled around in his pocket before pulling out the key and putting it into the lock.

"Is this yours?" Ryan asked him, watching as he pushed the large wooden door open.

"Kinda," Silas said quietly. He stepped to the side to let Ryan go in first.

"So, because of how my luck has been…you're not some creepy stalker cop who is really a serial killer are you?" Ryan half joked but lately it was very possible that it could be true.

"No," Silas said with a small smile coming to his lips.

It was mostly true - he wasn't a cop, he didn't technically kill anyone, he just reaped their souls. The

thought of kidnapping her and keeping her safe had crossed his mind, though.

"Ok," Ryan said as she stepped into the doorway.

She paused between the door and Silas and her body grew excited instantly at how close she was to him. He looked down at her. He studied her face.

"You're not going to hurt me are you?" The words just fell out of her mouth. Ryan didn't mean for them to, but it was too late now.

His hand reached out and cupped her cheek. He watched a raindrop fall from her hair and splash on to her cheek. He used his thumb to lightly brush it away.

"No, I can't hurt you." As he spoke he felt something in his chest feel like it was breaking.

"Are you ok?" Ryan asked. Her hand immediately went to the center of his chest almost like she knew what he was feeling.

He put his other hand on top of hers and held it to his chest. He had never felt anything like this before. This dull ache that somehow was causing him pain. Pain that couldn't even exist. The minute her hand touched his chest the pain was gone. He looked at her, trying to see if she had somehow felt the strange feeling he had in his chest. She looked from his chest to his face waiting for him to answer her. He felt his stomach turn. She didn't feel the connection. How was this one sided? He cleared his throat, chasing the thoughts away.

"Let's get out of the rain. Wouldn't want you getting sick." Silas nodded for her to finish walking the rest of the way into the building.

"Ok," Ryan whispered as she brushed past him and stepped into the dark building.

A familiar scent hit her and it triggered warm happy memories. She shut her eyes while inhaling. The door closed behind her, shutting her in the darkness. She was worried that even though she was locked in some strange building, with a stranger in the dark she didn't feel afraid. She shut her eyes listening and letting her other senses take control. A quick flip and lights slowly began to flicker on. She opened her eyes and was immediately filled with joy. They were in a library. It was old and dusty. There were bookshelves stretching towards the ceiling lined with books. She turned in a circle, her eyes amazed as she looked around.

"What is this place?" Ryan asked excitedly.

"It's an old library I kind of own." Silas shrugged slightly.

"It's amazing," Ryan said as she walked further into the building.

The vaulted ceilings were etched with swirling designs. In the center of the room was a large fireplace with a cozy couch and books stacked on the end table next to it. Ryan wandered to the couch and looked through the reading pile. She picked each book up in her hands.

"You don't really look like the nerdy type." Ryan smiled at him.

"Books are the closest thing I can get to the human world." Silas shrugged.

"Human world?" Ryan asked. Her eyebrows furrowed at his statement.

"I…I, I work so much that sometimes it feels like I am not a part of the outside world at all. Books let me take part in things I will never be able to," Silas said quickly to cover up his mistake.

"I get it. I've always been a loner. Books let you go on adventures and be anything you want. They let you escape," Ryan said and started putting the stack down.

"Your reading pile?" Ryan asked him. She still held some in her hand.

"When I'm not working." Silas smirked a little.

"Some of it is kind of dark…might want to travel down the mental health section, if you have one here," she teased.

"Not the first time I've been told that." He chuckled.

"Can I wander?" Ryan asked with a big smile on her face as she looked around.

"Go ahead." Silas smiled with a nod.

She looked like a kid in a candy shop. He watched her wander down aisles, her hand running over the books like she was searching for something. He couldn't help but smile as her eyes lit up every time she saw a book that she liked. How she took it carefully off of the shelf, blew the dust off of it, and flipped through the pages. The aisles were not labeled and before long she found herself down an aisle that caused her to smirk. She glanced back at him with mischief in her eyes.

"Hmm…let's see." She smirked wider as her gaze ran over the books on the shelves.

"More yoga in your life? Center your chi?" She grinned and pulled the book slightly off of the shelf.

"I'm pretty balanced." Silas smirked. He realized they had wandered down the self help aisle.

"Ok, balanced." Ryan nodded. She glanced back at him again.

"You're not a narcissist, are you?" Ryan raised an eyebrow at him. Her finger stopped at another book.

"Would a narcissist tell you if they were?" Silas rolled his eyes at her.

"Hmm, good point. Are you an empath and need help to protect yourself?" Ryan asked as she moved on to the next book.

"No," Silas said. He had lost all feelings for most things, except her.

He watched her move on to the next book. His eyes couldn't help but notice her shapely legs. His gaze traced them up from her calves to a pair of thick voluptuous thighs. He leaned against the bookshelf taking a moment as his eyes traveled to her perfectly round ass. Images flashed in his head of what it would look like to have her bent over. Her ass up in the air as his hand traveled from her thighs to her ass. He wanted to squeeze her ass cheeks, feel her beneath his hands. She shifted slightly, going from one book to another. His eyes were captivated by her hips. He imagined gripping them between his hands. He stepped closer to her as she read titles of books, trying to find one to tease him with. Thoughts of pushing her up against the bookshelf and letting his hands wander over her body as he buried himself in her flashed in his mind.

"Do you lack self discipline?" she asked, turning around. He was inches from her and she found herself staring at his lips and her heart sped up in her chest.

"Only recently," he whispered. His own eyes locked on her soft pouty lips.

"In what category?" she whispered as if she was having trouble finding her voice.

"Is dark brown hair, honey brown eyes and..." As he said the word and he stepped into her. His hand went to the side of her face.

"Pouty lips a category?" Silas asked as his thumb brushed her lips.

"I'm afraid there's no self help book for that category," Ryan said. She fought back the tingles spreading through her as her lower lip moved against his thumb.

"I guess I'm fucked." Silas smirked and then leaned into her.

She met him half way and her lips collided with his. Her back pressed into the shelf as his mouth moved against hers, pulling on her lower lip making her mouth open slightly. His tongue slipped into her mouth causing her to tremble as his tongue brushed against hers. His hand moved from the side of her face to the back of her neck as he deepened the kiss. Her tongue brushed back against his as they matched energy. His other hand moved to her hip and pinned her between his pelvis and the bookshelf. Her hand moved to his hips and she curled her fingers around his flesh holding him closer to her. He broke the kiss. Her eyes fluttered open as he pulled back.

"Don't," she whispered as she caught her breath.

"Don't?" Silas asked confusedly.

"Don't stop," Ryan murmured and then pulled him back into her. Her hand ran down his bare chest.

He hesitated in front of her. His eyes flashed yellow and caught Ryan by surprise. She blinked and he knew she saw. He went to step back before it was too late. She caught him by his pants and locked her fingers around his pant line. He was shocked by the action and looked at her. Silas expected her to question what his eyes just did.

"I said don't stop," she said and pulled him towards her.

He caught her wrist that was holding on to his pants and pulled it up above her head. He pinned her by her wrist to the bookshelf and stepped to her. His mouth inches from hers.

"Are you sure?" he asked. His mouth was so close to hers that as he spoke they brushed against each other.

She nodded slowly and her nose brushed against his. Her lips instinctively puckered, waiting for the kiss. His mouth moved the side and he began kissing her neck. The impact of his lips against the delicate flesh of her neck made her knees weak. Silas holding her was the only thing keeping her up. Warmness spread through her as his mouth moved down to her collar bone. A small gasp escaped her lips and his mouth moved over her collar bone. He let go of her wrist and moved to grasp her shirt. Her hands found the shirt first and pulled it up over her head. She dropped it on the floor. He looked over her and the remains of her tattered shirt from the alley still hung to her underneath his shirt. He clenched his jaw as images of the men holding her down flashed in his mind and he felt

100

anger burning inside of him. He wanted to go back and kill them again.

"Your eyes," Ryan whispered and touched his cheek.

He went to back away once more. He expected her to scream or be frightened but her hand on his hip kept him in place. She looked at him and then shook her head and pulled him back into a kiss. She pressed her lips to his and he was slow to respond.

"I don't care right now," she whispered and pulled on his bottom lip with her lips.

Her mouth touching his made him ache. Everything about her called to him and he needed her. From the moment he laid eyes on her, he was connected to her. He needed her. Touching her now was more than his mind could even understand. He kissed her back fiercely, like he couldn't get enough of her. Breaking the kiss only for air. She moaned against his lips as he broke the kiss moving down her neck and along her collar bone. He leaned down as he reached her chest. He placed warm wet kisses down the center of her chest and over the tops of her breasts. Her skin responded to his touch with goosebumps and chills. She leaned back into the book shelf as she tilted her head back and closed her eyes. His hand cupped it, squeezing it firmly as he took her nipple into his mouth. The sensation of his warm mouth over her breast was so intense she arched into him, craving more. His hand fumbled over her shorts as he continued to suck on her breast. She reached down to help him with the button and they dropped to the floor.

He ran his tongue down the middle of her stomach, slowly getting to his knees as his tongue reached her center. Her dark black panties hid it from him. He ran his tongue over the silk fabric and he watched her shiver. His fingers slipped inside the thin strings of the panties and slid them down exposing her to him. He ran his tongue over her center and she arched her hips trying to help him reach her. He grabbed her by the hips and pulled her off the bookshelf. Still holding her hips, he laid down on the ground and guided her as he moved until she was kneeling over his face. She let out a small moan as she straddled his face. He moved his tongue against her, licking her bud. She quivered against him as he used his tongue to rub against it. She lifted her hips trying to move. His hands came up and pushed her hips down, holding her to his mouth. His warm wet tongue began to rub against her and she tilted her head back in pleasure as the feeling overwhelmed her. A loud moan escaped her as he pulled her bud into his mouth and sucked on it. He moved his mouth from her bud and ran it down over her slit. He then pushed his tongue inside of her. She let out a cry of pleasure as he thrust his tongue in and out of her. She grabbed onto the bookshelf to steady herself as her body quivered from pleasure.

His hand moved over her ass and lifted her slightly. She scooted back and moved to his pants. She undid his pants button. Ryan pulled his pants back and exposed his member before he had a second to catch his breath. She grasped him in her hand and lowered herself down on to him. A low groan escaped him as he entered her. She pressed down on him, letting him fill her completely.

"Fuck," he whispered as she began to rock against him.

She began riding him with her hand pressing down on his chest keeping him in place. Her breasts bounced as she moved. He let out another groan. Her body clenched around him each time she moved. He let her have her moment of control. He pushed into her as she came down on him. His hands grabbed her hips as he sat up. He wanted to fuck her now. He pulled her against him as he sat up her, grabbed her legs and locked them around his torso. Then he slowly stood. Her eyes grew a little wide at his strength. He pressed her up against the book shelf and thrust into her. A loud moan escaped her as he pulled out and pushed back into her. Books began to fall off the shelf as he moved over and over again. Ryan held on to him as she felt his member begin to throb inside of her. Her own body tightened around him in a spasm of ecstasy. He could feel his release coming. A warm feeling washed over her as all her muscles began to contract. She let out a moan and clung to him as a wave of intensity rushed over her. He felt her orgasm and it instantly made him release.

She relaxed in his arms with a sigh of contentment as she pressed her head into his shoulder.

"You ok?" he asked quietly as he realized he had lost all control.

"Mhmm." Ryan said quietly, going to release herself from him.

Silas grunted in response, not letting her untangle herself with him. He moved away from the wall, letting her cling to him as he walked over to the couch, his member still inside her. He laid her back onto the couch and slowly

moved off of her. She let out another sigh and curled into herself happily. She patted the couch telling him to cuddle with her. He smiled at the gesture and sat down on the couch. He grabbed the blanket hanging over the back of the couch and draped it over her. She curled into him. Her hand reached up and grabbed his as she nodded out.

Chapter Eleven

She woke up curled in the blanket he had placed on her. She was still very naked and shivered slightly. She pulled the soft plaid blanket up around herself before sitting up. He had lit a fire in the fireplace and the glow around her made her feel cozy. She saw a small bag on the table with a note on it. She reached over, the plastic crinkling, as she pulled the white piece of note paper from the bag. Her heart sank. She knew it was a "hey, I had to leave" note. She crinkled the paper in her hand. She didn't want to read it. How could she have been so stupid? He seemed so nice. She was stupid. Everything lately had been chaos. Why did she think this would be any different? She shook her head as she took a deep breath and pulled her knees up to her chest, letting out a sigh.

"Coffee or tea?" His voice came from behind her and she looked over her shoulder.

He was standing there with two mugs waiting for her response. She looked at him in confusion. Her hand squeezed the note.

"I, um...tea," she answered, still looking confused.

"Tea," he said and held out a white flowered mug to her.

"You ok?" he asked as he watched her take the mug.

"Did you change your mind?" Ryan said, holding up the note.

"My mind…did you read it?" Silas asked. He sat down on the couch and raised an eyebrow at her as he took a sip of coffee.

"Isn't it the same note every guy leaves? Great time, it was fun, I had to leave," Ryan said, still squeezing it in her hand.

"Hmm, sounds like you sleep with assholes. It says, "went to get coffee, clothes in the bag." Silas smirked.

"What?" Ryan asked. She was a little embarrassed as she undid the very crinkled note in her hand.

"Went to get coffee, found some clothes for you. They're in the bag. Silas"

She really didn't know how to react. She reached over and grabbed the bag. She found a dark navy blue t-shirt with pink roses that covered the back of it. A dark lacey bra with panties to match and light blue jean shorts.

"How did you know my sizes?" Ryan asked as she held up the shirt.

"I'm a good guesser." He smirked.

"Mmmhmm," Ryan said. She grabbed the bag of clothes and looked around.

"Down the first aisle to the right, tucked back in a corner," Silas said. The smirk still remained on his lips.

"Uh?" Ryan asked, looking at him.

"The bathroom," Silas said as he put the coffee mug down on his end table.

"So, are you a mind reader or something?" Ryan said, as she raised her eyebrows at him.

"Yup, that sounds totally possible." He grinned.

"Oh, ok. Tell me what I am going to do now then?" Ryan smirked and mischief flashed in her eyes.

"You're going to clutch that plaid blanket to your chest, walking kind of sideways to that last book aisle. Hoping the blanket covers your very nice ass and then duck down it hurrying to the bathroom." Silas grinned.

Ryan pressed her lips together. She didn't say anything as she stood up clutching the blanket to herself, just like he said.

"Mhmm. I told -" Silas started to say but his eyes locked with Ryan's.

Ryan dropped the blanket just as Silas was about to tell her I told you so. The words stopped in his mouth as his eyes ran over her body.

"Why do I need the bathroom when you've seen everything?" she asked. Her voice dropped to a low sexy purr as she dumped the clothing on the ground.

Her eyes locked with his as she turned slightly and bent over to pick up the dark lacey bra. She stood back up slowly, her eyes not leaving his as she held the bra up.

"What's wrong…you didn't see that…coming?" she asked with a teasing smile playing on her lips.

Silas was up off the couch before she could tease him more. His hand went to her hip and pulled her against him. His eyes darkened as his lips stopped inches away from hers.

"You're playing with fire, love. Don't want you to get burned," he whispered.

"I think I'm holding the matches," she whispered back. She looped her finger through his belt loop, pulling him closer as she said it.

Silas let out a small growl as his hand went to the back of her neck. He wanted her again, wanted to taste

her, to feel her move against him. He craved her like nothing he had ever wanted before. He had been empty for so long, feeling nothing. Now that he had her, could hear, see, and touch her. It was like a drug; he may never let her leave. His eyes flashed yellow as he went to claim her mouth.

"Your eyes," she murmured and pulled back slightly.

"I thought I made it up," she said. Her eyes studied him.

His heart sank. How was he going to explain this? He gritted his teeth trying to think of anything to say that would be rational.

"Would you believe it was a birth defect?" He half laughed as he started to move away from her.

"I've been seeing things," Ryan whispered. Her voice was suddenly filled with fear.

"Hearing things," she continued as her hand went to his face.

"Are you real?" she asked and her voice shook slightly.

"Did I make this up? I've hit my head so many times in the last forty eight hours. What if I am still in the hospital? Or I've finally lost it?" Ryan asked. Tears filled her eyes, one slipped out and rolled down her cheek.

"I am real," Silas said as he put his hand on top of hers.

"You are, you're not made up. You're not like the things I've been seeing?" Ryan said. Her voice was so soft and vulnerable.

"What things?" Silas asked. He was becoming concerned, was something else coming for her?

"God, you're going to think I'm crazy." Ryan laughed as she wiped the tears from her eyes.

"I won't. Tell me," Silas said. His hand was still holding on to hers.

"There are these women. They are all dressed in black. They cry and wail. It's like they keep trying to take me somewhere." Ryan laughed and shook her head as another tear slipped out.

"You need to stay away from them. Leave when you hear the crying," Silas said firmly.

His voice bounced around in her head. She had heard something like that before. His eyes… She looked at them, narrowing hers. He was in her dream. The field. He warned her then about the crying.

"I…I need to get dressed," Ryan said with a rush of emotions going through her.

Silas pulled back as he watched her hurry over to the pile of clothes and begin getting dressed. He was becoming nervous, he wasn't sure what just happened.

"They're banshees," Silas said. He was trying to explain more but didn't want to scare her.

"Oh ok. Banshees, like from Irish folklore." Ryan laughed as she wiggled the shorts up and grabbed the shirt.

"Yes, but instead of warning you when death is near, They've started trying to do Death's job," Silas said. Words fell out of his mouth as he stumbled to explain.

"Oh..ok.." Ryan laughed again as her head popped through the shirt.

"Ryan, I am being serious. You need to be careful. You need-" he said. He was trying to get her to see she was in danger.

"I need to go home," Ryan cut him off. This was all spiraling and Silas sounded crazier than the things she had been seeing.

"You need to stay here," Silas said possessively.

"Umm, ok," Ryan said. She backed away from him slowly.

"When will this library open?" Ryan asked, trying to think of a way out.

"It doesn't. It's mine," Silas said quietly as he watched her move.

"Ok, this is a bit much. I am going home and if you are a detective you understand that keeping me here is against the law," Ryan said as she folded her arms across her chest.

"I'm not a detective." Silas smirked. His eyes darkened and a light ring of yellow began to form around his iris.

"What are you?" Ryan asked when she saw the yellow again. She began to back away slowly.

Silas took a deep breath. He had wanted to tell her at some point. He wanted to tell her everything, but he also wanted to protect her. The way she was looking at him right now made his stomach twist in knots.

"Silas! Answer me!" Ryan yelled. She was getting upset.

"I...I... can't" Silas answered.

"Tell me or I am leaving and you won't ever see or hear from me again," Ryan threatened.

"Ryan..." Silas said as he walked towards her. The thought of locking down this place and keeping her here forever was starting to sound really good.

"Silas!" she yelled back. Her chest rose and fell faster as she got angrier.

"I'm Death," Silas blurted out.

"What?" Ryan whispered as she tried to grasp what he had just said.

"I..am…Death." Silas said slowly.

"Mhmm…like the grim reaper. Like the person who comes and takes you after you die?" Ryan said. Her words became rapidly spoken as she continued.

"Yes," Silas answered, almost wincing.

"Am I dead?" Ryan asked with her voice barely above a whisper.

He started to say "you're supposed to be," but right now wasn't the time. Silas inhaled, trying to think of something to say.

"If you are Death…am I dead?!" Ryan yelled at him.

"This must be hell, that's why all these horrible things keep happening " Ryan muttered under her breath.

"No, you're not dead but you are in danger." Silas said seriously.

"This is the craziest thing I have ever heard. Ok, thanks for saving me in the alley. Um, thanks for the tea and the clothing. I am heading home," Ryan said calmly as she began inching out of the room.

Silas followed her, fighting with himself to just grab her and lock her away. He followed her to the front door, his stomach twisting. He had messed this whole thing up. He reached out and grabbed her hand and she froze.

"I am not going to keep you here. You need to be safe. I am not going to be able to always get to you to save you. Stay away from crying. If you hear their cries you need to leave. You have my number, call me," Silas said. His voice was soft and calm.

Ryan paused to look at him. The seriousness in his voice and the soft tone pulled at her heart. He really thought he was Death and that something was after her.

"Ok. I'm going to get a cab and go home," Ryan said quietly.

"Please be safe," he said as he let her hand go.

Ryan nodded slowly and her heart sank. This was crazy but her heart ached for him. He pulled the door open and let her walk out of it. He felt like he couldn't breath as she walked out. He watched her walk to the curb and throw her hand up and in seconds a yellow cab was pulling up.

He shook his head at himself. He should have lied; he should have let her think she was crazy. Maybe she would have stayed. He needed to stay with her. This was the second attempt on her life in less than a week. Something was up and someone was behind it. Watching the cab pull away from the curb he got the familiar tingle that tugged on him. A soul was waiting for him. He shut his eyes and sighed.

Ryan got in the cab and pressed her back into the seat, clutching the empty bag the clothes Silas had given her. The world was spinning. Her feelings were all over the place. She must be losing her mind because she wanted to stay with him. She watched him as the cab pulled away. Her heart sank with the regret of her choice. Why did she feel like she needed him? She almost felt whole again

112

being with him. She put her hand to her head feeling even more crazy. The bag fell off to the side and as it did a white tulip spilled out onto the seat. Ryan looked down at it and her heart felt a connection to it. She picked it up in her hand. Her mind immediately said his name, "Silas."

Chapter Twelve

He was pacing the apartment. His hands locked behind his neck as he wore a path on the wooden floor. It was dawn and she still wasn't home. Ever since the bar he had this rage in his stomach, like something or someone had put it there. It was eating him alive. He felt like he was uncontrollable. He needed her but he was angry she chose a stranger over him. How dare she! Then she didn't even come home. He swung his arm as the rage became overwhelming. His arm connected with the white "best friends" coffee mug on the counter. It was flung off and crashed onto the floor. The pieces shattered around the floor. Seeing the broken pieces on the ground just made him angrier. He walked over to the shards of broken mug and stood over them. It was a mug Ryan had gotten him. He stared at the broken letters of friends as if they symbolized everything going on. He stepped up when her mother died, he took her in, he cared for when she was sick, and she wasn't even home yet! His hands went into fists as he looked at the broken pieces.

"Will?" Ryan's voice came from the doorway of the apartment.

He had not heard the door unlock or open. He looked up at her and instantly became furious. His eyes ran over her new clothing and his jaw clenched.

"Hey, it's ok. It was a cheap mug. I can buy you a new one." Ryan smiled as she walked by to get the broom.

He wasn't sure what came over him but he caught her by her arm as she passed him. Ryan stopped short with a look of shock on her face as Will squeezed her arm.

"You have new clothes on?" Will snapped.

"Yes…hey, you're hurting my arm." Ryan said. She tried to pull her arm away.

"Where were you?" Will asked. He didn't let go.

"Will, let go of me," Ryan demanded as she locked eyes with him.

"Where were you?!" Will snapped. He pulled her into him and kept his hands on her.

"Will, if you don't let go of me right now..." Ryan threatened him.

"What, Ryan? What are you going to do? Leave? Where will you go? You have no family, no loved ones…no one cared about little old Ryan when her world fell apart. No one but me. Me, Ryan. I picked you up, got you back to somewhat normal but let's face it. You've never been normal. Then you pull shit like this? What the fuck are you thinking?" Will cut her off.

"Will, what the fuck is wrong with you? Are you still drunk? Fucking let go of me!" Ryan said and this time actually looked at him.

His eyes were foggy and glossed over. He was looking at her but it was like he wasn't there. She was now concerned that something was wrong with him.

"Will, are you ok?" she asked. As she looked at his face she reached her free hand toward his forehead.

He pulled back as her hand touched his forehead. She could feel how clammy he was. He looked past her

like she wasn't there any more. He would never touch her, never mind be mean like this.

"Why don't you love me?" Will asked, as he fought against the violent tremors of anger flooding his body.

"Will, I do," Ryan said. She tried to get him to look at her.

"You don't. You would have came home last night. You wouldn't have stayed with him. You come home in different clothing. You don't love me," Will said quietly.

"Will, that has nothing to do with me loving you or not. I love you, you were there through everything. Will, you are my best friend. I don't know how I would have made it without you," Ryan said. She touched his shoulder, desperately trying to get him to come back.

"Friend..." Will laughed. The laugh rolled out of his chest and slowly turned to a deep guttural noise.

"Friend!" He growled and his eyes narrowed.

"Best friend! I don't want to be your fucking friend," he snarled as he pulled her across the room.

"Will!" Ryan yelled. She struggled in his arms.

Will lifted her up off the ground. His arms wrapped around her as he made his room to his bedroom. Ryan's heart sank.

"Will! What are you doing!? Put me down! Will!" Ryan screamed and began kicking. She dug her fingernails into his forearms.

He let out a small growl as her nails dug into his flesh and caused him to bleed. He carried her to the bed. Ryan's mind screamed No! This can not be happening as the bed came into view. She kicked harder. Her legs were hitting him in the thighs. She scratched him more. He

116

groaned and almost stumbled. She leaned forward trying to get him to drop her but he squeezed tighter. She launched herself backwards. Her head hit his face as hard as she could. She heard a loud pop and he let out a groan but he didn't let go. He threw her down on the bed. She tried to crawl away but his hand captured her ankle and yanked her back.

"Will! Stop, please! Will!" Ryan screamed as she dug her hands into the bedding trying to stop from being pulled back.

He didn't say anything. The bedding slipped through her fingers as she was dragged backwards. He climbed onto the bed as he pulled her between his legs. His hands grabbed her hips and flipped her over to face him. His eyes were completely white now. Blood poured down his face from his nose and he acted like he couldn't feel it.

"You should have loved me," Will said robotically as he looked down at her.

"Will, stop. There's something wrong with you. Stop. You would never do this," Ryan pleaded, trying to get through to him one last time.

"You should have fucking loved me!!" he screamed and his hands wrapped around her throat.

Ryan's hands went to his as she tried to stop him from squeezing. He began to squeeze tighter. Her airway started to restrict. She dug her fingernails into his hand hard enough to draw blood as she tucked her chin trying to cut off his access to her throat.

"Why didn't you love me?!" Will yelled as pain, and rage flooded his system. It made his blood boil and his hand shook as he held on to Ryan.

Ryan tried to kick him in the groin. Her knee connected but he didn't react. It was like he wasn't feeling anything. She struggled as hard as she could with her air being cut off. Her sight was blocked by the tears filling them.

"That's enough of that." Ryan heard a voice from behind Will. She heard a sizzling noise and Will let go. He looked down in horror as his eyes cleared.

"Ryan?" he whispered as he realized he was straddling her.

Ryan lifted her knee connecting with his groin again. He let out a yell as the pain went through him. He fell backwards off the bed. Ryan began coughing as she rolled sideways trying to get far away from Will.

"I got you, darling," she heard the same voice coming from the side of the bed she was rolling to.

She felt hands on her as they helped her off the bed. She looked up to see who was there. His tousled red hair came into view and his warm brown eyes looked at her neck.

"Balor?" Ryan whispered. Her voice was hoarse.

"Just in time, it seems. Let me see," Balor said, going to touch her neck.

"I'm ok," Ryan said as she stepped back and looked around to see where Will was.

Will stood up. Hurt ran across his face as he saw his hand marks on Ryan's throat and his finger prints on her forearm.

"Ryan..I..I don't know. I -" Will started to say.

"You need fucking help. What the fuck is wrong with you? You..I.." Ryan said. She was trying to process what just happened.

"Ryan, I swear I would never hurt you. I don't even understand what just happened. I was in this trance and all I could see was hate," Will tried to plead his case. He reached out to her.

"Stay the fuck away from me," Ryan snapped and pushed by Balor.

Ryan rushed out of the room and to hers. She grabbed a backpack and began shoving clothing and anything she could think of that she would need in it. She could hear Will coming across the living room to follow her to her room.

"I wouldn't try it, lad." Balor's voice came from her doorway. He blocked Will from entering her room.

"I just need to explain," Will begged.

"Not now. I think you should go to your room and wait until she's gone," Balor said. His voice sounded deadly.

"I-" Will started to protest.

"Will, go. I don't want to see you, hear you or talk to you right now." Ryan yelled as she zipped her bag.

"Ryan-" Will started to say.

"Go!" Ryan screamed. Her voice cracked from the pain in her throat and the pain in her heart.

Will reluctantly retreated to the other side of the living room, still watching her door. He couldn't process what happened. He was there and he saw what he was

doing but it was like he wasn't in control. Like he was watching some weird movie.

Ryan finished packing and then tapped Balor on the shoulder to tell him to move. He moved out of her way and walked with her to the front door, almost blocking her from Will's view.

"Ryan, please., Will begged from the other side of the living room as Ryan got to the door.

Ryan paused at the door as she noticed how the wood was broken on the door frame. She opened the door and didn't look back to Will as she left. Balor followed behind her.

Will's heart sank as he watched her leave. He looked down at his hands. He did not understand how he could have possibly done all that. His nose hurt badly but he didn't mind. He felt like he deserved it and welcomed the pain. He reached up and touched the back of his neck. The small burn stung as his fingers brushed it. The burn was the only thing he had felt when he was in the trance. It was that pain that snapped him out of it. He had never experienced anything like that before. Something was wrong.

Chapter Thirteen

She rushed down the hall and to the door leading outside. She needed to get out. She needed air. She needed to stop her brain from rattling around. It had been one thing after another. Balor was still following her as she hit the door for the outside and rushed to the guard rail and took in a deep breath. He gritted his teeth. He was supposed to let her die. It was going to be a murder-suicide. He had set it all up. Planted the seed in Will's mind. It was supposed to be his clean up from the alley, but he couldn't do it. Before he knew what he was doing he had kicked the door open and was in the bedroom standing by watching Will choke the life out of Ryan. Something in him had awakened and he was starting to feel things he had never felt before. He pushed his cigarette into the back of Will's neck. Fire was the only thing to bring people out of a demon trance. He watched her take another deep breath and then start down the stairs. He followed closely behind her. As she reached the patio at the bottom she turned and looked at him.

"What are you doing here?" Ryan snapped. She turned around and narrowed her eyes at Balor.

"Easy, doll. I came to check on you, to make sure you made it home ok," Balor said as he threw his hands up.

"Yeah, it would have been great if you came into the alley. Where the fuck did you go?" Ryan said with anger now rising in her chest.

"I passed out in the gutter. What happened?" Balor lied. He knew exactly what happened.

"Nothing. Forget about it," Ryan said and tugged her bag up over her shoulder as she started for the stairs.

"Ryan, I'm sorry," Balor said. His chest felt like it caved inward for a second as the words came out.

"Do you know how often I hear that? Ryan, I'm sorry your dad died of cancer. Ryan, I'm sorry your mom died in the same car accident you were injured in but somehow walked away. Being thrown from a vehicle and just coming away scratched. Ryan, I'm sorry you're struggling with life. Ryan, I'm sorry you were attacked. Now it's gonna be sorry your best friend went psycho. You know what would have been so much easier. If the car accident actually killed me too," Ryan yelled. Her body shook and tears formed in her eyes.

"Shh, come here," Balor said as he held his arms open to her.

"Nope, no. No. I'm good," Ryan said as the shaking got worse. She was trying to hold it all in.

"Shh. It's ok," he whispered to her and he meant every part of it.

Balor pulled her in for the hug anyways. She went to pull back but when his arms closed around her, it was what she needed at that moment. She leaned into him. The hug felt good and for a second she forgot what had just happened. She sighed and let it take away the overwhelming emotion that was racing through her blood. She let out another breath before pulling back.

"Thanks," Ryan said. She raised her hand to catch a tear that had slipped out of her eye.

Balor's hand was quicker and his thumb brushed it away quickly. He left his hand on the side of her face, cupping it gently.

"Not a whole lot of girls can look beautiful when they're crying," he said with a small smile.

"Gee thanks! Lucky me!" Ryan chuckled.

He rubbed her cheek gently. Ryan paused. She felt her cheeks blush as his thumb caressed it. She didn't move as his thumb traveled across her cheek and down to her chin. He held her chin in his hand and then slowly moved towards her. His eyes fixated on her lips as he leaned in. Her heart sped up in her chest as she saw his lips coming towards her. She didn't pull away and a mixture of excitement and panic flipped in her stomach. She was unsure if she wanted to kiss him or wanted to pull away.

Suddenly Balor's hands were yanked away from her face and someone stepped in between them. Balor was hit hard in his chest and he was sent flying back into the stairs.

"Get the fuck away from her!" his voice boomed. It was low like the roar of thunder.

His whole body was tense as he stood in front of Ryan, blocking her from Balor. The rage pouring out from him caused his shoulders to tremble with each breath he took.

"Silas!" Ryan yelled as it took a second to process who was standing in front of her.

"Silas." Balor smirked as he let out a small grunt getting up off the stairs.

"What the fuck are you doing?" Silas growled. All of the muscles in his arms flexed.

"Oh, you know, the same old-same old." Balor taunted Silas with a grin.

"Wait, you know each other?" Ryan asked. She stepped off to the side.

"We're old friends." Balor grinned wider.

"We are not friends," Silas growled.

"Well, we were friends." Balor laughed as if he had just told a joke.

"Ok," Ryan said as she took another step away from both of them.

"How do you know her? What are you up to?" Silas demanded. He bowed up more to Balor, who was now casually leaning back into the stair railing.

"Ryan...me and her are friends." Balor smirked. His voice lingered on the word friends as if it meant something more.

Silas lost his control. He lunged at Balor and his hand wrapped around Balor's neck as he picked him up off the stairs. His other hand closed into a fist as it collided with Balor's face. A loud crack echoed through the stairwell as the skin on Balor's cheek bone split open.

"Silas!" Ryan yelled. She rushed forward and grabbed hold of his arm as he cranked back to deliver another blow.

The minute she touched his arm, he froze. He was still squeezing Balor's throat but he didn't want to risk hurting her.

"Let him go," Ryan said very calmly but she did not let Silas's hand go.

"Ryan, he's not what you think. You need to stay away from him. He's dangerous," Silas said. He turned slightly to look at her but kept Balor in his sight.

"The only one who looks dangerous right now is you," Ryan said, trying to keep her voice steady.

Silas's eyes flickered. He wanted to end Balor but he didn't want to scare Ryan. He needed her. He needed her to trust him. Silas let out a low growl as he slammed Balor into the railing and let him drop onto the stairs.

"You fucking stay away from her," Silas threatened.

"Silas!" Ryan snapped at him.

"Ryan-" Silas started to explain.

"No, he saved me. He doesn't need to stay away from me," Ryan said as she let go of Silas's arm.

"What?" Silas asked. He didn't understand the words saved and Balor in the same sentence.

"Balor saved me from a situation. He is a friend," Ryan said annoyedly.

"Saved you?" Silas whipped his head to Balor, looking at him as he stood up rubbing his throat.

"Yup…that's right. I saved her…hero here." Balor grinned.

"You don't save anyone," Silas said. He turned towards Balor, ready to rip him apart.

"If anything you cause the reason people need to be saved," Silas said as he clenched his fists.

"Ryan he is a…a -" Silas said. He turned to her as he tried to find a way to say the word without making Ryan scared.

"Demon." Balor grinned as he watched Silas stumble to say the word.

"Oh…funny," Ryan said, as she shifted further away from them.

"He is… He's a demon," Silas said quickly as he tried to get closer to her.

"Ok, so he's a demon and you're Death," Ryan said with a small nod.

"Demon?" Ryan asked Balor. She was trying to make sure he wasn't being funny.

"Guilty." Balor grinned.

"So did you two go to the same…school…or hospital?" Ryan asked. She started to move quickly towards the curb.

"Hospital?" Silas asked. His eyes left Balor and turned to Ryan.

She moved away from them slowly as if they were some kind of threat that she was trying to sneak away from.

"Ryan," Balor said. Now he was concerned as she backed towards the street.

It was a busy road and right now it was the middle of the day. The cars were driving steadily through. Most of the drivers were not paying attention.

"No, it's ok. I believe you guys. I just…you know… I need to, um, get to-" she started to say as her foot caught the curb.

"Ryan!" Silas yelled. He moved quickly towards her.

Ryan fell backwards. Her stomach dropped as she tried to catch herself. She could hear the cars coming as she fell into the road. Her back hit the cold hard cement as she heard a loud honking noise echo through the rumble of the road. She sat up and saw the headlights coming for

her. Silas raced for the curb. His stomach twisted as he tried to reach her.

Balor phased and got to her before he could even process what he did. He scooped her into his arms and pulled her safely against him before he phased once more. He appeared back on the sidewalk like he had never left with Ryan in his arms.

"You ok?" Balor asked. He looked down at her. Ryan blinked. She didn't understand how this all happened.

"I…yes," Ryan said as Balor slowly lowered her to the ground but kept his hands on her.

"How did you get there so quickly?" Ryan asked him as her feet touched the ground.

Silas turned and looked at Balor in confusion. He just saved Ryan. He walked back over to them slowly. A mixture of anger and concern rolled around in him like thunder ready to escape.

"What are you getting at?" Silas growled as he got to them.

"I saved her," Balor bragged with a small smirk on his lips.

"Why?" Silas growled.

"Silas," Ryan said shortly. She was confused about his anger.

"He doesn't do anything good, ever. He is not what you think he is. He only does things to serve his own purpose." Silas said. His eyes narrowed at Balor.

"Ok..." Ryan said. She stepped away from Balor.

"He's right, for the most part." Balor smirked and threw her a wink.

"He's a demon, Ryan. They only help themselves," Silas said firmly, trying to make her understand.

"Yes, and you're Death. It's been amazing meeting you and him. Maybe I can meet an angel next." Ryan laughed. She covered her mouth as the words came out.

"Pssh, angel. I'll treat you better than an angel, love. Don't need one of those." Balor winked at her.

Silas growled. His eyes flashed yellow quickly as he went to Balor. Balor laughed and put his hands up. Silas was too quick for him. Within seconds his hands were around Balor's neck. Silas grabbed his chin in one hand and then the back of his head and twisted. The snap echoed through the stairwell even louder than when he had hit him earlier. Balor dropped to the ground like a sack of potatoes.

"Silas! Holy fuck! You killed him!" Ryan yelled and covered her face.

"You can't kill a demon like that," Silas said as he pushed Balor's body with his foot.

"Oh my god. Oh shit. You're fucking insane. He is not a fucking demon. There is no such thing as demons," Ryan yelled at him. She searched her pockets for her phone to call for help.

"He is a demon. Just wait," Silas said. He stepped towards Ryan.

"Stay the fuck away from me," Ryan yelled at him.

"Just wait," Silas said again. He reached towards her but she pulled her arm away.

"Hello, hi. I am at the corner of 21st and 22nd Street. Like right on the curb. We need police and I don't

know…an ambulance. He's on the ground. He snapped his neck. I think he-" Ryan spoke rapidly into the phone.

Silas snatched the phone out of her hand and snapped it in half. He threw the phone down and pieces of it shattered on the ground. Ryan blinked as she looked at the broken pieces of her phone.

"Just wait!" Silas demanded. His eyes flashed yellow as he became more and more annoyed.

Ryan watched him carefully. She told herself that she got her location to the police. That they would be here any second and she just needed to stay calm until then.

"For the love of…come on, you piece of shit," Silas muttered as he kicked Balor's boot.

"Silas, we need to get help," Ryan said quietly. She winced as he kicked Balor again.

"He's taking longer on purpose," Silas growled. He was becoming angry with Balor.

"Silas…he's dead. We need to get you help," Ryan said. She glanced down the road, hoping to see red and blue lights.

"Ughhh." Balor's voice came from the ground as he rolled over getting to his knees.

"See," Silas said with an 'I told you so' look.

"What?" Ryan whispered. She looked confused.

Balor put his hands to his chin and straightened out his neck. There was a loud pop as everything snapped back into place. He stood up slowly and rolled his neck in a slow circle. Several more pops sounded as Ryan looked at him. She was dumbfounded.

"Well, that was fucking rude." Balor glared at Silas.

"See? He's fine," Silas said and turned to look at Ryan.

"He…you..dead," Ryan stuttered.

"He did say I was a demon." Balor shrugged with a smirk.

"How?" Ryan asked. She stumbled back a step as the world began to spin.

"It's ok. I was telling the truth. It's ok," Silas said reassuringly as he tried to get closer to her.

"Demon…Death," Ryan muttered. Her eyes darted back and forth between them and her legs began to feel like Jello.

"You better catch her." Balor sighed and shook his head.

"Huh?" Silas looked back at him quickly.

"Catch her or I will," Balor said and nodded to Ryan who began to wobble.

"Shit," Silas muttered as Ryan's legs gave out and she stumbled.

Silas caught her in his arms and pulled her into him. He glanced at Balor, still not sure how he played into all of this. Sirens were heard from down the road. He grumbled.

"Time to go," he said out loud.

"Where to?" Balor smirked. He knew it would get under Silas's skin.

"You're not fucking coming," Silas muttered as he swept Ryan's legs up and cradled her.

"You bet your ass I am. Not going to miss that." Balor's smirk slowly turned into a grin.

"Have fun finding me," Silas said. His eyes flashed yellow as he phased out with Ryan in his arms.

Chapter Fourteen

"**W**hat the hell is going on!" Nyx screamed as she watched Balor save Ryan from not only Will but also the car.

"Told you he wasn't the demon to trust," another woman snickered as she watched Nyx throw a fit.

"Don't you dare take that tone with me, Eurynomos," Nyx snapped. She reached out and grabbed Eurynomos by her throat.

"You might be a high ranking demon but I am still the ruler in this shit hole," Nyx growled. Her fingers closed around Eurynomos's iridescent dark blue skin.

"I am only saying that you should have me do it," Eurynomos said through gasps of air.

Nyx dropped her and she hit the ground. Nyx began pacing back and forth. Balor might be onto something. He had screwed up twice now but maybe it was part of a plan. She let out another yell. Eurynomos flinched as if expecting another blow.

"Balor may have something planned. I need him to come back." Nyx growled.

Eurynomos sunk further into the ground. Nyx looked down at her and then something clicked in her head. Something Balor had said. Ryan's body needed to be destroyed so Silas wouldn't be able to save her.

"Actually…go," Nyx said. Her voice was suddenly calm.

"Go?" Eurynomos asked as she looked up.

"Yeah and when you get the girl to die…do what you do," Nyx said and waved her hand dismissively at Eurynomos.

"Really?" Eurynomos asked brightly.

"Yes, devour her for all I care. She won't be able to be saved if she is just bones." Nyx grinned.

"**W**here is my brother?" Kere said as she sat on the dock dipping the tips of her toes into the water.

The white ghostly looking souls reached up and brushed against her feet. Her foot splashed at them as she pulled her toes away with a small giggle.

"You shouldn't tease them like that. It's honestly really sad," Charon scolded her as he rocked in his boat.

"Sad? Are you getting sentimental on me in your old age?" Kere snickered.

"There's just too many of them lately. Too many of them are going into the river and not enough are making it to the promised land," Charon said. He frowned as he looked into the water.

"When did the increase start?" Kere asked. She was concerned with the sadness she sensed in Charon.

"A year and a half ago." Charon shook his head as the words came out.

"Where is Silas?" Kere asked as she started to connect the dots.

"I don't know." Charon shrugged.

"Aren't you his best friend?" Kere asked annoyedly.

"Aren't you his sister?" Charon shot back at her.

"So Death has a secret life," Kere stated. She stood on the dock.

Charon had no response for her comment. He wasn't saying anything else. He never really knew where Kere stood with things. Kere studied his face waiting for some type of expression.

"And what do we have here?" Eurynomos snickered, seeing Kere and Charon.

"Just chatting," Kere snapped at Eurynomos.

"Hmm…Chatting," Eurynomos said with doubt in her voice as she paused to look at them.

"Just because no one wants to… chat… with you doesn't mean the rest of us don't enjoy company and chats," Kere said. Her face twisted in disgust as she looked at her.

"I don't need anyone to chat with me," Eurynomos snapped angrily.

"Where are you going?" Charon joined the conversation.

"I am going to tie up some loose ends for Nyx. Balor failed. Not that it's any of your concern," Eurynomos said proudly.

"What? Why would Nyx choose you? Who would let you out and about? What would Balor fail at?" Kere rambled.

"Because I am better. You all see me as less but I am the one thing down here that finishes my jobs and ensures everything is…consumed." Eurynomos giggled at her own pun.

"What loose end?" Charon asked curiously.

"A girl." Eurynomos laughed.

"What would Nyx want with a girl?" Kere scoffed at Eurynomos.

"Don't know. Don't care. This will bring me one step closer to being where I should be. You're just jealous that she no longer calls upon you," Eurynomos said. She flipped her phthalo green hair over her shoulder.

"How are you going to blend in, in the human world exactly?" Kere asked through her teeth.

"Easily. You're so small minded, Kere." Eurynomos laughed as she took her hands and ran them over her face.

As Eurynomos touched her skin it turned to a beautiful shade of olive. Running her hands over her face her lips turned from their blue black color to a deep plump red. Her eyes turned from their hollow inky color to bright green and her hair the color of fire. She twirled around to show off her transformation.

"Now, I will be back before sunset. After that I shall get my new title." Eurynomos laughed as she snapped her fingers and phased out.

"She is fucking crazy. Nyx…give her a title? Title of what? Guardian of the loonies? Of the buzzards? God, she is a buzzard after all," Kere said. She still stared at where Eurynomos once was.

"Kere…we need to talk. Your brother…I think, is in danger." Charon fought to get the words out. He prayed that Kere would care.

"What's wrong with Silas?" Kere stopped and turned to look at him as she spoke.

Relief rushed over Charon. He knew that she was not close with anyone and neither was Silas, but he had always felt there was a tie between these two.

"We need to get to him…well, you need to get to him. I can't leave," Charon said quietly.

"Why? What is going on, Charon?" Kere asked. Her voice was serious and deadly.

"It started a year and a half ago. There was this girl he was supposed to help cross over. He couldn't do it. We all know fate tries to correct itself. So he has been stopping her death ever since. I think Eurynomos is going after the girl. It's going to be bad. I don't know what Nyx wants with the girl but we need to get to Silas and maybe even talk to Balor. It's odd he didn't finish his assignment if Nyx sent him first." Charon rushed out in a hush tone. His eyes searched the perimeter as he spoke.

"What the fuck, Silas," Kere mumbled.

"Where would he be?" Kere asked. Her stomach twisted in knots.

"I didn't tell you this… and I am only telling you because of how important it is. There is an old library he bought years ago. It's where he goes to get away from all of this," Charon said to her.

"Do you know how many fucking old libraries there are?" Kere snapped as she grabbed Charon by his shirt.

"There can't be many in Salem," Charon blurted out.

"Salem?" Kere asked quietly. She let go of his shirt.

"Yes, that's where the girl is," Charon mumbled. He glared at her as he straightened out his shirt.

"He's a fool," Kere muttered and phased out.

"Well, this is just fucking lovely," Charon grumbled and walked back towards his ferry.

"If this keeps up I am just going to dive in there with you poor lost souls and float around for the rest of eternity," Charon grumbled to the river.

Chapter Fifteen

His fist slammed against the dark wooden door. His eyes watching the black hinges shake as he brought his hand down again.

"Silas! Open this fucking door!" Balor yelled as he continued to pound on the door.

He followed them here. Silas had phased, but it wasn't hard to track him. Balor was good at tracking people and his ability to phase was quicker than most. He had been doing it since the dawn of time. His fist hit the wood again angrily. A small split in the wood appeared. As he watched the wood crack he decided he would break the door down if he had to. Silas had done something to the building. Balor could not phase into it. He had tried three times when he first landed on its concrete steps.

A loud roar rumbled through the door as it was yanked open. A hand clasped around Balor's throat as he was pulled into the building.

"Fucking annoying ass. Making a goddamn scene out there. What the fuck do you want?!" Silas yelled in Balor's face. His eyes glowed bright yellow.

"I..." He didn't know. He wanted to be with Ryan. That's all he knew but he couldn't let Silas know that.

"I'm curious." Balor smirked as he quickly reverted back to his charming self.

"Curiosity killed the cat. It sounds like a perfect ending to you," Silas growled.

"We've done this several times. Let's just skip it, it stings. You win the fight. You're still annoyed, I will still exist. Why don't we just save energy? Now what is this place?" Balor said. He patted Silas's forearm.

"Shut up." Silas growled and shoved him backwards into the door as he let Balor go.

Ryan rolled over and groaned. Her head hurt. Why did she feel like she was still exhausted? She slowly sat up and opened her eyes. Silas narrowed his eyes at Balor silently telling him to stay put as he walked towards the couch.

"Hey," Silas said quietly as he approached the couch.

She looked around. She was on the couch. She ran her hand over it, trying to register why she was on the couch in Silas's library.

"A dream." Ryan laughed. Her hands covered her face as she laughed harder.

"Oh thank god. It was all a dream." She laughed again.

She had amazing sex with Silas and then had an awful nightmare. Thank god. She looked up at him and saw his confusion. She choked down her laughter. She reached up and touched his face in relief.

"I am so sorry. I am not laughing at you. I just had the most awful and ridiculous dream. Will tried to kill me. You thought you were Death-like the grim reaper-and this guy I met at the bar thought he was a demon. It was so

silly. I am so sorry." Ryan laughed again and shook her head.

"Mhmm, dream all right," Balor said. He leaned over the couch and looked at her.

"Balor? What? Uh?" Ryan asked. She looked at him confusedly.

"I will kill you," Silas growled at him. His eyes flashed yellow as he bowed up.

"Oh shit…it wasn't a dream," Ryan whispered. Her eyes grew wide as she moved away from Silas.

"Ryan." Silas spoke her name softly, trying to calm her.

"I mean, I am dreamy. He's a little more of a nightmare." Balor smirked as he nodded to Silas.

"Shut up," Silas growled.

"Woah…this is a lot," Ryan said. She stood up but then sat back down. She didn't know what to do with her body right now.

"I know," Silas said reassuringly as he sat down next to her. She didn't move away from him and it made him feel some hope.

"Maybe I'm sick. Maybe I hit my head too hard." Ryan laughed lightly.

"This is real… Life, Death, Heaven, and Hell. It's all real," Silas said quietly.

"So you're Death," she mused quietly as she turned to look at him.

"Yes," Silas said gently.

"Are you…I can see you because…Are you here for me?" Ryan asked with a quiver in her voice.

"No. I can't take you." Silas let a little bit of truth slip out.

"Can't?" Ryan questioned. Her hand slowly moved towards him. Her eyes were fixated on his face.

Her hand shook a little bit as she hesitated to touch his face. Her hand brushed his skin slowly as if she expected something to happen. She ran her thumb over his cheek. Small tingles rushed through him as he leaned into her hand. Balor let out a loud sigh and loudly walked over to the single chair across from them. He sat down with a huff.

"I swear to god I will kill you," Silas growled. His eyes flickered yellow again.

"The yellow..." Ryan murmured as her other hand caught his face and she cradled it in her hands.

"It's the reaper coming out," Silas explained quietly. He tried to hide the anger in his voice.

"Grim Reaper...so if folklore is right, you take souls," Ryan stated. She still gazed at the faint glow left in his eyes.

"I escort souls to the ferry which takes them to the afterlife," Silas explained. He hoped that telling her bits and pieces might make this all ok.

"So, you're a good guy," Ryan said quietly.

"Ha...good guy." Balor slapped his knee as he laughed out loud.

Ryan let go of Silas's face and turned to look at Balor. She narrowed her eyes at him as she frowned at his outburst.

"And you're a demon," Ryan said flatly.

"That would be correct." Balor grinned.

"So you work for the devil and do his bidding? Running around hurting people and things?" Ryan asked. She kept her voice level as she spoke.

"Yes and no," Balor answered. As he grinned his canine teeth seemed to become more pointed.

"Yes and no?" Ryan asked. She ignored that his eyes were now slowly glowing red.

"Balor..." Silas warned. His body tensed as the demon side of him slowly came out.

"Yes, I cause havoc, chaos and hurt things. Mostly I like to lead and persuade people to do what they really think or feel. No...I work for myself and do what I want, when I want and for my...own enjoyment." Balor grinned.

"So why am I being involved?" Ryan asked as she looked from Balor to Silas.

"Oooo, good question. I'll let you field this one death boy." Balor snickered.

"Because I... I..-" Silas struggled to find how to tell her what was going on.

"Silas!" The air in the room shifted. A dark cloud seemed to appear and a woman's voice boomed through it.

Silas stood defensively in front of Ryan. Balor stood up even though he was not sure what was going on. His eyes glowed red. The black dress that matched her hair shimmered about her. Her green eyes narrowed in on Silas.

"Kere," Silas said. He narrowed his own eyes on her.

"We need to talk now...Balor?" Kere said and then turned to see Balor.

"Kere…it's been a while." He smiled charmingly.

"Not long enough. Silas, I assume the girl you're standing in front of so protectively, is the one causing all the problems," Kere said. She tried to peek at Ryan.

"You don't know what you're talking about," Silas growled.

"I know enough. Charon told me about what you have done! How could you? You're messing with fate," Kere snapped.

"You don't get to tell me anything," Silas spat. All the muscles in his arms and back tensed as he stood straighter in front of Ryan.

"What is going on now?" Ryan yelled from behind Silas. She began to move out from behind him.

Kere cocked her head to the side. Her eyes ran over Ryan. There was something about her. She narrowed her eyes as she tried to figure it out.

"Family reunion." Balor smiled at Ryan. He hoped that was all the explanation she needed.

"Why is she talking about me?" Ryan demanded as she moved away from Silas.

Kere phased and was standing next to Ryan in a blink of an eye. Her hand wrapped around Ryan's arm as if she was going to yank her away. Silas felt the shift and his hand went to Kere's throat. Balor phased as well. He appeared behind Kere with a blade pressed into her back.

"Don't move. It's a demon blade," Balor whispered in Kere's ear.

"What is she?" Kere asked. She looked at Ryan.

"Let her go," Silas threatened. His hand squeezed her throat tighter.

"Silas, you don't understand. I am here to warn you. Nyx has found out what you have done and has sent Eurynomos," Kere said. She ignored the pressure from Silas's hand and the blade in her back.

"Eurynomos, that snake." Balor spat as he stepped away from Kere.

Kere released her grip on Ryan's arm. Once she had let go of Ryan, Silas let go of her. His face held no expression. Balor kept the blade pressed in Kere's back. He grinned as she turned to look at him.

"I dare you," Kere whispered with a fire in her eyes as she spoke.

"Not today love." Balor smirked, sheathing his blade.

"What the fuck is going on?" Ryan asked again as she stepped away.

"Ryan…I…" Silas started to say but glanced at Balor.

"Don't look at me, I ain't explaining shit," Balor said and shook his head.

"Someone better!" Ryan yelled.

"You've been touched by death and are still here. Death failed to do his job and now fate is trying to correct it. However, I am not sure what Nyx has to do with this all," Kere said looking at Ryan. Her expression was guarded as she tried to study her.

"Death…as in you." Ryan turned on Silas.

"Yes," Silas answered, becoming overwhelmed and angry.

"There's not more than one of you. So you were supposed to…what did you say, reap my soul and failed to

do so. So now I have essentially a target on me. Is that why all this horrible and weird shit has been happening to me? Oh and you just magically appear to save the fucking day!" Ryan yelled her hands in fists.

"Busted. She is pretty quick with all of this." Balor laughed watching the scene in front of him.

"And you! What's your angle in all of this? Mr. Demon. Why are you here?" Ryan snapped. Her eyes narrowed on Balor.

"Woah, easy," Balor yelled. He threw his hands up in defense.

"No, she's right," Kere said, looking at Balor.

"You're close with Nyx. Eurynomos mentioned something about you. What is your involvement?" Kere said quietly.

"Balor!" Silas growled. He strode across the room to him.

Balor quickly moved around the couch to put it between Silas and him. Silas's hands were in fists. His eyes glowing bright yellow as he stared Balor down, ready to tear him apart. Kere left Ryan's side and began making her way towards the other side of Balor ready to close in on him.

"Fucking fine!" Balor yelled as they ganged up on him.

"Talk!" Silas yelled. His low voice boomed off the walls around them.

"Nyx wants the girl. She sent me to make sure she…passed on." Balor's voice cracked slightly with regret as he locked eyes with Ryan. Hurt and betrayal flashed in her eyes.

"Ryan-" Balor started to explain.

Silas moved faster than Balor could talk and slammed him into the wall behind him. The wall cracked as Balor was pressed into it.

"Why does Nyx want her?!" Silas yelled as the skin on his face slowly started to crack away revealing the skull underneath as the reaper came out.

"She said she needs her. Something about the banshees she is always hanging out with. I don't know the connection but she believes Ryan is the missing piece," Balor said. He ignored Silas's peeling face.

Balor's eyes darkened and began to glow bright red as he glared at Silas. His own face began to morph. Ryan watched the scene unfold in front of her. Her stomach twisted tightly into knots. Demons and Death were actual things. Someone was after her. She was supposed to have died. She couldn't process it all. Everything was so overwhelming. Her chest tightened. Her breath became shallow and she could feel her heart pounding in her chest. Was this even real?

"The car accident." Ryan's voice broke through all the rage in the room.

Silas's voice softened hearing her voice. Kere watched the change in him. She was unsure of why this girl had such an effect on him.

"Where..did you…my mom." Ryan couldn't get the sentence out. It came out in broken words.

"Yes," Silas said as he let go of Balor and turned to face her.

"I need air," Ryan said. Her eyes shifted to the door.

"Ryan, you can't be alone right now," Balor said. He rubbed his throat as he spoke.

"We don't know what Nyx wants and Eurynomos is looking for you," Silas said. He stepped forward.

"I need air and space from you two," Ryan said firmly as she walked to the door.

"You can't be alone right now," Silas repeated what Balor said.

"You don't get to tell me anything right now," Ryan snapped at Silas. A small amount of rage leaked out into her voice.

"She can come with me," Ryan said, pointing at Kere.

"What?" Silas asked as he looked at Kere.

"You can't be serious," Balor grumbled.

"She can come or I'm going alone," Ryan said firmly.

Ryan started to walk to the door without giving Silas or Balor a second to protest. Ryan heard a small chuckle and footsteps began following her.

"I think I like her." Kere laughed to Silas as she followed Ryan outside.

Chapter Sixteen

She loved the hunt. The thrill of it, the drive. It had been so long. Eurynomos had evolved from just a scavenger to a hunter. She would no longer be taking others' scraps. She would no longer be cowering at the bottom. She would find this girl, deliver her to Nyx and become what she always wanted. A reaper. She would be the first female Death. Death itself called to her. She could sense when things were dying. Animals, people, the more they suffered the louder the pull was. She needed to be near it. The pain sent tingles and chills through her body. It was more euphoric the closer she was. Sitting on the other side was unbearable. She could feel the pull but was not able to chase it, to watch, to feel it. It was driving her insane. She was never going back to that.

The smell of the wet cement hit her nose as she stepped out of the alleyway onto the pavement. The street lights gave off an amber glow as she looked around. She knew Death had failed in taking her. The girl's scent would be different from most humans. She was using borrowed time. Eurynomos inhaled. She had tracked Balor's scent to this spot but it quickly went cold. She knew he would be close. She inhaled deeply. Her eyes opened and she locked eyes on a nursing home across the street. The smell was overpowering. She could smell the death leaking out into the streets. Her mouth began to water as the smell invaded her nose. Just one quick fix before she was back on her hunt. If she got it out of her system she would be more focused. It felt like her brian was itching and her skin crawled. She needed it.

She walked quickly across the street. Her hand out in front of her ready for the door to the nursing home well before she was close enough to open it. She pushed through the door and inhaled deeply. She shivered in delight as the smell overwhelmed her. It was delicious.

"Ma'am, I'm sorry but visiting hours are almost over." A sweet voice came from behind the counter.

"Oh, I will be quick." Eurynomos smiled brightly at her.

"Ok, but I need you to sign in on the sign in sheet right here," the girl said as she reached through the window and pushed a clipboard towards Eurynomos.

Eurynomos smiled brightly and walked over to the counter. She plucked an orange pen out of the metal cup holder on the counter and paused looking at the paper. First name, last name and phone number. She tilted her head at it.

"Is there a problem, ma'am?" the girl asked. her big blue eyes looking up at her from her seat.

"How old are you?" Eurynomos asked her.

"Twenty," the girl answered.

"Mmm. Twenty," Eurynomos said. She had to catch some of the drool with her tongue as it threatened to slip out of her mouth.

"Ma'am?" the girl asked as her expression turned to concern.

"Who were you visiting exactly?" She stood up.

"Mr. Smith." Eurynomos answered with a basic name.

"Smith-" the girl started to say but Eurynomos leaned on the counter.

"There's something wrong with your pen," Eurynomos said and shook the pen slightly.

"Oh. Here, I will get you another one." The girl opened a door and passed a blue pen out the window.

As soon as her hand was out from beneath the glass, Eurynomos snatched it. She bent down and smelled it. The girl let out a startled yell and tried to pull back. Her fear pouring into Eurynomos made her smell even better.

"What do you have?" Eurynomos asked as she yanked the girl's hand back towards her nose.

"Help!" the girl yelled while using all her might to pull away.

Eurynomos slid her long finger nail down the girl's forearm. The skin split easily beneath it. The girl flinched and tried her best to wiggle away.

"Stop! What are you doing?!" the girl yelled in hopes that someone would hear her.

Eurynomos bent forward and ran her tongue down the cut. Her eyes rolled back in her head as the blood tingled across her taste buds.

"What are you doing! You're a freak! Leave me alone. Someone help!" She screamed.

"Oh, that is lovely. Streptococcus. Been feeling sick suddenly?" Eurynomos giggled as she let her arm go.

"Excuse me!" The girl snatched her arm back and closed her free hand around the cut.

"Fever, chills? Achiness? Diarrhea, Vomiting?" Eurynomos grinned.

'Yeah, just suddenly. I've got locked in. This is my third shift and all of a sudden I feel really sick. I go home in two hours so I was trying to stick it out. I just thought it was because I had worked too long," the girl said as she stepped away from the window.

"Oh, what's this?" Eurynomos asked. She swished her mouth around as if sampling a fine wine.

"Diabetic, too. That's why it's happening so fast. Headache?" Eurynomos asked with laughter in her voice.

"Yeah, since yesterday. What do you know? What are you talking about? How can you taste that through my blood?" the girl demanded as the world started spinning.

"As a girl in the medical field you should know what streptococcus is. On your period, currently?" Eurynomos asked. She rolled her eyes as she propped her head up on her hand, leaning on the counter.

"Yes," the girl said, needing to sit down.

"Tampons?" Eurynomos smirked.

"Are you saying I have Toxic Shock-" the girl started to say but the world went black and she hit the ground.

"Perfect." Eurynomos giggled as she walked around to the office door.

She turned the silver door handle and pushed the steel gray door open. She closed it behind her, the door clicking into place. She slid the bolt across the top to lock the door. She glanced down at the girl's body as she began to twitch and convulse on the floor. Eurynomos grinned as she reached over and pulled the shade down on the window. She was going to enjoy this death, no one was going to interrupt to save this girl. She sat down on the floor and pulled the girl close to her. She inhaled deeply; the smells of decay and toxins floating out of the girl and into Eurynomos's nose made the eyes roll back in her head. How she missed the human world.

The cold air hit her face as she shut her eyes. She leaned against the rough brick of the building trying to get her bearings. The world was spinning and she couldn't handle it anymore. Nothing had been the same since the car accident.

"Tell me what he's not telling me. Explain more," Ryan said with her eyes still shut. She didn't hear Kere come out but she knew she was there with her.

"I really don't know a lot. I am just finding out about you. Silas is good at his job. He follows the rules. Doesn't care for anything or anyone until now. He's been doing it for centuries-" Kere was explaining.

"Centuries! How old is he?" Ryan snapped her eyes open.

"I don't even remember how old he is. Does that matter right now?" Kere looked at her confusedly.

"I guess not. He just looks like he couldn't be older than thirty." Ryan shrugged.

"He died when he was twenty six," Kere said quietly as if speaking of his death pained her.

"He died..." Ryan said. The thought of him dying hurt her and pulled at her heart.

"You're not really bright are you. I might be changing my mind about you." Kere sighed as if Ryan was now annoying her.

"Sorry, it's a lot." Ryan muttered.

"How did he die?" Ryan asked. She was not sure if she really wanted to know.

"Like all reapers," Kere replied. Her voice hardened as if it made her angry.

"I am not part of this world. Not sure what that means," Ryan said to her.

"He...He died saving his sister but because he knew it would kill him, they considered it suicide," Kere said bitterly.

"Reapers are men who commit suicide?" Ryan asked, confused.

"It needs to be done a certain way. In place of someone they love." Kere murmured.

"That's not, who says..how did he die?" Ryan stumbled over a number of questions trying to come out all at once.

"It's not mine to tell. And they, as in the almighty. God, gods, whoever you believe in is what judges you in the end," Kere said quietly.

"Were you human at one point?" Ryan asked her quietly.

"What are you?!" Kere snapped. The anger from bringing up Silas's past and then her own snapped in her.

Kere's hand collapsed down on Ryan's forearm and her fingers wrapped around it tightly. Ryan locked eyes with her. As she went to pull away the world around them went black.

Kere woke up in a field. It was like the field in the In-Between but instead of long tall grass that swayed in a ghostly wind, the ground was dark, green and rich. The sky was blue but dark as if it was going to rain.

"Ryan!" Kere yelled out enraged. Thegirl had something to do with this! Where was she?

A white tulip popped up out of the ground. Kere stepped back away from it. She tilted her head to look at it. She paused and within a few seconds another one popped up. A third and then a fourth. Before she could process what was happening, a full row of white tulips sprouted up. Kere took it as a sign and slowly began following them. The sky grew darker as she followed after the tulips. They

soon turned into a field and in the center of the field was a tree.

"It is a forgotten place," a voice whispered.

Kere narrowed her eyes; she was not one for games and she was not afraid of anything in any world. There was little that anything could do to her.

"So why am I here?" Kere asked. She tried to keep the annoyance out of her voice.

"Death is losing his touch, others will notice soon," the voice whispered around her.

"What? How do you know this?" Kere snapped. She quickly looked around.

"More souls are being put into the river and not getting to move on." The words were spoken viciously.

"That's not just Silas's fault." Kere defended him.

The tulips turned from white to black and began to wither and die as if it was predicting what would happen.

"What happens if Silas is no longer Death?" Kere whispered. She couldn't stop watching the tulips.

"Then she will be free to walk the earth and her army will be unleashed." The voice changed from being angry to monotone.

"She? Army? Nyx…She has an army?" Kere asked. She was still trying to find where the voice was coming from.

"There is one who will decide. Everything is depending on her. She will either save Death or cause destruction," it whispered softly.

"The girl. She is the key to all this?" Kere demanded as she spun around in a circle.

The world went dark and blacked out the ability to see all together. Haunting soulless screams filled the air. She knew those cries. They plagued the long grassy area in the In-Between. The light came back and she was surrounded by banshees. She saw Nyx wandering through them, lingering, whispering to them. Then as if everything clicked into place the scene faded out and she watched a banshee pull a soul who was kicking and screaming towards the river. It dropped the soul into the river and as the soul plunged into the river the banshee turned to ash. Nyx growled angrily in the distance.

"We need the girl to get this right! We can trade banshees for souls and everytime we gain a new one we get set back. The river will flood with trapped souls and I will ride it into the human world. Then I will reap all the souls I need. I will rule over both worlds and no one will stop me," Nyx yelled out over her black hooded army.

Lightning struck and Kere saw her. Ryan was moving through the sea of banshees. Her eyes had changed from their once warm brown to pure black. Her skin was pale white and the blue veins running over her body looked like cracks in her skin. She reached out for Nyx. Nyx smiled widely, took her by the hand, and led her to the river.

Another lightning strike and Silas was running towards them. He was fighting through the banshees to get to Ryan. He phased in front of them. Ryan locked eyes with him. He was begging her. He reached out and touched her cheek as if trying to connect to her in some way. Ryan leaned into his hand and then as if the moment was gone she reached out and shoved Silas. He fell

backwards into the river of lost souls. The souls reached up and wrapped around him. They pulled him into the depths.

As if the world blinked, She found herself standing in a field full of tulips. She stood at the back of the field and looked out over them. In the center of the field was a tall tree. She saw someone wandering around the base of the tree in the center of the field. They looked like they were lost. She narrowed her eyes.

"Silas!" Kere shouted. As she began to move towards him she was thrown back by a force.

"Silas!" she shouted again but she could not reach him.

"Where are you? What is this I am seeing!?" Kere tried to get the voice to speak again.

"He is lost in the forgotten place. He will never come out and he will forget everything, even himself," the voice whispered.

"Why? How do we stop this? Wasn't he just in the river of souls?" Kere demanded answers.

"These are all different outcomes," the voice whispered and then the world shifted.

The scene changed in front of her. A woman appeared in the field. She was making her way towards the tree. Each step the woman took the tulips seemed to glow.. Kere's eyes focused on her, Her long dark hair flowing behind her as she was able to reach the tree.

"Ryan?" Kere whispered as she squinted.

. "It is said a woman stands with Death as his last remaining link to the human world. To remind him how

precious life is. Without that link, he is nothing," the voice whispered and then Kere fell back.

"Let go of me!" Ryan yelled, slamming her hand into Kere's shoulder, sending her back into the door of the building.

"I am not doing this with any of you anymore!" Ryan yelled as she took off down the steps.

Kere's chest burned as if her lungs had exploded inside of her. She was shaky and couldn't move. She tried to get her body to respond. She needed to chase after Ryan but she was frozen. She managed to ball her hand into a fist,her vision tunneled. The world started to go black. She began to pound on the door as the world started to go black, she needed to tell Silas. As she fell backwards into the door the loud noise echoed inside the building. The world around Kere was fading fast. She took the last little bit of strength she had and began tapping on the door. After what felt like hours the door opened.

"Kere?" Silas rushed out the door.

"What's going on-woah." Balor said as he came out the door behind Silas and caught Kere as she slumped to the side.

"Ryan. She took off." Kere pointed down the road as she went limp in Balor's arm.

"Silas, go!" Balor yelled at him as Silas looked down at Kere.

"I got her, go get Ryan. Go!" Balor said and scooped Kere into his arms.

Silas nodded and took off down the stairs to follow after Ryan. Balor let out a loud sigh as he carried Kere back inside.

Chapter Seventeen

The sliding glass doors of the nursing home shut behind her as she exited. The rush of all the emotions from the girl's death sent chills through her. Euryonmos could not feel emotions of her own; so right now she was on a high and nothing would take her down. She walked down the road. She felt better than she had in a million years. A cool night breeze blew by her. She inhaled and a new scent hit her. It was not the smell she expected. It was sweet and pleasant all wrapped up in misery. It was painful, but bitter sweet. She knew in an instant this was the scent she had looked for; this was the smell that would lead her to the girl. She closed her eyes and phased to the far end of the street. As she reappeared she inhaled again. The scent was stronger. She phased quickly to the street light down the road. Once again, Eurynomos took a deep breath. She would find her and quickly.

Ryan rushed down the street, not sure where she was going. She just needed to get away. The world was falling apart and she had just found out things that she only heard of in stories actually existed. She didn't even realize the street lights were flickering as she ran past them. She needed to run. She couldn't go home and deal with Will or even see him after earlier. She couldn't understand anything that was happening and being around Silas and

158

Balor made her feel worse. Kere was a whole other story. Running made her mind clearer. She felt like she was fixing something when everything else right now was out of control.

She glanced to her right and saw an alley and debated running down it. She cringed at the thought of what happened the last time she went down one. She shut her eyes and continued running. Before long she had run to a place just outside the city limits. She recognized the house instantly. She was running home. Her stomach ached as she stopped in front of the white gate. The house was still empty. She walked slowly up the white wooden steps of the porch. She felt sadness and a sense of belonging as she sat down to catch her breath. The little garden boxes along the fence were now all overgrown with weeds. The grass had died and the yard was almost bare dirt. The cracks in the white painted stairs reminded her how long it had been.

She felt the air around her shift and she knew he was there. She kept silent as she waited for him to speak. Part of her had wanted him to find her, to tell her that it was going to be fine. Maybe she even belonged with him. Then a small piece of her wished that whatever creature looking for her would find her and then maybe she would be at peace.

"The car accident. Did…did my mother suffer?" Ryan asked quietly.

"No, she chose to go," Silas said. He came out of the shadows and sat next to her.

"She chose? There's a choice?" Ryan questioned. Several emotions rushed through her: anger, sadness, abandonment.

"Only one soul was supposed to be taken that night." Silas decided to come clean.

"Me..." Ryan whispered. Her stomach felt like it had completely twisted and her heart sank so far down she didn't know if it was inside her any longer.

"She asked me to take her in your place," Silas said quietly.

"Why? Why did you listen? You should have taken me!" Ryan yelled. She turned to face him with tears beading up in her eyes.

" I-" Silas started to say.

"You always do your job. That's what Kere said. Why? Why didn't you take me?" Ryan demanded as a tear rolled down her cheek.

"I couldn't. You were laying there on the cold ground. It was like any other death. But when I went to reap your soul, I couldn't. I reached out and grazed your soul and I felt something. This feeling rushed over me of belonging, want, and need. I had not felt anything in so long. I felt drawn and connected to you. I was torn between doing my job and rebelling against everything I stood for," Silas said, his voice raising and falling in tone as he spoke.

She knew what he meant. She felt it every time he was near. This warmth and acceptance. This peace like her soul had known him forever. His hand reached out and cupped her cheek. His thumb chased away the teardrop.

"Your mother was fading and could see me. She called out, begging me to take her in your place. She gave me the loophole I needed," Silas whispered.

"It's supposed to be me, not her. Me," Ryan whispered.

"I know. But your mother wanted you to live," Silas said. He was trying to figure out what Ryan was feeling.

"I don't know what to feel," Ryan said as she leaned into his hand.

Silas pulled her into him. His arms wrapped around her. She leaned into him with a mixture of emotions swirling through her.

"What are we going to do?" Ryan asked.

"I'm not sure," Silas said quietly. He was enjoying just being close to her.

"This is all happening so fast. I know nothing about you," Ryan muttered.

"I know. All I know is that I need to keep you safe," Silas responded in an effort to explain why he needed to be with her.

"Tell me something, something that's not about you being Death or demons or how I'm supposed to die. Tell me something about you." Ryan changed the subject quickly to have some semblance of control in this all.

"When I was alive my favorite color was brown, like the color of the earth, of the ground. It made me feel connected to something bigger, something more." Silas started talking and watched Ryan's face soften.

"I guess even way back then first date questions existed." Ryan chuckled a little bit.

"Never been on one." Silas laughed.

"You've never been on a date?" Ryan asked in amazement.

"We called it courting but no. I wanted to build a life for myself before I found the woman to spend forever with. I wanted to make sure she didn't have anything to worry about and I wanted...wanted a little bit of adventure before that," Silas said with a hint of sadness.

"The library, it's why you have all those books. You feel like you missed out on living." Ryan ran her hand down his forearm to comfort him.

"Well now you can go anywhere you want," Ryan said. She was trying to make a positive out of it.

"I don't feel anything." Silas murmured.

"What?" Ryan turned in his arms to look at him.

"Nothing. I am empty. Numb. I guess Death has to be, seeing people die and hearing their pleas all the time. But it's not just that, cold, heat...nothing." Silas looked down at her hand on his arm.

"But you said-" Ryan said, starting to bring up something he had said to her but he cut her off.

"Until you. The moment I saw you I felt this pull towards you. It was like something awoke in me and I could feel things again. Only when you're around. I can feel your touch and the cold night air. There's this bond to you, everything in me craves and calls to you," Silas said quietly. He was not sure how all of it was falling out of his mouth.

He watched her face trying not to regret saying it. She was just saying how everything was overwhelming and he goes and vomits all of that.

162

"I feel it, too," she whispered as if she was afraid to say it out loud.

"Hmm?" Silas asked as he took hold of her hand, and wove his fingers through hers.

"That feeling, those feelings that you said. Like we're connected. That I belong with you." Ryan said and closed her fingers around his.

This surge passed through both of them as their hands clasped. Ryan looked at him with a small smile spreading across her lips. Silas leaned down, his mouth moving towards hers. Chills interrupted the moment. Then another wave. Silas groaned. He was being paged.

"Fuck," Silas muttered. His mouth was only inches from Ryan's.

"Fuck?" Ryan asked. She pulled her head back and narrowed her eyebrows.

"A soul is calling," Silas said annoyedly.

"Where are we?" Silas asked as he finally looked around.

"My old home," Ryan said quietly.

"I will get this done quickly and be back. I will send Balor for you. You can't be out in the open," Silas said. The tone of his voice implied that he felt torn.

"It's ok. I can get back to the library quickly. It's not far." Ryan started to stand.

"Fuck. I hate this. Start now so at least I can watch you start." Silas clenched his fists as a strong chill passed through him.

"Ok." Ryan started to go but Silas caught her hand and pulled her back into him.

His mouth came down on hers. He kissed her fiercely. It was as if he had needed it for centuries. His mouth was warm and demanding against hers. Heat spread through her as she wrapped her hands around the back of his neck trying to keep him there. The kiss ended as quickly as it started, leaving them both out of breath.

"Go," he whispered as he leaned his forehead against hers.

"Hurry back," she said reluctantly and stepped back.

He watched her start jogging down the road. He waited until he couldn't see her anymore. Then he gave into the chills and phased.

He reappeared in a small room. The body was laying on the floor. Pieces of flesh and muscle were torn from the corpse. He looked down at the body confusedly. The soul was still trapped inside. He reached down and touched the hand of the girl. As he stood back up, the soul appeared. The girl instantly began sobbing. Silas stared down at the bizarre wounds.

"She ate me after I died," the girl cried to him.

Silas's blood ran cold as he turned back to the girl. Eurynomos was close. Ryan. His chest clenched. He didn't say anything to the girl, still holding her hand he phased. As they reached the In-Between he let go of her.

" Wait here," Silas said to the girl as he let go.

"What? Where am I? Don't leave me!" she cried as she reached out to touch him.

"I am sorry, I have to go. I'll be back. Wait here," Silas repeated. He phased before she could beg him again.

"*H*ey, are you alright?" A woman called to her from just up ahead.

"Fine," Ryan answered. She slowed her run into a jog.

"You don't look fine, sugar. Where are you running to…or from?" the woman asked as Ryan slowed down near her.

"A friend's." Ryan said. She stopped in front of the woman.,Ryan bent over at the waist with her hands on her thighs as she took a deep breath in.

"Are you ok?" Ryan asked. The woman was beautiful and was standing all alone in the dark.

"I'm better now." She smiled and walked towards Ryan.

"Eury." The woman smiled and held out her hand.

"Ryan." Ryan returned the smile and reached out her hand.

"No!" His voice screamed as he phased in between them.

Eurynomos's hand hit Silas's shoulder. He let out a small growl as her touch burned him. He scooted Ryan behind him while his other hand shoved Eurynomos hard in the chest. The force sent her flying back into the brick wall. The impact caused cracks and fractures in the bricks as her body sank into it. As Eurynomos hit the wall her skin slowly began to peel away and was replaced by her iridescent blue one. Ryan hit Silas in the shoulder to try and see around him. She didn't understand what was happening. As she glanced over his shoulder she saw the

woman transforming. Her eerie green eyes locked with Ryan's and she let out a horrid screech.

"Holy shit," Ryan whispered as she sank back behind Silas.

"What the hell is that?" Ryan panicked in her voice as she tried to back away from the creature.

"We need to go. Ryan, look at me. Ryan." Silas tried to get her attention.

"What?" Ryan finally pulled her eyes away from the creature peeling herself off of the wall.

"We need to get out of here," Silas said to her. He placed his hand on the side of her face to get her to focus on him.

"No shit," Ryan blurted out as she tried to see where the creature was. Silas touched her face gently and she locked eyes with him.

"Hold your breath," Silas ordered as he pulled her into him and wrapped his arms around her.

"What?" Ryan asked again as she wrapped her arms around him purely by instinct.

"Hold your breath," Silas repeated.

Eurynomos was up and moving fast. The screeching became louder and higher as she raced towards them. Silas focused all he had on the phase. He went to phase but it felt wrong. He clenched his jaw; it felt like trying to start a car with a low battery. This had never happened before. He had never had trouble shifting. He could hear her running at them. Ryan's panicked eyes looked for him to do something. He felt something click and prayed it worked right. His body wrapped around hers and he phased just as Eurynomos went to snatch them.

Eurynomos's hand went through the air as they were no longer standing there.

"Silas!!" She screeched at the top of her lungs.

Silas crashed to the ground of the library, his chest hitting the floor. He let out several loud coughs. He tried to breathe again as he turned to his side. He had never phased like that before. Silas pushed himself up to his knees and opened his eyes as he pushed past the pain.

"Ryan." He coughed from the impact as he looked for her..

"Woah, woah. Easy." Balor's voice came to his side.

"Ryan. Where is she?" Silas asked. Hevshoved Balor away from him.

"Ryan's not here. Did you find her? Did you lose her? Why the hell are you like this? What happened?" Balor asked the questions rapidly.

"She's not here? I...I phased with her," Silas said. He was now on his feet looking around the room.

"You phased with her!" Balor shouted.

"Eurynomos was going to hurt her, I reacted. Why the fuck do you care anyways. You were setting her up to kill her for Nyx until recently." Silas growled, bowing up at him.

"Well I'm not now and I do," Balor said, getting in his face.

"Idiots!" Kere yelled from the couch as she swung her legs off of it and stood.

"You shouldn't move so quickly." Balor went to her side to steady her.

"Am I in some alternate universe?" Kere asked. She moved her arm away from Balor.

"He phased with Ryan. I assume she was conscious, so she could be anywhere. And also I am done being helpful. Frankly, it's annoying and it sucks. I hope you fall on your face when you go to move again," Balor snapped at Kere.

"Enough. You phased with Ryan?" Kere questioned Silas.

"Yes," Silas responded. He shut his eyes to see if he could feel where she would have gone.

"I've done it before. Something... Something felt wrong this time," Silas said. He looked at his hands.

"You need to go now. She's-" Kere started to say.

"She's in the In-Between," Silas whispered.

"How?" Balor asked as he looked at them confusedly.

"I can feel her there," Silas said. He closed his eyes as he tried to gather his strength to phase.

"But ho-" Balor started to say.

"Part of her soul is already tainted from her near death experiences. She is able to be there because she is supposed to be there," Kere narrowed her eyes at Silas as if telling him.

"I know! Enough!" Silas yelled and then he went up in smoke.

"Well..." Balor said quietly before he walked away.

"Where are you going?" Kere snapped at him as she held onto the arm of the couch to steady herself.

"All this helping is making me feel sick. I figure visiting a local bar and stirring up some fights and chaos

will get rid of the ick," Balor said without looking back at her.

"You need to go with them," Kere ordered him.

Balor growled and shifted. His hand went to her throat as he phased in front of her. Kere didn't even move as she locked eyes with him. He squeezed gently as he moved into her.

"You do not tell me what I need to do," Balor growled. His eyes glowed as he spoke.

Kere flicked her wrist and a blade pressed against his groin. A small smirk appeared on her lips.

"You may have me by the throat but I have you by the balls," she said quietly.

"Want to see who gives first?" She snickered as Balor squeezed tighter.

She pressed her blade further into his groin and he grinned at her threat. He pulled her closer to him.

"I only play games I can win," Balor's lips brushed against Kere's as he spoke.

Kere watched his eyes for a second and then his lips pressed into hers. The kiss was hungry and demanding. His teeth pulled her lower lip into his mouth as his other hand grabbed her hip. She kissed him back and her tongue playfully demanded his tongue to submit to hers. She pulled his lip into her mouth and bit down.

"Ouch!" he yelped and pulled back from her.

Blood dribbled down his chin as he let go of Kere's throat. He touched his finger to his lip looking down at his own blood.

"That was cheap." Balor smirked.

"I play to win." Kere grinned.

"We've been playing this game for far too long, haven't we?" Balor asked. He reached around her and pulled a tissue out of the box sitting on the side table.

"Help us," Kere pleaded as she grabbed his wrist.

Balor paused and looked at her. He frowned then shook his head slightly.

"The In-Between is huge, add the banshees and Nyx... Silas is going to get himself in trouble," Kere whispered.

"I'm a demon," Balor said dismissively.

"So?" Kere started to say.

"I like to bargain." Balor grinned.

"We don't have time," Kere yelled as she clenched her hand into a fist.

"One night with me, you alone. I will help you save your brother and the girl. That's what I want in exchange for my help." Balor smirked.

"Are you fucking kidding me?" Kere snapped.

"Not at all." Balor's eyes danced in amusement watching her face.

"Fine, but we move now." Kere's eyes burned into his.

"After you." Balor grinned.

"I thought you liked the girl." Kere accused. She stepped away from him as she began to phase.

"I found her interesting. There's something otherworldly about her. But you. You are entirely different. You I..I have wanted for a very long time." Balor admitted. His voice dropped as he stepped back into her.

"And you have wanted me," he continued as he watched her struggle with her feelings.

170

“You're too weak to phase still, let me help,” Balor said and slipped his hand around her waist.

“I guess if I have to pay a fee for your services. I might as well take all the help you're supplying.” Kere said. It was meant to be an insult but her voice failed her.

“There you go.” Balor laughed as he pulled her closer up against him and phased.

Chapter Eighteen

"**S**he failed!" Nyx's voice vibrated off the walls of the cave she had made her home.

She was peering down into a small pool of water where she had watched Eurynomos fail. The greedy hungry thing only thought about feeding her own wants and needs. She let her own desire get the best of her. Nyx should have never sent her. Silas - if only she could sway him. He was utterly perfect. Strong, fierce, fearless. A soldier in every way. She had created him perfectly. Now this girl was ruining everything. The girl was meant to be hers! The key to letting Nyx release her army into the human world. She would make it her own realm. She had to take this into her own hands. Balor failed, Eurynomos failed…Kere. Where was that girl? She was always off doing her own thing. She wouldn't agree to it anyways. Nyx could never turn her fully against Silas. She grasped the stones of the pool and looked into the dark cool water for answers. A banshee's cry tore her away from the water.

It was lingering in the doorway of the cave, whining like a lost dog. Nyx groaned. She walked to the front of the cave entrance and then it hit her.

"Someone new is here," Nyx announced. She closed her eyes and drew on the new energy.

"She's here…" Nyx whispered, excitement oozing out of her as she rushed out of the cave.

She rolled over, the surface was hard and crunched underneath her. The smell of dirt floated up around her. She propped herself up on her forearms as she lifted her head up. Tall thin blades of beige grass swayed in front of her. She was completely concealed in it. She slowly pulled herself up to her knees. Even kneeling she was still covered by the grass. She looked around trying to figure out where she was. Her body felt strange, her limbs shaky like jello.

"Silas," she whispered as she touched her arms, trying to get them to stop feeling so strange.

She slowly stood up and ran her hand over the long grass. She had been here before. She looked around in her dreams, as she searched for the source of a sound in the distance. It started out low and quiet like a soft whisper. It was growing louder by the second. She recognized it now. It was crying.

Stay away from crying. Silas's words rang in her ears.

She dropped to her knees, ducking into the long grass. She didn't know where she was but she knew this was somewhere different. This was not like any place she had been. Was she dreaming again?

"Silas, where are you?" she whispered. She dropped closer to the ground as the cries became closer and louder.

"Ryan." Her name was sung out in a haunted tune.

Someone knew her here. She hesitates. Silas said to stay away from the crying but nothing about someone who called her name. She gritted her teeth, not sure what to do. The crying slowly turned into a humming noise.

"Ryan, come out," the voice called again.

Ryan stood slowly and looked out across the field. She locked eyes with a beautiful woman with stunning green eyes. She smiled brightly at her. She felt a connection to her. She knew her on some level. The longer she looked into her eyes the more she needed to go to her. Ryan felt the world around her fade and she began drifting towards her.

"That's it, come here child. Don't be afraid. We are one and the same," Nyx held out her hand.

Ryan was being pulled towards her and the humming from the banshees surrounding them turned into a song. It was haunting and like magic she was being pulled towards Nyx. Her hand stretched outward. Ryan needed her. There was something there, like she belonged.

"That's it. You must willingly choose me." Nyx smiled at her.

The humming began to rattle around in Ryan's mind; she paused as images flooded her mind. The world around her faded. She was watching it like a movie scene playing out in front of her.

"Please." The cry came from a woman with soft brown hair and honey colored eyes.

"What do you want, human?" Nyx grumbled as she stared down at her.

"Please, my daughter. Please save her, goddess of the night. Save her from the darkness," the woman holding a small limp child cried.

Nyx sneered and then her eyes glowed as a vision came to her. She was taken aback but silent about what she had seen.

"I will save your child but the price will be paid down the line. One of your descendents will help free me," Nyx said quietly.

"Free you, goddess?" the woman asked quietly.

"Yes. I got a glimpse of my future and I need your line to survive," Nyx said bitterly.

The world flashed back to normal and Ryan was left in a daze. What had she just seen?

"Ryan, come now." Nyx smiled, still holding out her hand to her.

---

*H*e phased into the In-Between with fear rushing through him. How was he going to find her? She was in danger here. He prayed that she remembered to stay away from the crying. The banshees were mindless without Nyx but under orders they were deadly. He raced down the dock and for the grassy field. Something was telling him she was there. Then he heard the banshees wailing and in the pit of his stomach he knew they had found her. He phased to the center of the field in a blink of an eye. He spun around trying to locate them and that's when he saw her.

Silas saw her across the long grass. The banshees circled around them blocking any interference between Ryan and Nyx. His stomach twisted and panic flooded him. He closed his eyes and shifted.

175

"Ryan!" he yelled as he appeared in front of her.

Ryan's eyes were glossed over as she walked into him like a zombie. Her eyes were fixated on Nyx.

"Stand aside, Silas. This has nothing to do with you. The girl is meant to be mine. Move." Nyx's voice screeched over the wailing of the banshees.

"Ryan!" Silas shouted as he physically blocked her way to Nyx.

"Come back!" he yelled. He placed his hands on her shoulders and shook her.

"Silas, this will be your last warning," Nyx threatened.

"Ryan, you can't go to her. You don't belong here," Silas begged as he reached out and cupped the side of her face.

A sharp piercing feeling went through his chest. Silas gasped as the tip of a blade poked out of the center of his chest. Blood started to drip down the front of him as Nyx's laughter filled the air. She pulled the blade back out of him. He gritted his teeth as he tasted blood in his mouth.

"Ryan…" Silas tried to form a sentence through the pain.

"Silas?" Ryan's voice sounded groggy as her eyes cleared. She looked at him as if she was just now realizing he was there.

"Silas!" Ryan yelled in concern when she saw the blood and the hole in his chest.

She immediately started to apply pressure to the wound as she tried to grasp what was happening.

"You need to get away from her," Silas said as blood started to drip out of his mouth.

"Who? We need help. Help!" Ryan yelled.

"Ryan dear, never mind him. He is fine. Come to me." Nyx said tried to lure her back into the trance.

"Help!" Ryan yelled again. She pulled Silas closer to her as she tried to still hold his chest.

"Ryan." Balor's voice came from behind her.

"Balor! Please!" she cried as Silas started to nod out.

"Balor, are you betraying me?!" Nyx screamed as she went to step forward.

She paused, angry she could not make the girl come to her. Nyx could not take her by force. Ryan had to choose her. She growled when Balor ignored her. Balor phased next to Ryan, seconds later Kere was on the other side of her. She placed a hand on Ryan with the other she grabbed Silas's shoulder. She locked eyes with Nyx, her eyes glowing bright red as she dared Nyx to come closer. Balor mimicked the same move. He nodded to Kere.

"Ryan, hold your breath and we all need to think of the same place. If we don't we can lose you again." Kere ordered.

"The place we all met," Kere said, hoping Ryan realized it was the library.

Balor nodded to Kere and with the small motion they phased with Nyx screamed in defeat as they faded out.

Chapter Nineteen

*H*er skin felt like she had been microwaved. Everything burned as she curled into a ball, suppressing a scream. Her body felt misplaced and like she couldn't communicate with her limbs. They were lifeless pieces of jello.

"It's ok, take a deep breath in." She heard a familiar voice.

She opened her eyes to see Kere rubbing her back. She faded back into reality as she came out of the haze. She took a deep breath in as her vision refocused.

"Fucking bleeding all over the place." Balor muttered, wiping his hands on his pants.

Bleeding... the word snapped inside Ryan's head. She jumped up to look for Silas. He was lying on the floor, eyes rolled back in his head. Balor was hovering over him with a look of annoyance on his face. Ryan skidded across the floor to him and grabbed either side of the hole where the blade had ripped the fabric. As she pulled, the black fabric shredded in her hands.

"We need medical supplies," she said quickly. The hole was through and through.

"We need a hospital. He's not going to make it like this." Ryan tried to keep the panic out of her voice.

"Doll, he's fine," Balor said as he looked down at his blood stained clothing.

"He's been stabbed through the chest. He's not fine. Kere tell him that he's not okay," Ryan snapped angrily.

"He's fine. He's Death. It takes more than a stab wound to kill Death." Kere smiled at how much Ryan cared.

"What? But all the blood... and he's not responding," Ryan said. She looked worriedly from Silas to Kere.

"Yeah, he's making a bloody mess all right," Balor muttered.

"Do you die if I stab you?" Ryan narrowed her eyes at Balor.

"Easy, doll." Balor laughed.

"Nyx probably has some type of poison on the blade. It will take longer to heal and that's probably the reason he's unconscious. Clever bitch," Kere grumbled while looking over the wound.

The wound's edge was black in color like it had been burnt. Kere frowned. Nyx had dipped the blade in something.

"It's nightshade," Balor said quietly.

"How do you know?" Kere asked.

"She likes the side effects, we're not alive but we're not dead so our bodies will be in pain and suffer. Nightshade blurs the vision, gives headaches, causes delirium, hallucinations, slows the heart and breathing. Lastly, paralysis." He gestured towards Silas as confirmation of his point.

"What do we do?" Ryan asked. Her eyes still studied the wound.

"Nothing." Balor shuddered.

"Nothing?!" Ryan snapped.

"It's poison; it has to work its way through his system. The wound will slowly heal. He's lucky he's unconscious," Balor said quietly.

"Paralyzed doesn't mean unconscious," Kere said bitterly.

"Right." Balor sighed. He looked at her and then Ryan.

"There's gotta be something," Ryan said. She got up and began walking down an aisle of books.

"Where are you going?" Kere yelled at her back.

"To do something," Ryan yelled.

"Help me get him up on the couch." Kere sighed and looked at Balor.

"He looks fine on the floor," Balor muttered as he bent over and grabbed Silas underneath his shoulder.

"Just lift him." Kere groaned as she grabbed Silas's feet.

They hoisted him onto the couch. Balor took a step back and let out another groan at having more blood on him.

"You're racking up a lot of favors." Balor smirked at Kere.

"Well I'd rather owe you then cheat you out of it," Kere said, rolling her eyes.

"I'm glad you acknowledge you owe me. I am going to hold you to it." Balor grinned. His eyes danced with mischief as he looked her up and down.

"You've always been a pervert," Kere said. She adjusted Silas's head.

"For you..yes." Balor chuckled.

"I found it!" Ryan announced. She walked back to them with a book in her hand.

"Found what?" Balor sighed and rubbed his temples as he sat down in a chair.

"How to fix him." Ryan rolled her eyes.

"What do you think you have?" Kere asked. She walked over to Ryan.

"Yarrow." Ryan smiled.

"Yarrow…" Kere repeated quietly.

"It's basically the opposite of nightshade. It can be used to treat wounds and fever. I figured if we are going all magical and supernatural. It should work," Ryan said with a shrug.

"Yarrow, really?" Balor said, shaking his head.

"It couldn't hurt to try," Ryan shrugged again.

"Love, light, protection. She's right, it's worth a shot," Kere said quietly.

"I'm going to go gather some things to at least clean the wound. If this is a hideout, I'm sure there's something here for that. With Eurynomos hunting me I should stay put. You two need to find the yarrow." Ryan said, folding her arms across chest.

"No." Balor sighed.

"Yes," Kere said and narrowed her eyes at Balor.

"He will be fine," Balor said, getting frustrated.

"We need him to be fine now," Ryan said. She clenched her hands into fists.

"I-" Balor started to say but Ryan put her hand up to stop him.

"I am going to go find stuff to clean the wound. You two figure out who's finding the yarrow," Ryan said as she turned on her heels and walked away.

"Balor-" Kere started to say but he was on his feet and in her face within a blink of an eye.

"Do you understand that leaving right now puts whoever walks out of this protected place in harm's way?" Balor said in a stern voice.

"Yes-" Kere started to say but Balor's finger landed on her lips.

"Do you understand that we all just crossed Nyx? Now we all have a bounty on our heads." Balor's voice dropped low as he spoke.

"Fine, I will go. Cow-" Kere was cut off as Balor's hand draped around the back of her neck and tilted her head upwards.

"You are staying put. I will go but it comes with a price," Balor whispered. He stared into her eyes.

"I am not playing your game," Kere whispered as she fought the excitement that was flipping around in her stomach.

"You enjoy our games more than you care to admit but the way your eyes gloss over and how your breath hitches in your chest tells me the truth," Balor whispered into her ear.

"What's the price?" Kere whispered.

"This one is simple," Balor said, moving away from her ear.

"And it is?" Kere questioned as her eyes searched his.

"Admit it." Balor smiled.

"Admit what?" Kere said. Her eyebrows furrowed in confusion.

"Admit that you want me." Balor grinned.

"Admit that I want you?" Kere said, trying to force a laugh.

"Admit that you want me and I will go get the yarrow." Balor said with his other hand pulling her hips against him.

"You think I want you when I could have anyone," Kere sneered.

"Yes." Balor grinned.

"I-" Kere started to say but Balor pinned her to the wall behind them.

"I want you. I've wanted you for decades. You are not the only one who can have anyone," Balor whispered to her.

Kere's skinned buzzed and her heart vibrated in her chest. It was true that they had been playing this love-hate game for years and she had wanted him to want her badly. She could feel her stomach tumbling with excitement as her eyes lingered on his lips.

"Admit it. I can see it." Balor grinned his fingertips tucked under her shirt and began tracing along her pants line, watching her shiver at the slightest touch.

"Fine," Kere whispered.

"Fine…" Balor smirked. He leaned closer to her while his fingertips still brushed her skin.

"I…I want you," Kere whispered and it felt like her chest had exploded. Fear mixed with the excitement of finally saying the words out loud oozed out of her. She was terrified of how he would react.

"I know." He grinned as his hand moved to the back of her head and pulled her lips into his.

His mouth claimed hers. The kiss was fierce and aggressive. His mouth demanded what he wanted from her and she gave in. His tongue slipped into her mouth, fighting for dominance. His hand squeezed her hip as he deepened the kiss and pressed her harder into the wall. Her body was lit up with chills as she trembled in his grasp.

"Umm…This is great and all. Happy for you two but Silas is bleeding and unconscious. There are also demons who want me dead, so, can we pause the sexy time and someone get the yarrow," Ryan said with frustration.

"Jealous babe?" Balor chuckled and pulled away from Kere.

"Not in the slightest." Ryan rolled her eyes.

"Balor is going to get the yarrow and he will be quick," Kere said breathlessly as she straightened her shirt.

"Of course love," Balor said to her. The way his voice deepened when he said the word love sent chills through her.

He locked eyes with her as he phased out. Kere let out a long breath as she tried to control her heart rate. Ryan kneeled on the floor with some medical supplies.

"Are you ok with him?" Kere asked quietly.

"Yeah. I'm just going to clean up this wound and try to do something to make him better," Ryan said as she dipped a clean cloth into the warm water.

"I need some air, if that's ok," Kere said quietly. Her eye lingered on the wall Balor had pushed her up against.

"I'm good," Ryan said quietly.

"Thanks. I won't be far." Kere closed her eyes as she phased as well.

"Must be nice, just poof and you're wherever you want to be," Ryan muttered as she pressed the cloth into Silas's wound gently.

She watched his face. His brows pulled together slightly as if he could feel the cloth against his skin. She frowned. The shirt really needed to come off so she could get better access. She grabbed a pair of scissors she had taken to cut the bandage material. She grabbed the bottom of his shirt and began cutting up the middle and peeled it away from his skin. She looked down at the wound. It was getting worse. She dipped the cloth back into the water and pressed it to the wound. She let the water seep into the wound to flush it the best she could. She repeated and this time Silas made a small hiss noise.

"Ryan?" he groaned as he struggled to come back to consciousness.

"I'm here. Shh, you're hurt," Ryan said and presed the cloth against his skin again.

"Ryan!" Silas yelled. He jumped up and grabbed her wrist.

"Silas, it's ok, you're safe," Ryan said. Her free hand brushed a lock of his dark hair out of his eyes.

"I'm safe?" Silas repeated what she said. He was confused; he wasn't the one that needed to be safe.

"Yes. I got you." Ryan smiled gently at him.

"You got me?" He smirked and tried to straighten himself up.

"Are you ok? Are you hurt?" Silas asked. He studied her face.

"I am fine." Ryan smiled.

"You're fine?" His voice was getting groggy.

"Yes, you made sure I was safe," Ryan said. Her thumb stroked his cheek.

"Where are we?" Silas asked, trying to scan the room to make sure they were safe.

"Your library," Ryan said. She tried to get him to lie back.

"Where is Kere? I need to tell her Nyx knows. We need to come up with a plan to keep you safe." Silas clenched his jaw as he tried to sit up more.

"No, what you need to do is lie down. You're wounded. Kere is just outside," Ryan said firmly.

"I'll heal," Silas said, though the pain surging through him told him something was different this time. He had been hurt before and it was painful but something else was going on.

"You're not just wounded, you're poisoned," Ryan said. She wouldn't budge on the fact that he needed to rest.

"Ryan I will-" Silas started to say but a wave of pain caught him off guard.

He squeezed his eyes shut as he leaned back. The more he fought the pain, the stronger the gnawing burning sensation spread. Sweat beaded across his forehead and he began to feel shaky. His limbs began to go numb.

"Nightshade," he whispered, pressing back into the couch.

"It's ok, Balor's gone to get yarrow. It will reverse it," Ryan said. She squeezed his hand Fear pitted in her stomach as she watched him get worse in front of her.

The black tint around the wound began to spread. He took in a shallow inhale of air as if it hurt to breathe.

"Please, rest," Ryan whispered and leaned her forehead against his.

"I can't, we need to make sure nothing can get you," Silas muttered.

As he tried to get up another ripple of pain went through him and he lost complete feeling of his legs. A small tinge of fear began eating away at him. He was Death…Death couldn't die, right?

"Stop," Ryan yelled at him. She put her hands on his shoulders and made him lie back down on the couch.

"Rest, we will figure it out after you're better," Ryan said firmly. She was trying to hold on to some hope as she ignored the poison spreading.

Silas groaned, lying back only because his strength was depleting once again.

"It's ok. You're gonna be fine. You're safe," he grunted. He placed his hand over the top of hers as his eyes shuttered closed.

Ryan felt her heart tangle into itself. He couldn't leave her. Her eyes scanned his face. His dark brows bunched in a frown as he tried to mask the pain he was feeling. She barely knew him but she couldn't imagine her life without him now. Whatever was going on between them was now on a deeper level. She couldn't- she would not- let this happen. If only she didn't freak out and take off, he would be ok right now. He let out another painful groan.

"I'm so sorry," Ryan whispered. She held his hand tightly.

He went to talk to her but his face scrunched up in pain as he fought back another groan.

"Damn it, where are you Balor?" Ryan cursed as she looked over her shoulder.

"Hang in there, ok. Please.....I need you," Ryan begged.

Ryan looked down at the wound and the skin around it had turned completely black. Black lines that looked like veins stretched out over his skin. The poison seeped further into him. He clenched his jaw as the black spider veins spread further up his chest.

"Damn it. Where the fuck are you Ba-" Ryan went to curse again.

"Ta-da," Balor announced as he phased into the room. He held up a green plant with feather-like leaves and small white flowers.

"About fucking time," Ryan muttered. She got up and snatched the plant out of his hand.

"Umm.. Thank you…Oh you're so welcomed Ryan, it was no trouble at all," Balor huffed at her and rolled his eyes.

"Shut up," Ryan muttered as she rushed off to the back room where she found the medical supplies.

"Where are you going?" Balor yelled after her.

"Just watch him," Ryan yelled back.

"When the hell did I become a babysitter and an errand boy," Balor grumbled. He looked down at Silas.

"Mmm, that's not good. She's a clever bitch. I'm sure her plan was to capture Ryan while you were incapacitated. Enough time to do whatever she was

planning with her." Balor reached down and touched Silas black poison skin.

Silas groaned and flinched as Balor touched him. His eyes fluttered slightly and upon seeing Balor he growled and launched forward grabbing him by the throat.

"Where is she?!" Silas yelled. Sweat started to bead across his forehead while he tried to fight through the pain to hurt Balor.

"All right, we all know that poisons spread quicker the faster your heart beats. So why don't you let go before you piss a very spicy brunette off and I have to deal with more problems," Balor said, prying Silas's hand from his neck.

"Where is she?" Silas demanded as he let go of Balor.

"She's fine, she went to go save you," Balor groaned,and rolled his eyes.

"You let her leave?!" Silashot back up.

"Fucking relax, she's somewhere in here doing something with a plant. It might be easier if we just let you be poisoned. You're super annoying." Balor shoved him back down into the couch.

"I hate you," Silas growled. His eyes closed as the pain became overwhelming.

"Yeah, me too, bud," Balor said, hitting him in the shoulder.

"What's wrong with you!" Ryan yelled. She got back just in time to see Balor hit Silas.

"Move," Ryan growled at Balor as she swatted him like a small child.

"Fine," he snapped as he got up. He shook his head and walked away.

"Silas," Ryan said, coming to his side and placing a bowl down on the end table.

"Silas. I need you to drink this." Ryan put a cup to his lips.

The warm liquid hit his lips and he forced himself to drink it. He felt it hit his stomach and a warm tingling went through his body. Ryan pulled the cup away and set it down on the end table. She grabbed the bowl taking the paste she made into her hand and pressed it into the wound. Silas hissed slightly as the paste stung. She reached down and rinsed her hands in the bowl that still had water from when she cleaned his wound. She dried them on a towel then grabbed bandage material and placed it gently on top of the wound.

"Silas, I need you to sit up," Ryan said. She needed to apply the paste to the other side of the hole and wrap the bandage around him.

He nodded slowly and tried to sit up. She tried to hold the bandage to his chest and hold him up but it didn't work out. She heard a sigh from behind her and then Silas was being pushed forward.

"Here I got him," Balor said quietly.

Ryan didn't question him but quickly applied the paste to the wound on his back and wrapped the bandage. She nodded to Balor when she was done and he gently laid him back.

"What do we do now?" Balor asked her.

"Kinda funny you're asking me." Ryan chuckled a little.

"Why?" Balor smirked.

"Well, he's Death and you're a demon but yet you're asking some girl who is supposed to be dead what to do next." Ryan laughed and shook her head.

"Yeah, I guess it is funny." Balor laughed a little.

"We wait. I'm going to sit with him. Get him to drink more. Hopefully it reverses everything quickly. I really didn't read anything else to help," Ryan said quietly.

"Ok. Silas has this place pretty guarded, no one unwelcomed can phase in," Balor answered the unasked question Ryan had in the back of her mind.

"I got him. You should go check on Kere. She needed air." Ryan nodded to the door.

"Ok. I'll go check on her." Balor nodded before he turned and walked away.

"Hey…he's Death. What happens if he's not there to take souls to the after life? I mean he's unconscious right now," Ryan asked quietly.

"He only takes the souls who have trouble passing. If they are ready to move on and know then they go…as you humans like to say "go into the light." Most of the souls Silas is taking are the ones who would struggle leaving, So let hope they're all ready to move on until he's better" Balor explained.

"Hmm," Ryan said understandingly. There would be alot of souls for one person but just ones that struggle made it seem a little less. She shook her head slightly at her thoughts.

Balor shrugged as if he heard her thoughts and moved towards the exit. Ryan grabbed the cup on the end table and held it in her hand for a second as she watched

the color in Silas's face slowly come back. She glanced at his chest and the black lines were beginning to retreat. It was working.

Chapter Twenty

"**C**haron." His voice was deep as he stood on the dock waiting for the ferry to come back.

Charon locked eyes with him and gritted his teeth. He didn't know what the other man wanted but it wasn't good. He cringed internally as the boat hit the dock. Charon took a deep breath before addressing him.

"Acheron. To what do I owe the pleasure of your visit?" Charon asked as he leaned on his oar.

Acheron was tall with eyes completely black and skin a ghostly white. He was the god of the very river Charon ferries souls across.

"I came here as a friendly warning. Only because we are essentially co-workers," Acheron said quietly.

"A warning? A warning for whom?" Charon shifted in the boat.

"A warning for your friend who unsurprisingly is gone again. You tell Death he left me no choice. My river is being flooded with more and more souls. Souls that do not deserve to be in the river of pain; innocents. He is slacking in his job and something or someone is dumping them in my river," Acheron bellowed, causing the river waters to shake rapidly.

"I will let him know," Charon said as he tried to keep his balance on the ferry.

" I have gone to Aeacus. He will be judged once he is found," Acheron warned him.

"Aeacus! You've gone to one of the three gods of judgment. You didn't even give him a chance to correct the issue," Charon snapped.

"Silence! He is a vital part of the underworld and the after life. This is not a joke. This is disgraceful. If he was doing his job there would be no innocents in my waters!" Acheron yelled, the water began to rise in an attempt to tip the boat.

"Acheron, be careful. With no Death and no ferryman, where do you think all the souls will go?" Charon warned.

"It's too late now. Warn your friend. I am telling you because you have never faltered from your task. Not even when it was your own from the human world. You have always been honorable. I am not so sure what happened with Death but it cannot continue. Fate will find a new soul worthy to guide the souls home," Acheron said as he turned his back on Charon and stepped into the black river.

The river formed around his ankles and as if he was on a platform ushered him away just as quickly as he came.

"Damn it," Charon muttered. He glanced around hoping to see Kere or Silas but the In-Between's dock was empty.

How was he going to warn them? He could not leave his post. Or could he? With no Death, there would be no souls. No souls meant no one to ferry. He would be quick. If Silas was not in the In-Between he was in his hideout. Charon had never been there but he knew where it was. He debated with himself as he had never left his post before. He took a shaky step from the ferry on to the

194

wooden dock. He paused as his foot pressed into the old
wood. He took a deep breath and stepped off the boat.

    Her screams echoed louder than moans of the
banshees that surrounded her. She was so close. The girl
was here and just out of reach.

"Damn them! Damn them all! How dare they
interfere! How dare they think they can keep me here," Nyx
yelled.

"I will not stay here! I am the goddess of the night!
Not limbo! I will leave this place," she vowed to herself.

It felt like centuries had passed since they had
gathered to banish her. She spun in a circle as she
screamed. Her black hair flew out around her and sparkled
as if the stars were in her hair. She sank to the dirt floor of
the field and looked up at the gray sky. She reached her
hand up to it, wanting to paint it black. She wanted to see
the moon and the lights from the stars. She missed
bringing the night every night.

"You worked beautiful magic when you were
allowed to bring the night." A deep voice came from behind
her.

She let out a loud condescending laugh and shook
her head. She rolled her eyes as she knew the voice.

"Augusyon. Why have you come here, to this gray
and dreadful place? Hell getting too cold for you?" Nyx
chuckled.

"They would have let you. You could have stayed
the goddess of the night. Painting the sky with your magic

every night but it wasn't enough for you. You wanted it to
be night, always. You lusted after power," Augusyon
explained.

"You…What do you know about anything? Your
place is in Hell. Why have you come to bother me?" Nyx
asked as she stood., Her eyes narrowed on him as a ring
around her iris began to glow.

"Unforunetly being a Duke of Hell means I have to
clean up other people's fuck ups," Augusyon snapped.

"Fuck ups?" Nyx asked curiously. She wondered if
word had gotten out about her plans.

"The river of pain is overflowing with lost souls,
souls that do not belong there. Normally, I would not care
but souls are not making it to after life or hell. Acheron is
angry and has complained. So now I have to find our grim
reaper. Death has not been doing his job. There's the
question of how the souls are getting into the river. Do you
know anything?" Augusyon asked.

"Not really, I know Silas has been hanging out too
long in the human world. He may finally have given in to
temptation." Nyx smiled. He had no clue that it was her and
the banshees.

"Anything else?" Augusyon asked as he eyed her
suspiciously.

"From what I am told he hangs out somewhere on
Hollow Road. Might check there." Nyx smiled.

Eurynomos had told her she had followed the girl's
scent there before she had run into her. Nyx held back her
grin; she might not have to do anything at all. It seemed
like the underworld was stepping up. They had no clue

how close she was to escaping this prison. She just needed the girl.

"Hollow Road. Thank you," Augusyon said. He continued to look at her. There was something off about all of this and she was being so helpful.

Augusyon phased in front of her his mind thinking of Hollow Road as he stared down Nyx. Something still wasn't right.

"Look, I don't have to do anything now. He will handle Silas and the girl will be unprotected." Nyx chuckled.

"What's so special about this girl?" Eurynomos asked as she stepped out of the shadows.

"What are you doing back? And empty handed?" Nyx sneered at her.

"There were too many bodies, too many smells. I wanted them all. I was trying to get the girl for you but-" Eurynomos started to explain.

"But your own gluttony took over. Pathetic," Nyx snapped.

"I just needed air. I know where the girl is." Eurynomos bowed her head.

"I need her. Her bloodline runs back to the original banshee. With her by my side I will be able to leave this place. We can open a portal to the human world. Her blood will break my curse," Nyx said quietly.

"You just need her blood? I can bring her blood," Eurynomos said like it was no big deal.

"No, in death she has to choose between light and dark. She needs to choose darkness and join me." Nyx sighed.

"Well then we kill her, take her blood and threaten her friends. If she doesn't choose, we hurt them." Eurynomos shrugged.

"That would be forcing her," Nyx said while shaking her head no.

"Well…we make her forget," Eurynomos said quietly, unsure of her statement.

"What?" Nyx turned to look at Eurynomos.

"Make it so I am the next Death. I will guide her to the In-Between and to you. But first…forget me not. We crush them and make her drink them once she arrives. We tell her it's a passage and she will not be able to enter without it. She will forget everything. You should be her guide and befriend her. She chooses you. You get your escape and I get to be Death." Eurynomos grinned.

"You know... people misjudge you. Go. I will be waiting." Nyx's laughter echoed above the moans of the banshees in the distance. Everything was slowly starting to weave together.

Ryan watched him slowly flutter his eyes open. It felt like hours. She kept catching herself clenching her jaw or holding her breath while she waited for some sign that things were going to be ok.

"Silas." Ryan leaned forward to look at him.

"Ryan?" Silas said as Ryan's face came into focus.

"Hey! Tell me you're ok?" Ryan said as she took his hand into hers.

"I'm ok." Silas smiled as he squeezed her hand.

198

"Does it hurt?" Ryan said looking at his chest, now that the poison was gone the wound had closed up like it never happened.

"No." Silas smirked. He watched her face that was filled with worry turn to suspicion.

"Promise." Silas said reassuringly.

Ryan narrowed her eyes at him in disbelief. She slowly reached out and poked the spot where the blade had pierced his chest. He fought back a wince but his eye twitched ever so slightly. Ryan frowned instantly.

"Lies." Ryan said as her lips pursed together and she shook her head.

"We need to get ready. We have to plan for something coming. I need to make sure you're protected. Nyx is up to something," Silas said as he slowly stood.

"Who is Nyx?" Ryan asked. She moved slightly so he could stand.

"She was the goddess of night. One of the most powerful goddesses. She was made at the dawn of time. She brings the night. She would create beautiful star shows and the moon always seemed to glow extra bright, but something happened. It wasn't enough for her. She grew jealous of day and wanted it to always be night. Several gods got together and joined forces and banished her to the only place that could hold her- the In-Between. The only thing I can think of is that she wants out," Silas said as he tried to sort through everything.

"Where's Kere and Balor?" Silas asked. He looked about the room.

"Kere went to get air and I sent Balor after her," Ryan explained.

"Ok, I'll go get them." Silas started to walk to the door.

"Are you ok? Can you-" Ryan started to say but Silas looked at her over his shoulder with a smirk on his lips.

"I've been around for centuries. A little poison and a stab wound is nothing," he said with a wink.

The smirk and wink made Ryan's knees feel weak. Her stomach flipped with excitement. She could feel the tips of her ears turning red as she watched him turn and walk out of the library.

Silas smiled as he walked away. He could see the tips of her ears turn red and he watched her lips twitch slightly as she fought the urge to smile. She was falling for him. As he reached for the door handle to the outside, dread pitted in his stomach. She was falling for him...how could he keep her alive? The anxiety gnawed away at him. He pulled the door open and stepped out onto the cement stairs then shut it quickly behind him.

"Kere..." Silas said. He turned around and quickly went on the defensive, his hands balled into fists.

"Silas." His deep voice purred as he held Kere by her hair.

Balor was unconscious at the bottom of the staircase. Kere's eyes were trying to warn him as Silas looked from her to him.

"Augusyon, what brings you to the human realm?" Silas tried to remain respectful.

"You" Augusyon's voice was filled with anger and he narrowed his eyes at Silas.

"Well here I am. How can I help you?" Silas asked in a tone that verged on threatening.

Augusyon yanked Kere's head back hard. He placed his hand on her chin as he looked at Silas, threatening him with snapping Kere's neck. His fingers tracing her jawline.

"You're coming back with me. You have neglected your duties for far too long. You have compromised the whole underworld and afterlife with your selfishness. You are heading for judgment." Augusyon snapped.

"Silas go!" Kere winced.

"I will rip her head from her body and place it on a spike in whatever place you end up so she can stare at you for eternity!" he bellowed at Silas and yanked Kere's head further back.

Silas gritted his teeth. Kere's eyes were filled with fear but she was trying her best to not show it.

"Fine, let Kere go. She had nothing to do with my indiscretions." Silas said.

"Come here," Augusyon ordered.

Silas glanced back to the door. Ryan was just inside. If he took any longer he knew she would wander out. Augusyon was not acting like he knew about her. If he found out he would end her instantly. He needed to make this quick but at the same time everything in him was telling him to fight. His stomach was twisting in on itself and the blood rushing through his limbs was telling him to not give in; that he could take Augusyon.

"Better move boy. I am not patient," Augusyon growled.

"Give me a second." Silas's shoulders folded in defeat.

"What?" Augusyon asked, baffled.

"You have Kere, I will not let anything happen to her. Give me one last second inside my sanctuary and I will willingly come with no fight," Silas said quietly.

"You know there is no escape from me. I will kill Kere and that fool down there. Everything and everyone you have ever cared for," Augusyon growled.

"I know," Silas muttered.

"Five minutes," Augusyon said reluctantly. Generosity was out of character, but up until now he had always admired the dedication Silas had for his job.

"Thank you," Silas said as he quickly phased.

"You have five minutes. If he is a minute late you will cease to exist," Augusyon whispered to Kere.

Silas phased back into the library to find Ryan pacing in front of the couch where he had left her. Her hands were clutching each other and her mind focused on everything racing thought. She saw him and she immediately lit up. She walked to him quickly and reached out to grab his forearm. She felt something was wrong deep in her gut. She could feel it rolling off of him even though his face said everything was fine.

"Ryan-" Silas began but she quickly cut him off.

"What's wrong?" Ryan asked, looking behind him as if the answer was there.

"I have to go for a little bit. There's something in the after world I need to fix. I need you to stay with Kere and Balor. Just until I fix everything," Silas said as his hand captured her chin.

"Why does it feel like there is something you're not telling?" Ryan said, searching his eyes.

"There's not but I have to leave now." Silas said and watched her mouth form a protest.

He leaned forward and his arms wrapped tightly around her as his lips pressed into hers. Her protest turned into her lips begging his lips for more. Chills rushed over her and her mind went completely blank. Everything she was thinking was gone. There was nothing but Silas and the rush and desire her body was feeling. He broke the kiss suddenly and ran his thumb down her cheek.

"I have to go, " Silas whispered. His lips still close enough that they brushed against hers.

"Silas," Ryan whispered back. Hearing her say his name made it harder for him to leave.

"I will be back." Silas stepped back quickly as Ryan tried to reach out to hold him in place just a little longer.

He waved his hand and a white tulip appeared. He held it out to her and she took it.

"Silas, why does this feel like goodbye?" Ryan asked as she looked down at the tulip in her hand.

Silas didn't answer. He clenched his jaw and phased out of sight.

"Silas!" Ryan yelled. She swatted at the air where he once stood.

Silas reappeared on the front steps just as Augusyon was holding Kere up by her hair. He looked at Silas.

"Put her down and let's go." Silas's voice was quiet but deadly.

Augusyon grumbled but grinned as he dropped Kere. He offered his arm out condescendingly to Silas.

"So I know where you're phasing to," Augusyon said with a grin.

Silas didn't say anything out loud but his face said it all. He thought all of this was utter bullshit but he was going to comply. He went to grab Augusyon's arm but Augusyon's hand squeezed his shoulder tightly. He attempted to make Silas buckle but Silas acted like nothing was happening. Kere gasped for air as she curled into herself on the ground.

"Silas!" The front door of the library was thrown open and Ryan stepped out onto the stairs.

"You?" Augusyon stopped. He looked at Ryan with his head tilted.

"Don't worry about her, let's go." Silas tried to draw attention away from Ryan.

"I'll let her be. This will be interesting," Augusyon said quietly.

"Silas, wait." Ryan rushed towards them.

Augusyon let out a sigh and ignored the girl. He shifted and pulled Silas with him.

"Look after her," Silas said to Kere as he was pulled away.

Chapter Twenty One

"**S**ilas!" Ryan screamed. She stopped just in front of the spot where they phased.

"Who was that? Where are they going? What is going on?" Ryan yelled. She turned to look at Kere whose face was pale. She looked like she was going to be sick.

"Kere! Answer me!" Ryan shouted.

"His name is Augusyon." Balor coughed from the pavement at the bottom of the stairs.

"That tells me nothing," Ryan said. She moved away from Kere and walked down the steps towards Balor.

"He's a Duke of Hell. He's supposed to see all things past, present, and future. He is also a ruler of demons as well as something about honor and loyalty. The guy has too many roles, if you ask me." Balor groaned.

"What does any of that have to do with Silas? Where is he taking him?" Ryan asked as panic rushed through her.

She needed to do something. Her stomach twisted inside of her. Her whole body was telling her something bad was going to happen; that she needed to stop whatever it was.

"He's taking him to be judged." A voice came from the doorway of the library.

"What?" Ryan said as she turned around.

"Charon," Balor said. He stood and shook the aches out of his limbs.

Ryan stepped closer to Balor, eyeing Charon. Balor smirked a little bit at the motion and then looked back at Charon.

"Left your post? Now that is unheard of. Ryan, Charon, Ryan. Charon ferries souls to the after life. He's…well he's not my friend. He's Silas's friend," Balor said quietly.

"I was trying to warn Silas but I see I'm too late." Charon's voice was full of defeat.

"Ok, let's go." Ryan demanded. She looked to Kere who was still stunned. Up until this moment Ryan had seen her as a fearless badass but right now she was frozen.

"Go?" Balor asked quietly.

"Yes, go save him," Ryan said. She looked at him dumbfounded.

"Ryan…You don't save people from Augusyon." Kere finally spoke. Her voice shook slightly.

"Augusyon? Acheron was the one who came to me asking about Silas," Charon said, confused.

"Well it looks like Acheron complained to Augusyon." Balor rolled his eyes.

"So what, we just do nothing?" Ryan asked angrily.

"I need to get back to my post," Charon said quietly.

"Are you fucking kidding me? You are demons. He is your friend. We can't…I won't." Ryan's eyes burned into them as she spoke.

"Ryan there is nothing we can do. We need to hope they do not judge him too harshly and he can-" Kere started explaining.

"I can't believe you all," Ryan said as she turned on her heels.

"Where are you going?" Balor called after her.

Ryan ignored them and began walking down the road. She wasn't sure what her plan was but if demons were after her maybe she could find a brave one.

"Let her go for a second. She needs air," Kere said quietly.

"I'm not so sure that's a good idea," Balor said as he watched her walk away.

"Let her go. If we need to, we can just phase to where she is." Kere said. Her voice lacked emotion.

"Kere." Charon knew what she was feeling: loss, hopelessness, defeat.

"I told him. I told him that girl would get him in trouble," Kere whispered.

"We all told him." Charon sighed and shook his head.

"He's not coming back." Kere could feel it.

"What? Of course he is…he's Death. How are lost souls going to get to their right places?" Balor shrugged.

"They'll appoint someone new." Kere's tone was flat as she felt her world begin to crumble.

She shut her eyes as an image flashed in front of them. She was out on the ice, laughing. She twirled in circles as she stared up at the bright cold sky.

"Get off the ice!" His voice yelled out to her. He was standing on the shore with his arms folded across his chest and his face in a frown.

"Silas! Come on, it's frozen. Look!" she yelled back and jumped.

"Kere! Off now!" Silas demanded. His heart dropped into the pit of his stomach when she jumped.

"You're just scared! I am afraid of nothing!" Kere laughed as she spun in another circle.

"Kere let's go, you've made your point. If you fall in I am not saving your ass," Silas lied.

"Duh, you can't swim." Kere laughed, spinning once again in a circle.

"It's so pretty. Come on Silas. It's not water, it's frozen. You will be fine." Kere giggled more.

"I'm leaving!" Silas shouted and turned his back as if he was going to walk away.

"Fine!" Kere shouted, stomping her foot.

As Kere's foot hit the ice a loud crack echoed around the pond. Silas's stomach twisted as he turned to look back to Kere. The ice was fracturing around her in tiny small cracks. The world around him went soundless as the loud cracking noise echoed.

"Silas!" Kere screamed as the ice gave way.

He didn't even think twice as he rushed out onto the ice. He plunged into the freezing water. She remembered floating in the cold dark water trying to get back to the break in the ice. It was a struggle to move her legs and arms. Her muscles contracted making them not want to move. The water felt like knives that cut and sliced against her skin. She gave into the pain. She was holding in the last little bit of air she had left. She felt his arms wrap around her and she was pulled towards the light.

Silas shoved her with all his might up out of the hole in the ice and away from the fragile edges. The adrenaline that pushed him to save her was slowly fading. So when the edge of the ice he clung to cracked more, he

fell in. He gave into the darkness quickly. He was fine with it as long as she was safe.

"Kere…" Balor's voice broke through to her.

"We didn't find his body until spring," Kere said quietly as a tear ran down her cheek.

"Kere." Balor walked to her side and wrapped his arm around her.

"It was my fault then and here I am doing nothing again," Kere whispered as she tried to hold back the tears.

"Kere you can't blame yourself. He was destined to become Death. They all die tragically. Heroically. Sacrificing themselves," Balor said. He made a yuck face at her trying to get her to smile.

"It's still all my fault." Kere said, shoving him.

"Stop it. I don't know anyone's sister who would go make herself a demon to find her brother," Balor said and he gently shoved her back.

Kere didn't say anything. Her frown deepened and her eyes looked like we're about to let loose all the tears they were holding in.

"Fine," Balor sighed.

"Fine, what?" Kere whispered.

"We will go save him…somehow," Balor said quietly.

"How?" Kere asked just as quietly.

"I don't know, we will think of something. Charon go back to the In-Between and try to find out information. Plus you need to be there," Balor addressed Charon.

"Let me know what I can do," Charon said with a nod before phasing.

"We need to go find little Miss Spitfire and figure something out. Maybe we can plead a case for him or

something. I mean they act like a court, so maybe," Balor thought out loud.

"You will really go speak on Silas's behalf with me?" Kere asked. She stepped back and looked at him.

"I'm not doing it for him," Balor grumbled.

"Balor, speaking up for him can result in the same fate, if not worse," Kere reminded him of the consequences.

"It's fine. I'm a chaos demon. I love chaos…it's probably why I love you," Balor said with a wink and held his hand out to her.

"What?" Kere asked as she took his hand in hers.

"Like you didn't know. Let's go." Balor laughed but Kere pulled back on his hand.

"Say it again," Kere said, pulling him towards her.

"I love you." Balor's hand captured her waist as he said it.

Kere felt a warmth rush through her as he spoke the words again. Her stomach tumbled with excitement. She had been waiting for this moment for a very long time and it was happening. Kere's hand wrapped around the back of his neck. Her fingers weaved into his hair as she pulled his head down for a kiss. He pulled her tightly against him as his mouth moved against hers demanding it open to him. She opened her mouth slightly to deepen the kiss. Chills spread through her body as their tongues danced against each other. She pulled back as reality hit her mid-kiss.

"Balor," she whispered. Her lips brushed softly against his lips.

"I know," he murmured. He did not want to let her go.

"Let's go find her." He sighed quietly.

---

*R*yan took off down the road. She wasn't really sure where she was going. She was so frustrated. How could they just give up on him? She needed to find a way to him. If they weren't going to help her, maybe she could find someone who would.

"Hello, darling." A familiar voice echoed out from an alleyway.

Ryan froze. In the alley was the redhead from before. She was grinning and Ryan thought that at any second she would transform into the monster she saw earlier.

"You're a demon." Ryan stopped and turned to her.

"Guilty." Eurynomos flashed a charming smile at her.

"I need help," Ryan said, not really sure what she was doing at this point.

"Asking a demon for help is ironic but color me intrigued. What do you need?" Eurynomos asked as she walked towards her.

"I need to get to Silas. Someone took him somewhere and I need to help him," Ryan said, though she kept her distance from Eurynomos.

"Well I know where he is. But I need something, too," Eurynomos said quietly.

"You can take me to Silas?" Ryan asked her cautiously.

"Mhmm " Eurynomos purred as she took a step closer to Ryan.

"What do you need?" Ryan asked suspiciously.

"It's actually quite simple. I need you to come with me. I help you get to where Silas is and then you come with me to meet a friend. That's it." Eurynomos smiled.

"That's it? I meet your friend and you take me to Silas?" Ryan repeated.

"Yup." Eurynomos grinned. Her perfectly straight white teeth turned into long sharp fangs.

"Fine. It's a deal." Ryan held out her hand to Eurynomos.

Euyrnomous wrapped her hand around one of Ryan's fingers and brought the tip of it to her mouth.

"Hey!" Ryan tried to pull her hand away from Eurynomos's mouth.

"Hush! Deals need to be sealed in blood. Can't have you backing out on me," Eurynomos snapped.

"Blood?" Ryan hesitated.

Eurynomos took her finger and pressed it into her sharp, long, white tooth. Her skin separated as the tooth punctured it. Eurynomos let go of her hand and then scraped her own finger against her tooth. She held her finger out to Ryan with a small blue black bead of blood pooled at the tip. She motioned for Ryan to press her bright red blood into hers. Ryan gritted her teeth but if Eurynomos could get her to Silas then she would do it. She pressed her finger tip to Eurynomos and they shook hands.

"There! Done deal. Let's go," Eurynomos said without letting go of Ryan's hand.

"Where are we going?" Ryan asked. She was unsure of the choice she had made.

"To where Silas is." Eurynomos smiled as she pulled Ryan into her.

"Ryan!" Balor's voice came from the sidewalk as he phased out of thin air.

"Sorry." Ryan said as she stepped back into Eurynomos.

"Ryan, don't! She can't be trusted," Balor yelled.

"You won't help him so I've found a way to," Ryan yelled back as Balor rushed towards them.

Eurynomos grinned as her eyes began to glow in preparation for the phase.

"Darkness is coming." Eurynomos grinned wider as she took Ryan.

Chapter Twenty Two

"**F**ucking damn it! Fucking great!" Balor cussed as he fought the urge to slam his fist into the brick wall of the alley.

"Where is she?" Kere stepped into the shadows with him.

"Eurynomos," Balor said her name as if it was venom coming out of his mouth.

Silas's voice echoed in Kere's mind, "look after her." Kere felt her stomach churn in on itself. She could feel her chest tightening.

"We need to go after them." Kere started to phase.

Balor reached out and caught her hand. There was something about what Eurynomos said that didn't sit well with him.

"Eurynomos said darkness is coming." Balorlooked Kere in the eye.

"Nyx," Kere whispered. Her skin began to crawl.

"They're going to break Nyx out of the In-Between," Balor voiced Kere's thoughts out loud.

"What does Ryan have to do with all of that?" Kere said quietly, trying to get her brain to work.

"This is what we use as leverage to get Silas out. A bigger problem. Come on, let's go!" Balor grabbed Kere by the hand.

Silas was thrown on the cold stone ground of the judgment hall. He skidded forward until he hit a platform. Three large marble chairs stretched towards the ceiling. Silas grunted as he got to his feet. The room was soundless and cold.

"Silas, the grim reaper, the embodiment of Death-you are summoned here today to be judged." A voice bellowed down from the first chair.

The three judges of the underworld, Minos, Aecus, and Rhadamanthus stared down at Silas as he looked up.

"Judged? Judged for what?" Silas smirked.

"You will receive judgment on your failure to uphold your duties and sacred position," Aeacus spoke with anger in his voice.

"Silas, you have failed. Souls are being lost. The river of pain is overflowing with them. This is a direct result of you stepping away from your duties," Minos said emotionlessly.

"I have not stepped away-" Silas started to say.

He was cut off when a loud snap echoed through the room. Silas turned slowly to his right and a girl's soul stood there weeping.

"Proof. This soul was wandering the In-Between looking for help," Aeacus said, his voice shook with anger.

"I was coming back," he said to them.

"I was coming back to get you." Silas turned to her with guilt pitted in his gut.

"But you didn't," the girl weeped.

"We've seen all we need to. Silas you are to be condemned." Minos announced.

"Condemned? You cannot judge me," Silas snapped back, his hands in fists at his sides.

"How dare you-" Aeacus started to say harshly.

"I have been judged. The day I died, I was judged and sentenced to be Death for the remainder of time. You can only judge the ones who have passed and place sentencing on them. I have been dead for centuries, you cannot revoke or judge me again." Silas's Voice was calm and collected.

A hush fell over the room as the truth Silas spoke made the air feel thick with tension. The judges exchanged looks with each other. Silas was right; they had no right to judge him again.

"Come on," Silas said as he held his hand out to the girl.

"Where do you think you're going?" Acheron snapped.

"To do my job. To bring her soul to the ferryman." Silas walked towards the door.

"Silas!" Rhadamanthus shouted. He had been quiet this whole time.

Silas stopped in his tracks. He turned slightly to match eyes with him.

"You are correct, you cannot be judged again," Rhadamanthus spoke. He paused to watch Silas reaction.

"You are to be banished," Rhadamanthus announced.

"Banished?" Silas dropped the girl's hand and squared up with the platform.

"You are going to the forgotten place. Seems fitting since you forgot how important your role is. You will be

216

returned when we see fit," Rhadamanthus said with a small smirk.

"You cannot pass judgment on me," Silas growled.

"We're not. We are sentencing you." Aeacus grinned.

"It is the same thing," Silas demanded.

"The wording is different and no one here cares." Minos grinned

"You bastards. You say I'm not doing my job but look at all of you, bending the rules to fit your schemes," Silas snapped.

"Bye, bye." Minos chuckled and snapped his fingers.

In an instant, Silas was gone. The girl looked around the room with fear in her eyes. The judges sighed and shook their heads.

"What's going to happen to me now?" the girl whimpered.

"Ugh…souls." Minos waved his hand at the girl and she went up in smoke.

"What did you do?" Aeacus asked quietly.

"Sent her back to the In-Between. She can wander there until she finds Charon. Not our problem," Minos said.

"What about a new Death?" Aeacus asked. He began to feel the weight of what they had just done.

"Again, not our problem," Minos said and with that he disappeared.

"The world needs a Death. We cannot punish one for not doing their job and not to appoint someone in their place," Aeacus said, hoping to get Rhadamanthus on his side.

"Find one then," Rhadamanthus said and disappeared as well.

Aeacus let out a long sigh and shut his eyes as he disappeared too.

Balor phased just outside the hall of judgment. The hall of judgment was just beyond the entrance of the underworld. Kere appeared next to him. She took one look at the door and went to head in. Balor caught her arm to stop her.

"Just hang on a second," Balor said. He could feel eyes on them and was not sure if they were in danger or not.

"We need to stop them," Kere said as she tugged her arm away from him.

"It's done." A voice came from behind them.

"Augusyon." Balor sneered as he pushed Kere behind him to shield her.

"You're too late, they broke rules and sentenced Silas to the forgotten place." Augusyon sighed.

"Why are you telling you this?" Kere asked from behind Balor.

"I've seen all things and all outcomes. There is only one that benefits us all. Nyx must not escape this realm. The human world would be overcome with darkness and chaos. Souls will never find their way home," Augusyon began explaining.

"Souls will not find their way home now without Silas." Kere snapped.

"Unfortunately this part has to happen." Augusyon's voice did not waver, regardless of how Kere spat at him.

"Unfortunately?!" Kere said, her anger rising as she moved forward to threaten Augusyon.

"What do you want us to do now?" Balor asked catching Kere.

"Balor!" Kere protested but Balor pulled her against him and placed a hand over her mouth.

"In order for you to save Silas you must save the girl and the human world," Augusyon said nonchalantly.

"This is some bullshit. Do you know what I am? Demo - ouch!" Balor yelled as Kere bit down on his hand.

Balor shook out the pain as he stared at Kere's teeth mark. He went to give her a look as to say what the hell but her glare was set on Augusyon.

"How do you know about the girl?" Kere asked Augusyon with her eyes narrowed at him.

"I saw her. That's all it took and all the pieces came together." Augusyon shrugged.

"Where is she?" Kere asked him. Her stance and tone became threatening.

"I can answer that. Eurynomos is taking her to Nyx. That's what I was supposed to do. Damn it! You freaking drew blood." Balor said, still carrying on about his hand.

"Let's go cry baby." Kere hit Balor in the shoulder.

"Wait…there's one more thing," Augusyon said quietly.

"Why are you even helping?" Balor's tone now sounded deadly.

"I like order. There is an order about the world, from the beginning of time. I don't like things that mess with

order." Augusyon stated as he waved his hand at Balor as if he was some sort of bug.

"Let's go." Balor said to Kere but his eyes narrowed at Augusyon in annoyance.

"What's the one more thing?" Kere sighed and stopped Balor from leaving.

"You need light. Opposite of Nyx. She is darkness, you'll need light to stop her." Augusyon phased out before they asked any more questions.

"So what I need go get some fucking candles? A fucking flash light?" Balor growled frustratedly.

"Oh, I know... a damn Christmas tree!" Balor snapped. He shook his head.

"Hemera," Kere said quietly. She ignored Balor's ridiculous comments.

"Hemera….The goddess." Balor said as Kere's comment finally registered in his head.

"She is the opposite of Nyx. She is light and day. Nyx is darkness and night." Kere said quietly. A small frown came to her face.

"Fuck…A Christmas tree would have been easier. It would have been a great fucking Christmas tree." Balor shook his head.

He grabbed hold of Kere's hand as she rolled her eyes at him. Dread pitted in her stomach as she doubted they could pull this off. Without even discussing where they were going they both phased.

Silas hit the cold ground for a second time in what felt like a matter of minutes. The only difference was this time he was alone. He stood in an open field. The knee high grass blew in a soft breeze. He reached down and ran his hand over it. As he brushed his hands over the seeds that gathered at the tops of the blades they fell off one by one almost floating to the ground. He watched it mindlessly, staring at it because he knew something was wrong. Something was off. A tall tree was settled on top of a small hill. The branches of the tree stretched upwards and reached out to the sky. Silas took a step towards it, his foot crunched down into the grass. He paused to look down at his foot. Although he could feel it, the grass made no noise as his foot pressed it into the dirt. Then as if everything snapped into place it hit him. There was no sound here.

"Ahhhh!" he screamed but nothing came out.

The world around him was muted, even the colors were all soft gray tones. Nothing was bright or vibrant. Silas fixated on the tree and began moving towards it. They say the world was void of sound made him feel uneasy. He dug his feet into the ground walking up the hill and reached the tree. He ran his hands over the rough bark and got lost in its texture.

He was supposed to be doing something, he thought as he traced the tree with his fingers. Something important. There was someone, someone he needed? Someone who needed him?

"They call it the forgotten place because you forget. Not only does no one know where it is but once you're here

you forget. You forget who you are, well you forget everything." The voice laughed around him.

Silas whipped around trying to find where the voice was coming from. It's laughter surrounding him.

"Don't even try, I've been doing this way too long. I know all the tricks and how to survive here. Plus I am here to torment you." The voice snickered.

Silas watched the dark forest at the edge of the field. It had to be coming from there. He knew about the forgotten place, once you stepped into the field that's when all of its power began taking control. He had to get the edge of the field. Ryan. It was starting to come back to him. He had to get to Ryan.

"You can try. You'll get just into the field and get lost in the grass. You'll end up right back here looking at the tree." The voice chuckled.

Silas clenched his fists and locked his eyes on the closest section of the forest and took off running. The grass brushed against his legs as he ran. His eyes locked on the one spot he was focused on. He slowed his pace. Why was he running? The grass was really tall. He reached out and ran his hand over the grass: watched the seeds fall from the top of it one by one. He looked around. Where was he? He spotted the tree in the center of the field and it called to him. He began moving towards it.

"Epiales. Why are you tormenting him so?" Augusyon's voice came from behind him.

"Why do you care? Aren't you the one who brought him back for judgment. Shouldn't he be tormented for leaving his post?" Epiales grumbled.

"I didn't think a demon of nightmares would waste time watching this poor disappointing show. He is going to keep trying to cross the field over and over again," Augusyon said quietly.

"Ah, but I am going to see if I can bring some nightmares to life out there. Make him see horrors." Epiales chuckled as he saw Silas start making his way towards the forest again.

"Speaking of demons leaving their post. It will be nightfall soon in the human world. Don't you have nightmares to be handed out," Augusyon said softly.

"I will do my job unlike others who so carelessly left theirs. Don't you worry. I will have fun and then go to work." Epiales smiled.

"See that you do or there might be someone joining Silas in the forgotten place," Augusyon threatened.

"Yes, my Duke." Epiales bowed cautiously.

Augusyon did not want to leave but he could not interfere any further. This needed to play out as it was intended to.

"**W**here are we going?" Ryan asked Eurynomos.

"I told you, to see my friend." Eurynomos grinned at Ryan over her shoulder as she pulled her through the tall grass.

"You don't need to drag me! I said I would come," Ryan snapped and with all the force she had yanked her hand away from Eurynomos.

Eurynomos looked at her confused as Ryan slipped through her grasp. Ryan squared up and locked eyes with her.

"Fine," Eurynomos sneered as she turned and walked ahead of her.

Ryan walked into the grass; she had been here before. The tall grass brushed against her waist. She squinted as she tried to see exactly where Eurynomos was taking her. The crunch of the grass echoed around her until it was suddenly overpowered by the sound of crying.

Stay away from the crying. Silas's voice chimed in her head as she stopped and chills went through her. In an instant they swarmed around her. She was surrounded by a sea of black mourning dresses and sobbing. She covered her ears and tried to back away from them but they were all around her. She ducked down in the center of them with her hands over her ears. The sound was piercing and made her head hurt. The pain made her vision blur and she felt a small drip coming out of her nose. She let go of her ear and wiped it. Blood streaked the back of her hand. Cold hands wrapped around her arms and soon they were everywhere. They tugged and pulled on her. Their long nails dug in the flesh of her arms, cutting and scraping her. She went to yell but her sound was drowned out by their wails.

"Enough!" A voice pierced through the crying.

The cries stopped and Ryan was let go. The sea of black began to ebb away from her. Ryan stood up slowly and watched the figures move and part ways. They revealed a woman standing amongst them. She looked up and locked eyes with Ryan. Her eyes glowed the brightest

224

shade of jade. She began to move and as she walked past the figures her long back hair wrapped around her. Her hair shimmered like the night sky with each movement she made. Ryan stood still, captivated by her as the woman stopped in front of Ryan.

"Ryan." She grinned and offered her hand.

Ryan cautiously took it and the woman pulled her closer. She looked over her shoulder to see Eurynomos standing just past her.

"I've waited so long to meet you. I'm Nyx." Nyx squeezed her hand.

"Who are you?" Ryan asked quietly. She looked down at the hand that Nyx still held.

"Nyx…I am the goddess of night." She smiled brightly.

"Goddess?" Ryan looked at her with suspicion.

"Yes. I am older than time itself." Nyx still held on to Ryan tightly.

Ryan glanced down to her hand. The way Nyx hung on to it for dear life gave her a bad feeling.

"Are you Eurynomos's friend?" Ryan asked her as she looked back to Eurynomos.

"Yes." Nyx smiled wide again.

"What do you want with me?" Ryan tried to pull her hand away.

"I need your help," Nyx purred and wrapped her other hand around Ryan's forearm.

"My help? You're a goddess. Eurynomos, you said I just needed to meet her and you would take me to Silas." Ryan could feel the adrenaline rush through her as her body registered the danger she was in.

"Yes, you see you're special," Nyx said calmly and tightened her grip.

"Yes... special. Alright, I think you have the wrong person." Ryan said and tugged hard to free her arm.

"I need you. You need to take my place here in this nothing land. I am meant for more than this. You. You will take my place," Nyx growled, her fingernails dug into flesh as she squeezed Ryan's wrist.

"Hey!" Ryan yelled as Nyx's fingernail punctured her skin. A small bead of ruby red blood balled up.

Nyx looked at Ryan and then with her other hand slid her finger over the blood. She scooped up the droplet of blood, brought it to her lips and then slid her tongue over it.

"What the fuck." Ryan exclaimed as she watched her.

"Let go of me!" Ryan yelled. She pulled away hard. Nyx's fingers scraped down the rest of her arm as Ryan broke free.

She grabbed her arm as blood slowly leaked from the scratches. She clutched it and looked for a way out. The ladies dressed in black were still circling around them blocking her escape.

"Your blood. It's perfect." Nyx laughed as she placed her hands together.

"I was right. You are from the original bloodline. Your people go back to my time." Nyx clapped.

"This will work," Nyx said. Sheturned and smiled at Eurynomos.

"This is not what I agreed to," Ryan snapped and stared down Eurynomos.

226

"It is. You stay here and you can see Silas all you want. This is part of his realm," Nyx said as she held her hands out to Ryan.

"Where is Silas?" Ryan demanded.

"He's here." Nyx matched Ryan's stare.

"Then let me see him." Ryan watched the black ladies start creeping closer to her.

"Well, the thing is, you can't," Nyx said as she dropped her hands.

"Eurynomos! This is not what we agreed to!" Ryan yelled. Her hands clenched into fists at her side.

"You can't see him because you need to drink something. This isn't the human world. Everything is smoke and mirrors. This is a place for…souls," Nyx said quietly.

"Are you saying I need to die?" Ryan took a step back.

"No…no. No. The drink will fool this world into thinking you're a soul. You will not die," Nyx explained.

"How can I trust you?" Ryan narrowed her eyes at Nyx and still kept her distance.

"Honestly, you can't. But can you afford not to?" Nyx snickered.

"Eurynomos, the drink," Nyx ordered as she watched Ryan study her.

Eurynomos slithered up to Nyx and held out a wooden cup. Nyx's hand grasped around it. She held it carefully in her hand as if it was something so special. She offered it to Ryan.

"What is in it?" Ryan asked. The image of Silas lying on the couch with his skin turning black from nightshade ran through her head.

"Forget me nots." Nyx smiled and pressed the cup into her Ryan's hand.

"Just forget me not?" Ryan cautiously looked at the cup.

"Yup. They are not poisonous and here they have a mythical meaning. They will make the world forget you're human and that you're just a soul here," Nyx said almost too casually.

"I drink this, you take me to Silas," Ryan demanded and squeezed her hand tightly.

"Yup, done deal," Nyx said quickly. Her eyes flicked between the cup and Ryan's mouth.

Ryan looked down into the dark liquid, her stomach twisting in on itself. She slowly brought the cup to her lips. Ryan could see Nyx trying to keep her cool as a small vein bulged from the side of Nyx's neck. Everything was telling her this was a bad idea but Silas needed her. If this was the only way to get him she would do it. She tipped her head back and the warm liquid spilled to her mouth. The bitter taste was overwhelming as she swallowed quickly. She felt the liquid rush down her throat and land in her empty stomach.

"Perfect!" Nyx clapped excitedly.

"Take me to Silas," Ryan demanded as she threw the cup on the ground at Nyx's feet.

"Oh, just wait," Nyx sang the words as she swayed in her spot.

"No. You said-" Ryan started to say but a pain shot through her chest which caused her to drop to her knees.

Her whole body began to stiffen up. She couldn't move. The pain was overbearing. She fell backwards as her body began to shake.

"Sorry, love…you're gonna have a little seizure and then your heart will give out. It's fine and it's fast. We'll talk when your soul is ready." Nyx giggled as Ryan began to convulse.

"What is in it?" Eurynomos asked. She came forward to watch Ryan twitch on the ground.

"Forget me nots, some water from the river of pain and the fate sealer - oleander." Nyx laughed wickedly as Ryan's eyes rolled back in her head and her breathing stopped.

"Do you think the forget me nots are going to work once she's dead?" Eurynomos watched Ryan die, the rush of emotions feeding her. She shut her eyes and enjoyed the pain from the moment.

"It should," Nyx said quietly. She hoped it would but she didn't know for sure.

Nyx closed her eyes and listened. Ryan's heart sped up quickly and then clenched before it stopped in her chest. Ryan's whole body became rigid as a loud gasp of air escaped Ryan's mouth. Her whole body relaxed as her eyes dilated. Nyx stared at her lifeless body waiting to see what would happen. Nothing.

"We need her soul to be pulled from her body." Nyx sighed in frustration.

"Why are the banshees not doing it!" Nyx snapped as she looked at them.

"Silas…" Eurynomos said quietly. He was the only option she could think of.

"No, he was judged. Who knows what happened to him?" Nyx growled in anger. She looked down at Ryan's body.

She was so close and this little tiny technicality was going to keep her from her freedom. She looked at one of the banshees and tilted her head.

"You reach for her soul," Nyx yelled and glared at them.

The banshee cried out in pain as if the death saddened her greatly.

"One of you will do it!" Nyx bellowed.

One banshee stepped forward and looked down at the body of Ryan. A wave of overwhelming sadness was pushed forward as the banshee kneeled down. She placed her hand into Ryan's. She squeezed tightly and placed her other hand on her chest. The banshee ran her hand across her chest where Ryan's heart would be and then down over her arm. As her fingertips reached her wrist she released the hand holding Ryan's. As she stood up slowly a ghostly white hand was wrapped around the banshee's hand. The banshee pulled and Ryan's spirit was now standing in front of them.

"Perfect! Eurynomos, the body. Send it back to the human world," Nyx ordered. She looked at Ryan as her soul took full form.

"Where am I?" Ryan looked around, confused.

Eurynomos moved quickly so Ryan's soul would not see her own dead body laying there. She looked at Nyx

230

before she phased out. Nyx's look told her not to harm Ryan's body.

"My child. I have been waiting for you." Nyx held her hands out to Ryan.

"Who are you?" Ryan asked. She put her hand into Nyx's, completely mesmerized by her.

"I am the goddess Nyx and I've been waiting for your arrival. You were meant to be here in this realm." Nyx squeezed her hand gently.

"Realm? What is this place?" Ryan asked. She felt lost.

She couldn't remember anything or anyone. Something was…wrong. She couldn't put her finger on it.

"You are in the In-Between." Nyx smiled at her.

"Am I…dead?" Ryan asked. She looked around at the women in black that surrounded her.

"Yes." Nyx said calmly. She waited for the reaction but Ryan didn't show any.

Ryan looked down at the banshee that was still holding her hand. She felt familiar. Ryan took her hand away from Nyx and slowly put it on top of the banshee's hand that was holding hers. The banshee tilted her head up slowly. As the black hood tilted back Ryan was met with a face that looked exactly like hers. Ryan stared at it dumbfounded. It was like looking in a mirror. The crying from the surrounding banshees stopped. They went silent. Nyx looked around in amazement. It had been over a year and a half since they were quiet.

Suddenly a tendril of black smoke began wrapping around her arm that was still touching the banshee. Nyx moved back with a shocked look on her face. The black

smoke engulfed Ryan. Ryan felt a cold rush through her body as a strange electricity ran through her bones. The blackness engulfed her and suddenly everything meant nothing. The world went still as power filled the void. A loud wind kicked up. It blew the tall grass fiercely and as the wind faded the smoke cleared.

Ryan stood where the smoke was. The banshee that was holding her hand was gone. Ryan was cloaked in black from head to toe. Her eyes were no longer a warm brown but a deep, cold black. They were so dark you could not see the pupil. Her skin was pale and her lips were blue. Thick black lines swirled up her arms and neck. She turned to look at Nyx.

"Well, this is interesting," Nyx said as she looked at her. She could feel the power radiating off of Ryan.

"Not only was I right about your blood but you are the original banshee." Nyx laughed excitedly.

"Come, we have much to do!" Nyx announced and held her hand out to Ryan.

Ryan studied her hand. She could feel all this power rushing through her. She reached out and took Nyx's hand. She felt connected to her but something was off. There was a small piece of herself deep down inside that was telling her she was forgetting something…or someone.

Chapter Twenty Three

  Eurynomos dropped Ryan's body on the front steps of the library. She wanted it to be known the dumb girl was dead. She was a nuisance this whole time and terribly naive. The rush of watching her die was gone and Eurynomos felt drained. She needed another pick me up. The world needed more sorrow and she wanted to watch them find the body. She needed the perfect hiding spot. She walked calmly across the street and crept into the shadows.

  Will roamed the streets endlessly looking for her. She wasn't at work, she didn't go to her favorite little cafe. He needed to apologise. He didn't understand what happened. Deep down under all the jealous he knew that she was his friend but in that moment jealous and thought of her being just a friend consumed him. He had loved her all these years and she didn't love him like that. It hurt but what would hurt more is if he never got to tell her sorry. He had been calling her phone off and on night and day, praying she would answer. It had been two days since everything happened and he still hadn't heard from her. He paused on the sidewalk and looked up at the dark night sky. He reached into his back pocket and pulled out his phone then scrolled to her name. One last attempt to connect with her before he called it a night. He pressed the call button and watched his phone light up as it began calling her.

A soft chime caught his ear. He knew the noise. Before his mind could connect the dots his feet moved quickly towards the sound. A tall stone building stood out on the curb. The noise rang louder as his eyes followed the sound up the steps.

"Ryan!" Will yelled as he raced up the stairs. He dropped to his knees as he reached her side.

Her body was cold as he reached out and turned her head. Her lips were blue and she felt like ice. He panicked when he did not see her chest rise and fall. She wasn't breathing. He pressed his fingers to the side of her neck looking for a pulse. His heart broke when he found none. He second guessed himself and reached out to touch her chest. He pressed into it searching for her heartbeat. Nothing.

"No! Oh god! No!" His voice broke out over the ringtone still playing from her phone.

He scooped her up into his arms and shook her gently. Her body was limp and cold. He squeezed her body tightly to his and a heart shattering cry escaped him.

"Ryan?" a voice asked behind him.

Will turned slowly and looked at them. His eyes narrowed at the sight of Balor and Kere at the bottom of the stairs.

"You! You did this, didn't you! She's dead!" he screamed at them as he gently placed Ryan's body down.

"She's…dead?" Kere's voice whispered. She moved up the stairs.

"Stay away! I know you and that Silas had something to do with this," Will shouted.

Balor growled, getting angry as he heard Will scream. He moved towards Ryan's body and stepped around Kere. Will bowed up in front of her body.

"Don't touch her!" Will hit Balor in the chest.

Balor growled and hit him back. Will went to swing at him again but paused when he saw Balor's eyes. They glowed bright red. Will stepped back. He looked at Kere, whose face had gone pale white and her eyes glowed red as well. Will stumbled more looking back to Balor. Balor's face had morphed into this horrific looking creature. The bones of his eyebrows were protruded, his cheeks were sunk in and his face looked like ash.

"What are you!?" Will screamed in terror as he took off down the stairs, eyes still locked on Balor.

"Will, wait!" Balor shouted. The anger had set him off and made his demon face come forward.

"Stop!" Kere yelled as Will stepped out onto the road. He was still looking at them and did not see the bright headlights coming for him.

"Will!" Balor yelled. He tried to phase to him but the car hit him.

Will was thrown up in the air and behind the car. The vehicle didn't stop and was gone before Will hit the ground. Will crashed to the ground. He landed on his head, his neck snapped sideways as a long bone crunching sound echoed around them. His neck twisted and broke instantly as body crumpled down around it. Will was dead before the rest of his body hit the ground.

"Fuck! Fuck! Fuck," Balor yelled as he rushed out into the street.

235

Kere stood on the patio. She looked from Ryan's dead body to Will's. She watched Balor scoop Will up and carry his body up the stairs. He set Will gently down next to Ryan's body. He took a step back and ran his hands over his face.

"What the hell are we going to do?" Balor asked out loud.

"I..I don't know. He said to look after her." Kere's voice filled with pain as she realized she had let down her brother.

"What about their souls?" Balor said quietly.

"I…this is traumatic..I don't think they would move on by themselves." Kere tried to hold back the panic in her voice.

"Great. Fucking great." Balor muttered. He glanced up at the sky as if it would give him answers.

The sky was turning a strange color, the stars were completely gone and the moon looked like it was slowly being pulled from the sky. There were strange hues of green etched in the darkness.

"Everything has to be over the fucking top. Can't just enjoy what we have. All I want to do is be a god damn demon and torment the occasional human and cause a little bit of chaos. No, that's not enough for some people. Fuckng take over worlds and shit," Balor said as he looked at the sky.

"She's already starting," Kere whispered.

"You…you're Silas's sister, the soul stuff has to be in you as well. See if you can pull their souls out. Maybe they will move on. It's the least we can do for Silas." Balor looked down at Ryan.

"Damn it. When did I start caring?" Balor muttered, shaking his head.

"I don't know what to do," Kere whispered. She bent down to look at Will's dead body.

"What does he do?" Balor squatted down as well.

"He just touches them," Kere said. Her heart hurt as she thought of her brother.

"Then try it. You got it," Balor said with a small smile of encouragement.

"Ok." Kere let out a small breath of air before she reached out and touched Will's hand.

She felt a small surge of energy pass through her and go into Will. There was a small zap and she pulled her hand back. As she did, Will's soul appeared in front of his body. Kere looked at him amazed that she was able to do it.

"I'm…I'm…Dead." Will said quietly as he looked down at his body.

"Will…I am so sorry. There was a car, you didn't see it," Kere said quietly.

"Ryan? Will I be able to see her?" Will looked at Ryan's dead body.

"I'm gonna try," Kere said softly as she moved over to Ryan's body.

Will nodded and watched Kere reach out and touch Ryan's hand. Kere looked confused when she felt nothing. She squeezed Ryan's hand tighter. There was no spark, there was nothing.

"There's nothing. I don't think her soul is in her body anymore." Kere pulled her hand back.

"Her soul isn't there?" Balor was confused.

237

"When I touched Will I felt a spark. There's nothing." Kere said, defeated.

"So, her soul moved on?" Will asked as he came closer.

"I think so. I don't know. I am not Death. Her soul is not with her body. Will, we need to get you to the In-Between so you can cross over." Kere shook her head and stood up.

"Will Ryan be there?" Will asked.

"I am not sure of anything right now, Will. I need to get you to the ferryman so you can cross. So your soul does not become trapped. The after life is yours. Whatever you make it." Kere held her hand out to Will.

Will nodded slowly and took her hand. Kere looked to Balor and then to the sky.

"Something is happening. I need to get Will to Charon. Can you find where Hermera would be? If darkness is coming we are going to need light. Silas has to have something with all those books in there," Kere said before she phased.

"Ughhh, I clearly chose the side that is more work. Couldn't have just stayed a happy chaos demon, no, had to all of a sudden be the errand and research demon," Balor muttered as he walked to the front doors of Silas's library.

𝓃yx led Ryan to the river of souls. She gestured for Ryan to come stand beside her. Ryan looked down at the dark murky water. She could see white shimmers

throughout it. She looked down into the water and the white shimmers had faces. They were all screaming in pain. Ryan knew she should feel something, sorrow, sadness, pain for the poor lost souls in the water but she felt nothing.

"Lost souls. They are doomed to float in this river forever suffering." Nyx knelt down and swirled her finger tip in the water.

"Why are they in there?" Ryan kneeled next to her.

"They were lost and didn't make it to the ferry to the afterlife. They've been waiting for you." Nyx smiled at her as one of the souls reached up and grabbed on to her fingers.

"For me?" Ryan asked almost monotonically. She was in this haze where nothing mattered.

"You can set them free." Nyx said to her and held her hand out to Ryan.

"How?" Ryan watched the water swirl around the soul that clung to Nyx.

Nyx snapped her fingers and a blade appeared in her hand. The blade was black and ran up to a deep iron colored handle adorned with snakes and thorns. A ruby was set in the center of the handle with a snake curled around it. Nyx held her hand open, silently asking Ryan to place her hand into it. Ryan watched her as she placed her hand into Nyx's. Nyx flipped her hand over so it was palm up. Nyx slid the blade across Ryan's palm. A thin line split in her flesh. Red began to ooze out of the cut but as the blood hit the air it turned black. Nyx stood up holding on to Ryan's hand to make her stand as well. She held Ryan's hand over the river. Nyx made her close her hand into a fist

and squeeze. Several droplets of blood fell into the river. As the drops of blood hit the river water the river began to bubble. A loud noise began to rumble through the water. The bubbles turned into waves and the river began to swirl. The world around them darkened and lightning began to strike.

"It won't be too much longer." Nyx smiled brightly.

Ryan stared into the water as the souls began to swirl like they were stuck in a typhoon. Three lightning strikes hit the ground around them, burning the grass. The sky turned completely black as thick clouds began to roll in.

"It's time for the last part." Nyx looked up at the sky.

"We need to exchange…places," Nyx said, looking at Ryan.

"Only one who is as cursed as I am can take my place." Nyx grinned as her eyes began to glow a vibrant green.

"Cursed?" Ryan looked at her. She wasn't processing the words.

"From the time of your birth you were destined to die. You were not made for the earth, you were made for here," Nyx said as she took the blade and ran it across her palm.

"We need to seal our fate." Nyx held her palm out and moved her fingers in a curling motion, beckoning for Ryan's hand.

Ryan's hand was nearly to Nyx when she heard a noise.. She moved her hand back away from Nyx and turned around to the noise. Nyx looked down at her empty

hand and she curled her fingers inward in anger. She told herself to remain calm and not grab a hold of Ryan.

"Ryan?" The voice called out across the long grassy field.

Ryan turned and locked eyes with Will. She knew him. She felt a small spark toward him. He was supposed to be something to her. She turned from Nyx and moved towards him. His blue eyes called out to hers and she began walking faster. His name came into her mind as she got closer.

"Will!" Ryan yelled as she slowly remembered.

Kere appeared next to Will and locked eyes with Ryan. She was taken aback by the sight of her. Her eyes were no longer the color of honey but the color of onyx. She had black swirling tattoos running up her arms and her skin was so white.

"Ryan?" Kere whispered in shock.

"No!" Nyx wailed. She waved her hand and sent a rush of wind towards them. It knocked Will and Kere further across the grassy field and sucked Ryan back to her.

As she was pulled back she realized the only reason why Will would be here was because he had died. A pain shot through her as she was thrown back into Nyx.

"I am not losing when I am this close!" Nyx screamed. She clasped her hand onto Ryan's bloody hand.

A dark light wrapped around Nyx and Ryan as the transfer began. Ryan locked eyes with Kere as she slowly got lost in the power.

"Get him to the ferryman!" Ryan yelled. She was worried about Will's soul becoming like the ones in the river.

Another wave of power hit and Ryan's eyes went completely dark. A dark cloud wrapped around them and Ryan and Nyx were blocked from sight.

"Let's go. I need to get you there before whatever is happening happens." Kere tugged on Will's hand.

"We have to help her!" Will yelled at her.

"We are! I can't help her if you don't move on," Kere begged, squeezing his hand.

"Fine," Will said reluctantly and let Kere take him.

Kere pulled him faster as the cloud began to clear. Kere was afraid they wouldn't make it in time so she phased. They landed on the dock with Will's hand still in hers.

"Kere? What's happening?" Charon asked quickly as he looked at her wide-eyed.

"Take him!" Kere said and pushed Will into the ferry.

"Quickly, go. Nyx has done something. Get him to the afterlife now," Kere ordered.

"Where's Silas?" Charon asked. He took his oar in his hand as Will tried to steady himself in the boat.

"The forgotten place. Go!" Kere pushed the boat away from the dock.

"Kere. What are you going to do?" Charon asked as he started to paddle away.

"Whatever it takes." Kere said before she closed her eyes and phased.

Chapter Twenty Four

Eurynomos phased back into the In-Between. She arrived just in time to see the cloud clear and Ryan standing hand in hand with Nyx. Ryan was struggling to pull her hand away from Nyx. Eurynomos locked eyes with Nyx and anger flushed through her. She was supposed to be the next Death. That's what Nyx had said. She had watched Kere pull the soul from the dead body and then phase with it to the In-Between. She had helped Nyx gain everything she had wanted and she had nothing she promised.

"Nyx!" Eurynomos yelled as she rushed across the field.

Nyx ignored her, turned to the river and watched as the water began to swirl more fiercely. Nyx laughed, letting go of Ryan, and stood on the shore. A small light began to glow out of the middle of the swirling water. Ryan tried to see if Will made it. She felt a rush of relief when she saw the ferry was gone from the river. There was something more. She remembered Will and the girl vaguely. She knew she was something otherworldly. She remembered how souls crossed. Someone told her all about it.

"You said I could be Death!" Eurynomos yelled as she grabbed Nyx by the shoulder.

The word Death hit Ryan. Silas. She remembered Silas. She had to find him. She could feel every piece of this place since she was now connected to it. She could feel the pulling of the river and something strong coming. She began to slowly try to move across the field.

"Eurynomos, I do not have time for you now!" Nyx threw Eurynomos off of her.

Eurynomos hit the ground with a thud. Rage rushed through her as she looked up at Nyx. Nyx was focused on the water. The light was not growing; something was wrong. There was not enough power in the river to open the portal. Nyx let out a growl as her eyes scanned the field. She spotted Ryan trying to leave.

"No." Nyx snapped her fingers and Ryan was pulled back to her.

"No, no, no. You stay with me until I can cross." Nyx grabbed Ryan by the neck.

A low growl came from the ground and Eurynomos was up on her feet. She charged at Nyx. Ryan locked eyes with Nyx and anger started to flood through her. She needed to get to Silas.

"Where is Silas?" Ryan demanded as she stepped away from her.

"Hmm, the forget me not didn't work as long as I hoped," Nyx sighed.

Eurynomos let out a growl as she lunged at Nyx. Nyx caught Eurynomos by the throat and picked her up. Ryan backed away. Nyx's eyes glowed a bright emerald green as she squeezed her hand tightly around Eurynomos's neck. Eurynomos began to kick her legs back and forth as Nyx hung her in the air. Nyx's eyes flashed over to Ryan. When she saw her trying to escape she pointed to her then the ground next to her. Ryan was dragged back to the spot by an invisible force. Her feet dug into the soil as she came to a stop right by Nyx.

"I am so tired of listening to you whine all these years. I don't know how you're a demon at all. You are worthless," Nyx snapped. She looked at the river and how it struggled to keep the light in the middle of the typhoon going.

That was her way out and she needed more power. Power, she thought as she looked at Eurynomos. A demon had more power than regular souls. Nyx turned swiftly.

"Bye. Bye." Nyx laughed and threw Eurynomos into the river.

Eurynomos's eyes grew wide with anger as she sailed through the air towards the river of pain. She wasn't going alone and she would ruin Nyx's plan if it was the last thing she did. Eurynomos's long claws dug into Ryan, pulling her with her. Nyx panicked seeing what was happening and grabbed Ryan's hand. Eurynomos tumbled backwards and hit the water. The water wrapped around Eurynomos and instantly was sucked into the hole. Ryan tried to hang on to Nyx but she slipped through her grasp and landed in the water.

"No!" Nyx yelled but as Eurynomos was sucked into the middle of the typhoon a light erupted into the In-Between from the water.

When the light faded a perfect looking glass hole appeared in the river. Nyx let out a laugh. This was her way out. She didn't see where Ryan went but she couldn't be bothered with that now. She didn't notice Ryan's body being pushed down the river by lost souls away from the glass reflecting hole.

Silas sank to the ground and there was no way out. No matter how many times he tried, he couldn't reach the forest. He kept forgetting.

"Ahhhh!!" he screamed. He sunk to the ground, his fingers threaded through his hair as he grabbed fist full of it and pulled as he battled against his frustration.

"Silas." He heard her say his name. It was the sweetest sound he had ever heard.

"You're not her." Silas knew it was just the place taunting him.

"You didn't save me," Ryan's voice cried.

"I...I tried," Silas curled into a ball. This scene had been happening over and over again.

"You didn't try hard enough!" her voice screamed at him.

"I'm dead now and a lost soul. This is all your fault." Ryan's voice echoed around him.

"I'm sorry. I'm sorry." He whimpered and curled deeper into himself.

"Silas?" A new voice entered the field.

"Kere?" Silas let go of his hair and looked up.

"Kere!" he yelled at the top of his lungs. If anyone was going to find him it was her.

"Kere, don't come into the field. You'll forget. You'll get stuck," Silas shouted towards where her voice was coming from.

"You left me." Kere's voice whipped around him, circling him.

"What?" Silas asked. He turned around in a circle.

"You didn't save me at the lake. You were too scared. The ice broke and you let me drown. Freeze and drown." Kere's voice whispered harshly to him.

"No...No. I jumped in. I saved you. You, you lived. I died. I died in your place." Silas yelled back, confused.

"I became a demon because of you!" Kere shouted across the field. Her voice shook the world around him.

"No. I didn't want that. You shouldn't have done that. Kere, I regret that you did that." Silas's voice dropped low.

"It's all your fault," Kere sneered.

"You have saved no one and nothing," Kere whispered.

"You're not real. This isn't real," Silas said, growing angry.

"Giving up so soon?" Balor's voice taunted him.

"What?" Silas looked around for him.

"Fuck, it happened again." Silas found himself back in the middle of the field.

"Pathetic." Balor laughed.

"Don't you worry. I will make sure your girl is very well taken care of," Balor snickered into his ear.

"I will kill you!" Silas whipped around still trying to find where Balor's voice was coming from.

Silas let out a loud blood curdling scream and ran towards the forest. He would get out. He needed to get to them. He could see the edge of the forest; he was so close. He could feel himself fading out. No, he screamed in his mind. He slowed his pace. Why was he running? The grass was really tall. He reached out and ran his hand over the grass watching the seeds fall from the top of it one by

one. He looked around. Where was he? He spotted the tree in the center of the field and it called to him. He moved towards it.

$\boldsymbol{a}$loud thump echoed throughout the library as Kere hit the ground. She let out a loud groan that turned into a frustrated yell.

"Kere!" Balor rushed towards the sound.

Kere was curled up on the ground slamming her fist into the wooden floor over and over again.

"Kere, stop. Stop. Stop!" Balor said as he dropped down and grabbed Kere.

"She's gone!" Kere yelled as she tried to punch the floor again.

"Who's gone?" Balor winced as she struggled in his arms.

"Ryan's gone. She fell into the river of pain. Nyx is opening a portal. Silas…I couldn't even feel him while I was in the In-Between," Kere said angrily as tears welled up in her eyes.

"She fell into the river of pain?" Balor asked. He tried to hide the dread in his voice.

"Yes…Just as Nyx created her escape." Kere leaned into Balor.

"Shit." Balor said quietly.

"Fucking shit is right." Kere laughed and wiped away the tear that escaped the corner of her eye.

"Everything is fucked." Kere laughed again. She covered her hands with her face.

"No. No. Only one of us is allowed to do that. Ok. Ryan falling into the river doesn't mean she is gone. Lost

souls can float around in there forever. We will get her out. Silas is in the forgotten place. We will get someone to tell us where it is and then we will get him. Right now we need to stop Nyx." Balor mapped out everything as he talked.

"How?" Kere leaned back and studied Balor's face.

"We get Hemera. Light conquers Dark," Balor said as he put his hand on her cheek.

"We do not even know where to begin to look for her." Kere sighed.

"You give up so easily, love. And your faith in me is a little depressing." Balor laughed. He shook his head and held up an old leather bound book.

"We go to where the sun rises first in the world." Balor winked at her.

"Where is that?" Kere asked. Hope slowly returned to her eyes.

"Caroline Island just off the coast of Kiribati. It's where the sun touches the earth first." Balor smirked.

"I could kiss you," Kere said as she grabbed his face.

"Well shit… the world's ending, don't hold back." Balor pulled her in for a quick kiss.

"But honestly…I know I'm irresistible and this new hero look might be a good one for me but we gotta go. Sunrise is coming, we can't miss it." Balor let Kere's face go and grabbed her hand.

"Ok, let's do this." Kere nodded to Balor and squeezed his hand as they phased.

Chapter Twenty Five

Kere's feet touched down on soft white sand. She stumbled backwards as Balor phased through. Kere landed neatly in the sand and Balor came down on top of her. She was pinned beneath him, his arms on either side of her head and his face inches from hers.

"You know, we could just stay here. Let the world end?" Balor smirked.

"Get up." Kere pushed him gently even though she so badly did not want to move.

"I want you to know that me playing the hero is just for you. Do you understand that?" Balor bragged.

"After we save everyone, I'm taking you…..for all the favors you owe me." Balor said. He held his hand out to her.

Kere blushed for the first time in years as she grabbed his hand and let him pull her up. Balor's other hand went to her waist to steady for a second. His finger pressed into her hip as if he wanted to hold on just a little longer, a little tighter. Kere's breathing slowed as she felt a rush of emotions run through her. She wanted him, had wanted him for centuries.

"Let's go find this goddess so I can hurry up and collect." Balor's voice dropped low as he spoke and his eyes filled with lust as he looked down at her.

"Mhmm," was all Kere could manage to get out as she let Balor release her.

As soon as he took a few steps back she could breathe again. She looked across the ocean to the horizon where the stars were fading. Dawn was coming.

"So what exactly does your book say?" Kere asked, trying to keep her wits about her.

"It doesn't say a whole lot. Apparently she's a pretty simple goddess. No blood sacrifice needed." Balor winked.

"Can you never just answer a damn question?" Kere growled at him.

"Why? I love the fire that annoyance brings out in you." Balor grinned.

"What does it say?!" Kere snapped at him as the sky slowly lightened.

"Fine. All it says is when the first light touches the earth all you need to do is call upon her," Balor said with a shrug.

"Call upon her?" Kere asked. Her eyes went back to the horizon.

"I guess we say her name?" Balor shrugged.

"Ok, she better hurry," Kere whispered. She could feel something coming and she knew the power was Nyx.

It was getting too close. She wrung her hands as she fixated on where the sun should start coming up.

---

*H*e had watched her go in. Her head had bounced off the bank of the river, impacting on the hard rock. She was completely unconscious. He should have kept going. He was not supposed to interfere but he couldn't leave her. Silas was his only friend in the world. Maybe this girl was something else, something more? Maybe she could help

him? Seeing her effects in the In-Between already told him this had to be true. Maybe she was bound to Silas. He turned the ferry around. He pushed the oar into the water as quickly as he could. The lost souls pushed her body along as if they were helping. He was completely confused by this action. They normally pulled things down into them; wanting them to suffer and be in pain like them. Instead they kept her afloat. They moved her towards the dock. Charon pushed the ferry to the dock and quickly got off the boat. He rushed towards the shore as one soul pushed Ryan up onto the dirt. Charon grabbed her wrist and pulled her the rest of the way out. Ryan collapsed on the shore, coughing as liquid expelled from her. She looked up and locked eyes with Charon.

"Are you ok?" He offered her his hand up.

She stood up shakily. Her body felt poisoned. Nyx had done something to her. She felt this angry, gnawing feeling in the pit of her stomach. This dark rage that was begging her to give into it. To forget everything and become something vengeful. She shut her eyes and pushed it down, thinking of Silas.

"Silas," Ryan coughed.

"They banished him," Charon said with pain in his voice.

"Where?" Ryan demanded as she stood up straight.

"The forgotten place," Charon whispered as if it was something to be afraid of.

"Where?!" Ryan yelled at him. The power that radiated from her made him step back.

"No one knows….what are you?" Charon studied her.

"Angry," she muttered, walking past him. Her soaked black dress clung to her.

"Where are you going?" Charon called after her.

"To get him." Ryan started down the path away from the dock.

"They won't let you, " Charon called to her back. Ryan stopped and turned to look at him. Her black onyx eyes began to glow with a gold hue around them. Charon was taken aback

"They can try and stop me," Ryan said. She turned her back on Charon and began walking down the path.

Ryan closed her eyes and thought of him. She thought of his cold dark eyes and how they seemed warm to her. His jet black hair that had silver streaks throughout it. They way his hand felt in hers. The small curve of a smile his lips made when he resisted the urge to smile. She could feel him. She knew he was here somewhere. She just had to keep going.

As she walked down the long curved path the trees surrounding it became almost black in color. They reached over the top of the path on either side, their branch reaching towards each other. As she stopped to look at them, the feeling of being watched suddenly overwhelmed her. She heard a soft cry. She turned to the tree and narrowed her eyes.

"Come out," she ordered. Ryan held her hands in fists by her side.

"Please. Don't. Hurt me," the small fragile voice said as the girl slowly stepped out from behind the tree.

The darkness in the pit of Ryan began to crawl upwards. "Hurt her. Let her stay lost. She is nothing and worthless. She deserves nothing," it whispered into her brain. She clenched her jaw and focused on the girl's eyes and the fear in them. She thought of how she felt when Silas came to rescue her and focused on him.

"I'm not going to hurt you…you're lost?" Ryan asked quietly.

"I don't know. I died and she…the creature ate my body and this man appeared and took me here saying he would come back for me but he never did. Then-" The girl suddenly blurted everything out.

"Silas?" Ryan cut her off quickly.

"He was Death, he said he was going to take me to the afterlife but he had to go. He told me to wait and then I was suddenly in this place that felt empty and dark. He was there and it was a trial. One minute he was there, the next he was gone. They didn't even care about me. They sent me back here. I don't know where to go," the girl sobbed.

"Can you tell me which way it is?" Ryan asked her quietly. Maybe if she could get closer to where Silas had been last she could guide herself to him.

"Somewhere that way. I've been roaming for so long I don't know anymore. The ground was different. It was ash and hard black rock." The girl tried to hold back another cry.

"I will help you. I know where you have to go," Ryan said softly. She held a hand out to her.

The girl nodded slowly and took Ryan's hand. As she did, a surge went through Ryan. The power it sent

through her made her head tilt back as if a wind pushed through her. She looked down and some of the dark black ink on her forearm had disappeared. Ryan studied the girl and then nodded for her to follow her. She did not know what was happening but it felt right. The girl was still crying softly as she walked her back down the path to the dock.

"You're back?" Charon asked. He looked confused and then seeing the girl he tilted his head.

"She's a lost soul. She was supposed to meet you a while ago and got lost. You need to take her." Ryan pulled the girl forward.

"He's safe. He is the ferryman. He will guide you to the afterlife." Ryan smiled at her comfortingly.

"Are you sure?" the girl asked timidly.

"Positive. He is a friend of mine. He will take you and he will not abandon you." Ryan offered the girl's hand to Charon.

"It's my sworn duty to make sure you make it to the afterlife. I will take you." Charon took the girl's hand.

"Will you come with me?" The girl refused to let Ryan's hand go.

"I can't. My place is here. I need to save my…my…Silas." Ryan said, not sure what she was supposed to call him.

"He is lucky and you will." The girl said as she let go of Ryan and took Charon's hand.

"Follow the path until it turns to ash. That's all I remember," the girl said to her.

"Thank you," she said once she was on the ferry.

Charon looked at Ryan, amazed and intrigued. He lit his lantern and stepped into the boat, pushing it from the

dock. Ryan watched them for a second and when they got just barely out of sight a shimmer appeared on the river and they were gone. Ryan turned to walk and was hit by another surge of power. It made her fall to her knees. She braced herself as energy ran through her bones. She felt energized, like the force had pushed the darkness from her. She could still feel it but it was faint. She was able to keep it down. All she knew was it had to stay away from her heart.

She caught her breath and stood slowly. She noticed one arm was completely back to normal and the other still had swirls of black. Her dress was turning slowly from jet black to faded black. Something was happening but she didn't have any time to figure this out. She needed Silas and he needed her. She hurried down the path.

She came to a stop as the trees suddenly turned from black bark to white bark. She reached out and touched it. There was something about the color white. She was trying hard to remember when suddenly she felt something brush against her leg. She looked down and saw a white tulip had sprouted out of the soil. She reached down and touched the tulip. A flash of images rushed through her mind as she touched the tulip. She saw the first time she held one after she woke from her dream of the In-Between, and her last moment with Silas as he gave her one before he vanished with Augusyon.

"Silas," she whispered yearningly as she touched the tulip.

As she said his name another white tulip sprouted nearby. She eyed them suspiciously. But deep down in her

gut, passed the hate and rage, something was telling her to follow them. Another white tulip popped up and another. A line of bright white tulips called to her, blowing in the breeze. She stood slowly and began following.

"You all will meet me on the other side." Nyx's voice rang out over the sea of black hooded women.

They swayed but were unphased by what she said. Nyx looked at them a little confused. They usually responded more to her but with the excitement of being so close to freedom she ignored their apathy. She looked out into the river. She needed to get to the portal without touching the river of pain. If she touched the water she would be pulled in and lost with the wretched lost souls. Her eyes spotted a flat river rock that stood tall out of the water. It would be her stepping stone to the portal. She would not need to risk touching the water.

"I will need you on the other side before me. I need to send my darkness in first. I will make nightfall over the land and Then I will follow. You must guard the opening." Nyx said to the banshee as she prepared herself to step out onto river rock.

"What are you waiting for? Shift! Phase! Be gone!" Nyx commanded.

The banshees began to phase out of the In-Between moving like ash in the wind as they disappeared. Nyx stepped forward onto the river rock, nervously slipping. She saw the river coming up at her but she was able to maintain her balance. She grinned as she stood up straight. She was too wrapped up in her success

to see only a handful of banshees had left like she commanded; the others were slowly drifting out of the long grassy field. They were looking for something or someone still in the In-Between.

Nyx called upon her power. She had waited so long to do this. She had not been able to call upon night and darkness since she had been trapped and banished to this place. Now that Ryan had taken her place she was regaining everything she once had. She shut her eyes and threw her head back as the surge went through her. Her eyes glowed bright green as she opened them. Black smoke wrapped down around her arm, slithering like a snake as she locked eyes on the portal.

"Go, my darkness. Flood the human world. Take away their light so that everything becomes night. Forever!" she yelled as the black smoke shot towards the portal.

The darkness hit the shimmery surface of the water. It floated on top of the water portal until it slowly began leaking into the human world.

Chapter Twenty Six

Gold light began to shimmer from beneath the horizon. It danced and shimmered happily upon the crests of the waves. The sky glowed warm shades of pink and orange as dawn began approaching.

"This is it." Balor stood up and faced the sun rise.

"How do we call upon her?" Kere asked quickly.

"Hemera, Goddess of Light! We call upon you at first sunrise, at first light!" Balor shouted towards the sunrise,

They were met with silence. Nothing happened. More gold rays of sun spread out over the top of the ocean.

"Balor..." Kere looked at him. The fear of them not saying it right and running out of time twisted in her gut.

"Goddess Hemera, I call upon you! Show yourself!" Balor bellowed out over the water, his voice echoing in the early morning silence.

"Kere...I..I-" Balor started to say when a high pitch noise and burst of energy hit them like a wave.

A blinding light came as Balor and Kere shielded their eyes. They struggled to maintain their balance as vibrations shook the sand they stood on.

"How dare you call upon me!" Her voice bellowed as she floated just above the water.

Kere looked up at her, her hair was gold and she was wrapped in light, her white dress draping just above

the water . Everything on her glowed the warmest shades of yellow and white. Her eyes narrowed on them as she floated over the ocean.

"We need your help, goddess." Kere bowed her head respectfully as she addressed her.

"A child of darkness, children of the night need help from the goddess of light?" Hermera's voice shifted from anger to curiosity.

"Yes. Please...darkness is coming." Kere heard what sounded like music and realized the goddess was laughing at her.

"Darkness always comes but I arise every morning and chase it away. Fear not confused child of the depths," Hemera said almost dismissively.

"Hey! She's not kidding. We know you bring the sun rise, but this is not your normal night and day. Nyx is escaping the In-Between and she is bringing darkness to drown out your light." Balor growled.

"How dare you-" Hemera began but then as if she caught what Balor said, stopped.

She waved her hands suddenly and the world around them began to slow as if everything was paused. The sunlight dimmed a little as she pressed her foot down onto the surface of the water. As she walked towards Kere and Balor her body dimmed like the sun had.

"Nyx, she is coming?" Hemera asked quietly as she reached them.

"She is coming any minute. She has found a loophole to escape the In-Between and nothing is stopping her. We need your help," Kere said respectfully to Hemera.

"Why does a child of the night want to stop the darkness from coming?" Hermera looked confusedly at Balor.

"A girl," Balor chuckled at his answer.

"My brother, he is Death and he has fallen. He has been banished to the forgotten place and I-" Kere started to explain.

"Hmm so you're the girl this one is following hopelessly around. If you weren't already dead I would say she might be the death of you." Hemera chuckled.

"You say Death has fallen? Did he neglect his duties and receive punishment for it? He..he was always so righteous. A girl?" Hemera asked with a smirk at Balor.

"Yes, a girl for him too." Balor shrugged.

"She must save him. No one else can. This has been written by the fates long ago. As far as Nyx goes, we play this game every so often. I can only help you in the smallest way. I can give you some light. You can only use it when the world becomes darkest," Hemera said solemnly.

"Well, that ain't cryptic at all." Balor said and let out a loud sigh.

Kere reached back and slapped Balor's arm. She waited for Hemera to continue but the goddess had stopped and stared off for a minute.

"She's moving now. I can feel the darkness entering the world. You need to act quickly. Here... give me something." Hemera's eyes were not focused on them but on the dark horizon in the distance.

"Something?" Kere felt her pockets and looked around.

"Hurry. I need to try to get the sunrise to happen faster," Hemera demanded.

"For fuck sake," Balor muttered and reached up to grab a gold hair pin out of Kere's hair.

Her jet black hair fell down around her in soft waves as Balor chucked the hair pin towards Hemera. Hemera grabbed the hair pin and closed her fist around it. She shut her eyes and her body began to glow. A small ball of light came out of Hemera's chest. The glowing ball floated down into the hair pin. The pin flared brightly and then faded. Hemera held it out to Kere.

"Keep it safe and use it only when you have to," Hemera said.

"That's it? One tiny speck of light?" Baylor muttered in frustration.

"There can be all the darkness in the world but it will not be dark if there is one speck of light." Hemera glared at Balor.

Kere took The bright shiny hairpin in her hand. Gold swirls wrapped around the pin and on the very end sat a bright white stone. Kere gathered her hair up into her hands and swirled the hair pin back around it.

"Remember to use it in the darkest place," Hemera said as she floated up towards the sky.

When she reached the sky she shone brightly and burst into thousands of tiny pieces of light. As the glare faded the sun was shining brightly in the sky. Kere looked at Balor with a frown on her face.

"Any idea where the darkest place is?" Kere shook her head.

"So did she mean on earth or are we going to hell?" Balor shrugged.

"Well, Hemera comes through at the place where the lights first touch the earth, it would make sense that Nyx could exit the In-Between and appear at the darkest place on earth." Kere rubbed her forehead as she thought out loud.

"The darkest place on Earth is…The Canary Islands. Roque de los Muchachos Observatory to be exact." Balor muttered as if he was talking to himself.

Kere turned back to see him looking down at a book. His eyes scanned the page as his finger underlined what he had just read.

"You brought the book?" Kere asked with a small laugh hidden in her voice.

"Well, no. This is just a geography book. The legend book I found about Hemera is back at Silas's. I figured we might need to know more about places so I kept this book. Plus I kind of like it," Balor said defensively.

"Ok then- to Roque de los." Kere laughed and shook her head.

"You better stop laughing at me or you will be sorry when it's time to pay back all these favors." Balor smirked at her with a wink.

"I'm not laughing." Kere put her hands up in surrender.

"I actually think it's kind of cute." Kere smiled and held her hand out to him.

"You just called me cute? Now you really are in so much trouble." Balor grabbed her hand and pulled her body into his.

Kere let out a small laugh as she wrapped her arms around him. He leaned down like he was going to kiss her and then his eyes flashed with mischief and he phased.

"Tease." Kere laughed as she phased after him.

Ryan followed the trail until the dirt path turned to ash and rock. The tulips still continued to sprout through the rocky path. She paused at a fork in the road, one path continued through the ash and rock and the other led into a dark forest. The world around her flickered as if the color was being drained from it. A tulip sprouted up in the middle of the two cross roads. Ryan clenched her jaw as she waited for the tulips to show her which way she should go. Nothing happened. She could feel the In-Between beginning to slip as if something had pulled a plug, like everything was slipping away. She kneeled down in front of the tulip as she begged it to continue. She reached out and her fingertips grazed the tulip's petals. The flower seemed to lean to her and as they touched another flower sprouted up going into the forest.

Ryan's feet touched the dark dirt path and a row of tulips sprouted up. The sound of them popping out of the ground echoed down into the dark. It was as if the tulips were telling her to run. She took the hint and grabbed the side of her dress, balling into her fist as she began running after the tulips. The path curved; the trees grew thicker and taller until they blocked out any source of light. She narrowed her eyes and watched the bend and weave of the tulips as she ran. The bright white tulips stood out in the darkness. The path narrowed as she continued to run. She felt like she was suffocating as the trees closed in

264

around her. She tried to push it to the back of her mind and focus on the tulips. The darkness slowly wrapped around her. Then the tulips stopped. She dug her heels into the ground to stop herself before she hit the wall of darkness that stood in front of her. It was thick and looked solid. "How could darkness be solid?" Ryan thought. She tilted her head to the side and looked at it. She slowly reached her hand out to touch it.

As she extended her hand, the tulip on the ground in front of her caught her eye. The tulip was vibrating. Was the tulip scared? Ryan looked confused and slowly kneeled to look at it closer. She reached out and touched it. As she did the wall began to crumble and on the other side of it was a creature of night. Her eyes narrowed with anger as she watched the creature duck down muttering to itself. It was looking out over a field and its deep dark eyes sparkled with enjoyment. The creature didn't notice her as it was fixated on something in the distance. Ryan followed the gaze of the creature and her heart sped up with excitement and then worry.

Silas. He hunched down with his hands over his ears as he rocked in the middle of the field. She could tell he was screaming by the way his body moved but there was no sound. She knew this thing in front of her was the cause of Silas's pain. Ryan crossed the distance to the creature and grabbed it by its long stringy black hair. Ryan pulled hard and the creature let out a shriek as she yanked it to its feet.

"Leave him alone!" Ryan yelled and grabbed the thing's arm.

"How dare you touch me, you…you..What are you?" Epiales whimpered.

"Your worst nightmare," Ryan whispered as the darkness swirled out of her and around him.

Her eyes glowed an eerie yellow as the black cloud wrapped around Epiales until he was completely covered. When Ryan let go of him and the cloud cleared, all that was left was a small pile of ash. Ryan shook her shoulders as a chill ran through her. That felt good. She liked the power that rushed through her. The arm that was once clear of the black swirl had a small swirl of black reappear on her upper arm. The darkness leaked out just a little more and pushed back the progress that saving the girl's soul made. She picked up a handful of the ash that had once been Epiales and let it drop slowly out of her hand. A small giggle came out as she watched the black dust float away. She picked up another handful, holding her hand flat she brought her lips to her palm and blew. She watched it scatter until her eyes caught sight of him.

A part of her said to leave him to suffer. He had been meddling with her life far too long.

Leave him there. Let him rot away. A dark voice snickered in her mind.

She stepped back from the entrance to the field and a white tulip brushed her leg. She looked down at it and the tulip reminded her of everything Silas and her had been through. Every moment he had left her a white tulip came to her. She looked back across the field and to Silas. She watched Silas stand and her body buckled.

"Silas!" she yelled as he caught sight of her.

"Ryan!" he called back in confusion. He wasn't sure if she was real. Had he really lost his mind?

Before he could process if she was real or not Ryan bolted into the field towards him. Her feet crunched across the long grass.

"No!" Silas screamed as he tried to stop her.

"Ryan! Go back! No!" Silas screamed as his heart sank. He knew she had already ran to far in.

"No? What do you mean? Silas, I found you!" Ryan's smile faltered as she stopped. She was confused that he didn't seem happy to see her.

"This is the forgotten place. You're going to forget. You'll be trapped." Silas said. He felt anguish as he realized it was already too late.

"Forget?" Ryan asked as she walked the rest of the way to him.

"Yeah. I don't know how I've managed to stay like this for this long. Ryan what happened to you?" Silas grabbed her arm and looked at the black tattoo swirls.

"I..I don't know-" Ryan started to say but Silas cut her off as his hand went to the side of her face.

"Ryan, your eyes. What happened?" Silas tried to mask the panic in his voice.

"Nyx promised to take me to you. I had to drink this stuff that would make this world not realize I wasn't a soul. So it's just the drink. I'm ok." Ryan said quickly.

Silas clenched his jaw tightly as the realization hit him. He closed his eyes and took a deep breath to prepare himself to tell her she was not pretending to be a soul, she was one. She was dead. He opened his eyes and dropped his hand from her face. He took a step back and looked at

267

her. As he was getting ready to tell her a fog came over him and his eyes went dull. Where was he? He had something important he was doing.

"I was doing something," he muttered as he turned from her.

"Sil-" As he let go of her the fog set in around her, too.

She turned from him and walked through the tall grass. She ran her hand over the top of it. She was looking for something. She hummed slightly to herself as she forgot.

She roamed the endless grassy field still looking. There was something here that pulled on her heart. She just needed to focus. She stopped wandering in the field and closed her eyes. She took a deep breath in as she tried to remember. She could feel the thing that her heart was pulling her too. She turned slightly, keeping her eyes closed. She could feel herself being pulled the opposite way. She opened her eyes and began to feel foggy again. She spotted someone on the other side of the field.

"Hello!" Ryan shouted to the person. She spotted the tree in the middle of the field.

She forgot about the person and walked slowly towards it. She was lost in a trance as she walked through the tall grass.

The voice hit his ears. He knew it. He turned to find where it came from. He couldn't remember why the voice was important. He knew the sound of it and it made his heart sped up. He needed to find the source of it. He turned and saw a woman dressed in black wander towards the tree in the center of the field. His eyes moved from the

woman to the tree. He began walking mindlessly towards it. When he reached the tree he found the girl running her fingers over its rough bark. She took a deep breath in and he found himself doing the same. The fog seemed to shift. With each breath he took in his mind became clearer.

"Silas!" she yelled and then he felt her hands wrap around his forearm.

"Ryan?" he whispered as he looked at her. There was something wrong.

"Ryan, how are you here? What happened?" Silas said. He tried to search through all the missing pieces.

"I…I can't remember, I did something to get here, to get to you." Ryan filled with frustration as she tried to remember.

"Your eyes," Silas said. They were a deep onyx in color that matched his own.

"My eyes?" Ryan looked around as if somehow she would be able to see them.

"They are no longer their warm brown color. They're my color." Silas said as if piecing something together.

"Oh…I..Nyx. There's a woman named Nyx. She needed me to drink something too... I can't remember. Where are we?" Ryan looked around.

"Nyx," Silas growled. He knew that this couldn't be good.

"We need to get out of here as soon as possible." Silas grabbed Ryan by her hand.

He stepped out into the long grass away from the tree and paused. He was struggling with walking further, something told him he had done this before. No. He had

not done this before.., she wasn't here before. He squeezed her hand gently, reminding himself that she was real.

"The longer we stay the more we will forget until there is nothing," Silas said, trying to give himself the push to move forward.

"It's ok. We can do this." Ryan squeezed his hand. She was not sure why Silas was hesitating.

"Don't let go of me and run," Silas ordered. He entwined his fingers with hers tightly.

"Let's do this." Ryan smiled at him with a small nod.

Silas looked back at her before stepping into the grass. She nodded and they took off. Silas's eyes locked on the exit of the forest. A small smile broke his face as they ran past the halfway mark. He began breathing hard as he slowed his pace. The grass swaying in the wind caught his attention. He felt his hand drop and he turned away from Ryan as he focused on the grass. He ran his hands over the top of it.

"Sil-" Ryan started to say but became entranced with the grass blowing in the breeze.

She reached out and touched the top of it. It was so pretty and peaceful. She wanted to be one of the blades of grass blowing lightly in the breeze. She turned slightly and saw his back as he began walking away.

"Hey!" she yelled at him.

"You! Hey!" Ryan walked towards him.

"Me?" Silas turned to face her, his face riddled with confusion.

"Who are you?" they said to each other at the same time.

"Me? Who are you? Where are we?" Ryan asked back at him with her eyes narrowed.

"We…we're in a field. Do I know you?" Silas looked around then looked back at her.

"Maybe…you look familiar." Ryan inched towards him.

He stepped closer to her. One of his hands cupped her face, the other captured hers as his fingers looped around hers. They interlocked like they were made to fit together.

"Silas," Ryan whispered as she felt a chill of electricity run through her when they touched.

"How do you know my name?" Silas's voice bordered on defensive.

"Silas, it's me. Ryan," Ryan said with a small smile on her face. her stomach twisted as she tried to fight against the anxious feelings.

"Ryan? Ryan…I don't know you. Why are you here?" Sila snapped. His grip on her tightened and pain shot through her wrist as she winced.

"Silas! I came for you. Stop!" Ryan yelled as she tried to yank her hand away.

"For me! I am Death, no one comes for me," Silas growled.

A small dark voice creeped up from inside of her as the pain in her arm rippled through her. Turn him to dust like we did that lowly demon. She clenched her jaw, trying to ignore its whispering.

"Don't let him hurt us. Hurt him!" it screamed in her head.

She shut her eyes and took a step back even though he was still squeezing her wrist.

"Let go of me now, Silas," Ryan ordered as she fought against the urge to give into the snickering voice inside of her.

"Who do you think you are?" Silas growled.

"Let go!" Ryan screamed and as she opened her eyes she shoved her other hand into his chest.

Silas let go as he stumbled backwards nearly toppling into the grass. He gained his stance and squared off with her. Ryan's eyes began to glow as she waited for Silas to react. He ran at her in blind rage.

"Silas, don't!" Ryan yelled at him as his fingers clasped around her throat and he began to squeeze.

Ryan let out a yell and a force was sent out from her. The force ripped Silas from her and sent him flying. He hit the ground and skidded to a stop. He jumped back to his feet and shook off the grass and dirt that clung to him.

"What are you?" Silas demanded as he stepped towards her.

"I am darkness," Ryan growled. Her eyes glowed brighter as the black swirl descended back down her arm.

The darkness quickly took over her as she prepared herself to fight Silas. Ryan stood waiting for Silas to come for her.

"You might be darkness but I am Death." Silas growled. His arms flexed tightly as he marched towards her.

"Even Death is lost in the darkness." Ryan snickered.

Silas ran at her across the field and Ryan began moving towards him. She laughed as she walked to meet him. Silas let out a yell that rumbled the ground around them. Ryan slammed into his chest with all her might. He fell backwards into the dirt. His hands stretched outwards towards her throat. Ryan landed on top of him with Silas's back pressed into the dirt. Ryan's hand's wrapped around his throat and she squeezed tightly as Silas did the same.

Ryan felt the air being cut off from her and she narrowed her eyes. She could feel the darkness slipping down her arms and into her finger tips. She squeezed tighter and pushed the darkness into him. The skin on his neck began to turn the color of ash as she forced more into him. His grip around her neck became loose and his hands fell away from her throat as the ash color began to spread up into his face.

"And just like ash you blow away, into nothing." Ryan laughed.

The darkness poured into him; his skin turning completely gray. She laughed, seeing him about to turn into nothing. Something caught the corner of her eye. It was white and shiny. She paused and looked to her right. A single white tulip sprouted up out of the ground next to her. It seemed familiar. She let go of Silas and looked at it. Why did she want it? Silas took a breath in. He followed her gaze. He was confused at her change in actions. His eyes fell upon the white tulip and something pulled at him. He reached out for it at the same time Ryan did. Their hands touched the white tulip at the same time. Silas's eyes caught Ryan's and a bright flash lit up the field. As the light dimmed Ryan's black dress was turned to white. The black

swirling tattoos on her arms were gone and her eyes faded back to their warm brown. Silas's skin was no longer ash colored.

"Ryan?" Silas whispered. His hand cupped the side of her face.

"Silas! I found you!" She pressed her lips into his.

Silas kissed her back and his hand wrapped around her, grateful to once again be holding her. She pulled back suddenly and looked around quickly.

"What happened?" Silas asked. He looked her over with cornered.

"Nyx. We need to get out of here," Ryan said quickly. They had been doing this over and over.

"We're in The forgotten place." Silas said as he remembered.

"Can you phase?" Ryan asked him. She looked to see how far they were from the edge of the forest.

"No, this place is enchanted. There has to be a way to get out. The further you walk into the grass something happens and you forget. You end up back at that tree," Silas explained frustratedly.

"The tree." Ryan smiled brightly as an idea came to her.

"The tree?" Silas looked to where the tree would be if he could see it through the grass.

"Trees filter the air. There must be something in the air that makes you forget and the further you get from the tree the less filtered the air is," Ryan said excitedly.

"We'll hold our breath." Silas connected the dots.

"Let's get out of here." Ryan scooted off of Silas and stood up.

She took a huge breath in and offered her hand to him. He mimicked her actions and together they began walking to the edge of the field.

Chapter Twenty Seven

Sunlight flooded the world. Kere held tightly onto Balor's hand when they phased. She knew the second they arrived because of how the air felt. It was thick and chilled you to the bone. She saw the darkness leaking out of the glass looking portal in the sky. It slowly devoured all of the sunlight it touched. The world began to quickly darken the more it spilled into the world. Once the darkness was here Nyx would lay claim to this world. Darkness would plague the earth forever.

"Ready?" Balor asked her as she squeezed her hand tightly.

"I guess." Kere looked at the dark hole in the sky.

The light slowly began to dim as darkness fell over the area. She gritted her teeth and clenched her hand tightly around Balor's.

"So what's the plan, hot stuff?" Balor smirked. He was trying to make light of the situation.

"I don't know. There's no instruction manual." Kere snapped at Balor.

"Well love, time is an issue here." Balor grinned at her and then reached up like he had before and snatched the hair pin out of her hair.

The hair pin glowed warmly as he held it out to Kere. She let out a long breath and looked from him and to the hair pin.Her stomach was a bundle of nerves as she

shut her eyes and gripped the hair pin tightly. She held it up towards the darkness and waited. Nothing happened.

"Umm. Maybe you need to say something?" Balor shrugged.

"What did she say…the darkest point? Aren't we at the darkest point?" Kere growled as she waved the hair pin at the sky.

"I…I.."Balor tried to come up with something but he didn't have any ideas. This was all new to him, he was never the good guy.

"Damn it!" Kere clenched the hair pin in her fist.

"This is worthless and pointless! Here I am failing him again!" Kere yelled angrily.

"Kere." Balor spoke softly. He stepped towards her, wanting to comfort her.

"No. Don't. You can go. I'll just stand here and wait for Nyx to show up." Kere's voice was full of self hatred.

Balor started to reach for her and the world around them went dark. He couldn't see anything in front of him. The darkness consumed the air around them and made it feel heavy and thick, as if it held weight. He tried to navigate through it to reach her but he became breathless.

"Kere." He said loudly but he felt like he was losing his breath.

A small glow came from just in front of him. Kere opened her hand and the hairpin grew brighter. A spark went up into the air as if guiding Kere to the portal. She looked down at the hair pin. The crack she had made in it when she squeezed it was letting more light out. She grabbed both ends of the hair pin and snapped. With the snap of the hair pin a light shot out of it and Kere threw the

277

hair pin towards the portal. The hair pin sailed through the air. It shattered into tiny pieces and let all the light Hemera had placed inside of it free. A light as bright as the sun spread out over the land. Balor and Kere covered their eyes to the brightness.

"What the hell's happening?" Balor yelled to Kere.

The light dimmed and dawn was back. The warm, glowing sunrise sky shimmered on the horizon. The portal had closed.

"You did it," Balor whispered as he touched Kere's shoulders.

"I did?" Kere looked at the sky in disbelief.

"Hell yeah you did. You saved the earth." Balor laughed.

"Those are words I never thought someone would say to me." Kere laughed and shook her head.

"Let's get back to the In-Between and find your brother." Balor held out his hand to Kere.

𝑛yx laughed as she looked down into the portal and saw her darkness spread and squeeze out the little bit of light left in that small area. She would slowly take over the world one piece at a time. She just needed an entrance and she had it. She laughed again as she began to slowly step into the portal.

"Nyx!" Silas yelled as he phased inches from her. Nyx turned to see him.

"Silas! How?" Nyx was confused and angry. Her eyes then caught sight of Ryan behind him.

278

She was glowing white and her eyes were the warmest, shimmering shade of brown. There was a light inside of her. How? She was supposed to become darkness. She was supposed to be poisoned. Nyx growled at the sight of her walking towards her with Silas.

"Step away from that portal Nyx." Ryan commanded her. Power rolled off her with each step she took.

"You cannot command me. I am a Goddess and you are nothing." Nyx laughed and turned her attention back to the portal.

Silas moved forward as Nyx went to step through and grabbed her arm to pull her back. They struggled for a minute.

"Let go of me!" Nyx screamed as she tried to shake Silas off of her.

"No. You're not leaving." Silas tightened his hold on her.

Nyx turned and placed a finger to her Silas's forehead and began to send darkness into him. He felt it flood through him with a piercing pain. He clenched his jaw as his forehead felt like it was going to burst open. Ryan came towards Nyx to pry her away from Silas. As she reached them a light came through the portal and threw them all back. Nyx let go of Silas and was thrown into the field. Ryan hit the dirt but was quickly back on her feet. The adrenaline and urge to make sure Silas was ok pushed her forward. As she stood, the light that flooded the portal shot straight into her. The force lifted her off the ground and she hovered in the air as the light pulsed through her. She felt it run through her body as it vibrated in her bones. She could

feel more power being pushed through her to the point where she thought she was going to be crushed by it. She felt like it would burst through her skin and she would become nothing but dust.

The light faded and Ryan descended back down the ground. Nyx stood up and looked at a glowing Ryan in confusion. The portal sealed up and the world around them was dark. The only visible light came from Ryan. Nyx looked to the portal and fell to her knees. A wail erupted from her.

"Nooo!" Nyx shouted at the top of her lungs.

"You all will die for this!" she screamed as she buried her nails into her hands.

"Ryan!" Silas ignored Nyx and ran towards her.

He had to shield his eyes because of the light coming off of Ryan. Nyx stood up quickly and let out a low growl. She locked her eyes on Ryan and Silas and charged towards them. She was going to rip them to pieces. Silas didn't notice Nyx because he was so focused on Ryan; he needed to make sure she was ok. Silas went to reach out and touch her but Ryan gripped his arm first and pushed him off to the side. As Ryan moved Silas out of the way her eyes flew open. A light beamed out of her eyes. As Nyx went to grab Ryan she was hit with the beam of light. She was thrown backwards as the light penetrated her. Nyx's skin began to crack like broken glass. Shafts of light began to come through the cracks in her skin. A loud humming noise echoed around them as the light came bursting out of Nyx. In one bright flash, Nyx turned into a shimmery dust. The glow faded from Ryan. She was unconscious when she hit the ground.

280

She was surrounded by darkness. She curled into it, bringing her knees up to her chest. She felt alone and lost. She couldn't move the feeling of sorrow and fear that filled her. Where was she? How had she gotten here? She shut her eyes feeling paralyzed by the overwhelming emotions spreading through her.

"Silas," Ryan whispered out into the darkness. Her body felt cold as she curled further into herself.

"What are you doing sunshine?" A warm voice fluttered around her as a small light began to glow near her.

"Mom?" Ryanwhispered and looked towards the light.

"Mhmm, now why are you all balled up like that?" The light gleamed brighter and an outline of her mother appeared.

"Why did you go in my place?" Ryan asked as she stood.

"I'm your mother, there were no questions asked. There was no choosing. It was always me," her mother murmured.

"You should have let me go. It has been nothing but a mess." Ryan sighed. Emotions of sadness, hurt and pain ran through her.

"You were still needed and now you have a choice to make," her mother said quietly.

"Choice? What do you mean?" Ryan asked. Her body ached to reach out and wrap her arms around the lighted outline of her mother.

She was always so warm. Her arms would wrap around Ryan and no matter what was wrong, the minute

she was in her mother's arms the world felt lighter. It always felt like everything was going to be ok.

"You can come with me or you can continue your journey with Silas. The choice is yours," Her mother said as the light around her flared brighter.

"I don't want to lose you again." Ryan's voice cracked as she stepped towards her mother.

"You need to know that your soul has always been entwined with his. You are meant to be his link to the living. Remind him exactly what he has and what he needs to be doing. Without you he will fade. It has already started," her mother said cautiously.

Her mother waved her hand and a mirror-like opening appeared in the air. In it Ryan saw a broken Silas holding her in his lap. His face buried in her neck as he muttered things. Kere appeared behind him and went to pull him away from her. Silas let out a heart breaking yell as he swatted Kere away from them.

"Silas," Ryan whispered. The scene tugged at her heart as she watched him break.

"If you choose to come with me, he will break. Souls will wander aimlessly. There will be no reaper," her mother whispered.

"Ryan, I will always be with you. You need to know all the information before you make your choice," her mother said calmly.

Ryan smiled softly as countless conversations about life choice flashed through her mind. Her mother was always telling her to get all the information and then make a decision.

"Mom." Ryan's voice cracked. She turned to look at her. Her chest hurt from knowing the choice she was going to make.

"I know and I love you with everything in me," her mother whispered softly.

The light around her faded and her mother stood there with her long dark hair falling down around her. She looked at Ryan with her deep brown eyes. She held her arms out wide. Ryan didn't think twice and rushed into her mother's arms. Just like she remembered, all the hurt washed away.

"I don't want to leave you but-" Ryan choked on the sadness that creeped up from her chest.

"I know sunshine, I know. You're needed there and you will always have me." Her mother looked down at her.

"I'm sorry." Ryan pulled back as a tear slipped down her cheek.

"Shh. It's ok. I've got your father here with me. You go do what you were meant to." She reached out and wiped the tears away.

"I love you." Ryan smiled., She reached up and took her mother's hand.

"I love you always." She smiled as she squeezed Ryan's hand back tightly.

"Now go." She smiled brightly and motioned to the mirror-like hole in the room.

"How do I get back?" Ryan took a deep breath and followed her gaze back to the mirror.

"Your favorite book…through the looking glass." Ryan's mom laughed and nodded to the mirror.

Ryan looked to the mirror with a small smile on her face as she fondly remembered her father reading to her before bed. She looked back from the mirror to her mom and stepped into her arms again.

"One more," Ryan whispered as her mother's arms enveloped her. Ryan squeezed her tightly. This was the last hug she was ever going to get from her.

As she hugged her Ryan's mother slowly turned to light and faded softly away. Ryan looked at her empty arms. Her heart felt like it had the night of the accident when she lost her the first time. The ache and pain returned as she lost her for a second time.

"Ryan. Ryan, don't give up. Fight it. You come back." Silas's voice from the mirror caught her attention.

"I'm coming," Ryan said to the darkness as she walked slowly to the mirror.

The mirror shimmered as she stood in front of it. She was unsure how to do this. Alice had fallen through the mirror if she remembered correctly. This mirror was floating in the air. How could she fall through it? She let out a small sigh and adjusted her stance. She was just going to reach out and touch it; see what would happen. She stretched her arm slowly out and her fingers brushed the glass of the mirror and her fingers passed right through. Suddenly she was pulled in. With one strong tug she went falling through the mirror.

Chapter Twenty Eight

"Ryan. Ryan. Hey!" Silas yelled as he crashed to his knees on the ground next to her.

He reached out and gripped her shoulders as he pulled her into his lap. He didn't understand what was going on. She was a soul; the only thing that could happen to her was she could move on. What if she didn't move on? What if whatever happened to Nyx happened to her? The thought settled deep into his stomach and made him nauseous.

"Ryan," he whispered. He shook her softly trying to get a response from her.

"You need to come back. You hear me, you have been fighting for so long. You're not leaving like this." Silas whispered quietly as he buried his face in her neck.

"Silas." Kere's voice came up from behind him.

"Ryan?" Balor's voice echoed behind Kere as he looked at the scene in front of him.

"Where's Nyx?" Balor looked around, ready for a fight.

"Ryan... she did something and Nyx turned to dust. Now she's not responding." Anger flooded through Silas.

He looked down at her and her body seemed to flicker as she became even more limp. The flickering

285

reminded him of a bulb dimming and slowly dying out. He gritted his teeth and held her tighter.

"Ryan. Ryan, don't give up. Fight it. You come back." Silas begged quietly.

If he lost her he was going to burn this place to the ground. There would be no more In-Between. He would find each one of those judges of hell and make each one of them pay. If he had been with her sooner; if he had been able to protect her she would not be gone. This would not be happening. He felt darkness beginning to pool into him. His eyes turned an even deeper, colder black. His reaper face slowly started to come out. The skin on his face began to peel away and reveal his bright white jaw bone. More pieces of his flesh began to melt away, his collarbone and tips of his fingers were now bone.

"Silas." Kere placed her arm on his shoulder to try to make him stop.

He growled and moved away from her. He felt fire running through his blood. Everyone was going to pay. He slowly put Ryan down and stood. Half of his face was now bone and this eerie smoke seemed to be floating around him.

"Silas, what are you doing? You need to stop." Kere tried to reason with him.

"Everyone is going to pay. Even those who stand in my way…so don't," Silas warned her as he began walking away.

With each step he took the grass turned black and shriveled up. The blades shrunk into the ground like the life was sucked out of them.

"Silas, wait. Let me come!" Balor started to follow him.

"You stay!" Silas yelled and a wave of force hit Balor sending him backwards.

"I am only sparing you because you actually helped her," Silas snapped as he continued walking away.

"What the hell is going on? How does he have power like that?" Balor asked Kere as he rubbed his chest.

"We are descendents of Nyx. If she is gone there is no one to be the god or goddess of darkness," Kere whispered as if it was something she had been trying to hide forever.

"Make sense." Balor shrugged like everything was fine.

"What are we going to do about him?" Balor watched Silas power walk across the field killing everything that touched him.

"Ryan…Ryan needs to wake up." Kere said. She dropped to her knees and shook Ryan.

"He's going to start a war. Walking into the underworld and trying to kill the judges. They are already going to be angry that he escaped the forgotten place, never mind that he is going to kill them," Kere said and shook Ryan some more.

"Why is she not waking?!" Panic set in as she watched Silas fade into the distance .

"Do you think he can?" Balor watched the power in him increase with each step.

"Can what?" Kere asked harshly. She was angry that he just stood there watching Silas walk to his doom.

"He's draining the life out of things. That's how he's getting stronger," Balor said, connecting the dots.

"What?" Kere asked as she looked to see where Silas was.

"The grass. He's killing it with each step he takes and with each step he gets stronger. Can't you feel it?" Balor said as if he was amazed by it.

"Balor, shut up and help me! He's walking to his death! They are the three judges of hell!" Kere snapped as she reached over and tried to sit Ryan up.

Silas could feel the energy surging in him with each step he took. He was drawing on the world around him. There would be nothing left. He would drain everything in this realm and then move on to hell. Images of the three judges on their knees in front of him, begging to be spared, set his soul on fire. It was their fault. They stepped out of line; they crossed boundaries when they judged him. He had reached the forest. The trees tried to bend away from him as he walked by. He smirked and reached his boney fingers out to touch them as he went by. The trees cracked and snapped as the life in them immediately faded.

"Silas?" A voice came from behind him.

"Acheron, you should stay away from me. I am in no mood for chit chat." Silas turned to face him.

"What are you doing?" Acheron's eyes filled with anger as he looked at the trees and the ground.

"Paying someone a visit." Silas laughed and began to turn away from Acheron.

"A visit? How did you escape The forgotten place." Acheron asked him.

288

Rage set in as the words' forgotten place hit Silas's ears. How would Acheron know unless he was a part of it; a part of the reason Ryan was no longer here. He locked eyes with Acheron. His face was cold as he stepped towards him.

"You…you were part of this," Silas said quietly but his voice was deadly.

"I…A part of what?" Acheron asked innocently but tried to take as many steps back as he could.

"She's not here anymore because of you," Silas growled as the ground began to shake around him.

"Who? Who is she?" Acheron scrambled to keep distance between him and Silas.

"Ryan." The name was full of hurt and pain as it left his mouth.

In an instant Silas was in front of Acheron with his hand wrapped around his throat as he hoisted him in the air. Acheron kicked his feet as Silas dangled him in the air. His eyes widened with shock that Silas was able to do this.

"She's not here," he growled. His eyes glowed yellow as his hands squeezed tighter and Acheron began gasping.

Acheron's hand grasped around Silas's as his eyes started rolling back in his head. Silas's rage boiled up from the pit of his stomach and exploded out of his chest the more he thought about Ryan's lifeless body. Suddenly the darkness that was slowly running through his body began pouring out into Acheron. The skin around Acheron's throat turned black. Black vein-like marks started spreading up through his face. Acheron's lips turned black as the dark ash spread across his face. As the darkness reached

Acheron's eyes, they turned completely ink black. Acheron's skin began to crack and black smoke leaked out of the small cracks. His whole body turned ash gray and cracked beneath Silas's hand. In one hard squeeze Acheron's body crumbed to the ground. Silas looked down at the pile of ash and stepped on it. The crunching noise of his foot squashing the remains of Acheron into the ground echoed around him as he continued into the forest.

The sky darkened. Deep shades of purple and black swirled around each other as a storm began to brew. The cloud in the sky began to spin as thunder echoed in the In-Between.

"Is that a storm?" Balor looked at the sky in confusion.

"It doesn't storm here," Balor muttered as he watched lightning start to streak across the sky.

"Balor," Kere whispered as she watched the banshees appear and close in around them.

"Hey! Back away you freaks." Balor I swatted at them as he backed towards Kere and Ryan.

Kere scooped up Ryan's body and held it protectively as the banshees creeped closer. They reached out for Ryan. Balor slapped one of them away as he drew his demon blade. He held it out threateningly in front of him.

"Get back!" Balor yelled as his grip on the blade tightened.

"Give us the girl." An eerie whisper began to spread through the crowd of banshees, it started out as a plea and then began to turn into a chant.

"No!" Balor yelled and slashed his blade at them as they attempted to come forward.

One banshee stepped forward and raised her hand out to Balor as if telling him to stop. He paused when he noticed there was something different about this one.

"If you want your friend to come back, give her to us," the banshee said quietly.

"How can she? She is a soul." Kere was confused at the statement.

"She is lost in another realm. We can bring that part of her soul back to this form of her soul," the banshee said firmly.

"You don't trust them, do you Kere?" Balor whispered as Kere's stance shifted.

"What if they can? What do we have to lose to let them try? Silas is already gone off the deep end. Ryan is lifeless." Kere looked down at Ryan.

"Why not let them try?" Kere asked quietly.

A loud crack sounded as lightning struck the ferry dock. The wood on the dock scorched. Balor let out a loud sigh. He shook his head but stepped back to let Kere come into the view of the banshees. Kere stepped forward and held Ryan's body out to them. The banshee in the front took Ryan into her arms and Kere stepped back. A mixture of fear and adrenaline rushed through her. The banshees moved past Kere and Balor and surrounded Ryan and the one banshee holding her. A light glowed from the middle of the group and then faded. The banshee placed Ryan on

the ground and the crowd moved away. The banshee who had held Ryan motioned for Kere to come closer. Kere walked over to Ryan and knelt at her side.

"It's up to her now." The banshee slowly began to walk away. The others were already gone.

"What the fuck does that mean? How is that helpful? Everyone is always so fucking helpful." Balor said angrily. Helooked from Kere to the sky as a strong wind picked up around them.

"Silas is going to destroy this realm. If this realm goes there's no telling what's going to happen to the rest of the world. The whole order of everything will be ruined," Balor whispered.

"We need to go." Balor turned to look back at Kere.

"Go? Go where? We can't go!" Kere snapped. She could not believe she was hearing Balor say those words.

"We need to. This place is going to be nothing in a few short minutes. Look around Kere." Balor matched her anger.

"Balor!" Kere let him know by her tone that she was not going anywhere.

"Kere. I will not sit here and let you be destroyed too!" Balor growled. His eyes narrowed. He would make sure she was safe no matter what.

"We can't. There's gotta be a way." Kere her head. She tried to find some way to make him see that it was the only way.

"God…don't you guys ever stop." Ryan groaned as she slowly opened her eyes.

"Ryan!" Kere exclaimed. She bent down and scooped her into a hug.

"Oh ok." Ryan said slowly as she hugged Kere back.

"What's going on?" Ryan asked. She was confused at the hug but then she saw the sky and the chaos brewing,

"Silas. Where is Silas?" Ryan asked quickly as she noticed he wasn't there.

"He is currently on a warpath because..." Balor said quietly. He wasn't sure how to tell Ryan Silas lost it because she was dead.

"Because? And warpath? Explain..." Ryan asked as she tapped Kere to have her let go of her and slowly got to her feet.

"Because you weren't coming back. He's gone to punish those he thinks are responsible," Kere whispered.

"He's going to destroy this whole realm. We need to go." Balor hoped Ryan would side with him so they could leave.

"No, we need to stop him." Ryan searched for the path he took off on. Her eyes landed on a path of scorched black earth.

"I can phase you close to him." Kere held her hand out to Ryan.

"Let's go." Ryan nodded and grabbed Kere's hand.

"Let's hope it's not too fucking late," Balor muttered as he grabbed Kere's other hand.

Chapter Twenty Nine

*H*e stood with his boney fingers curled into his palm, squeezing his fists shut with everything he had in him. He was at the edge of the forest looking out into the next realm. He would find them there and he would judge them. He shivered as he thought about draining them like he did Acheron. Let them disintegrate into nothing; what remained of them blowing away in the wind.

"Silas." The ground around him shook as the voice spoke his name.

"You won't stop me." Silas didn't even turn to acknowledge his presence.

"Think about what you're doing," he said as he came forward.

"I'm not the one who needs to think about what they're doing. It's you who needs to be cautious. Do not come any closer and do not try to stop me, Augusyon," Silas demanded.

"Silas, do you forget who I am?" Augusyon chuckled.

"No, you're the Duke of Hell. I do not care if you were the King of Hell. Nothing and no one is stopping me." His voice was cold as he went to step forward into the underworld.

Augusyon grabbed Silas by the shoulder and yanked him back. Silas brought his elbow forward as he was ripped backward and he sent it flying into Augusyon's

face. The impact mimicked the thunder in the background. Augusyon let go and stumbled back. He was surprised that Silas touched him.

"You dare strike me?" Augusyon bellowed while his hand touched his face as if he was still in shock.

"I warned you." Silas laughed and narrowed his gaze as he slowly started walking towards him.

"What do you think you're going to do?" Augusyon to shake the bad feeling in his stomach.

Silas didn't speak but he walked slowly towards Augusyon, who straightened up as he tried to match stares with Silas. He watched the ground as Silas walked to him, everything he was touched was dying. How? Before he could react Silas had Augusyon by the throat and lifted him off the ground.

"Silas. Stop." Augusyon coughed out. He inhaled sharply when he felt the darkness spreading into him.

"Shh... you will be ash soon. Everything is going to be ash." Silas laughed as he watched the darkness start to devour Augusyon.

"Silas, no!" Kere yelled as she hit the ground after the phase first.

Silas didn't hear her. He was focused on ending Augusyon. Kere quickly crossed the small distance between them and grabbed Silas by his shoulders. Kere tried to pull him away but it didn't work. Silas acted like she was some bug that annoyed him and swatted her away. She stumbled backwards and lost her footing. The small swat was stronger than she expected. Balor phased in with Ryan and growled when he saw Kere on the ground. He ran at Silas and slipped his forearm between Augusyon

and Silas. Balor pushed his forearm into Silas's throat and locked his arms together.

"Let go, Silas!" Balor yelled in his ear as he watched Augusyon struggle to fight the darkness infecting him.

"Balor." Silas chuckled as he released Augusyon.

Augusyon dropped to the ground like a sack of potatoes. He collapsed into himself. Silas grabbed Balor's forearm and pulled down. Balor's arm gave away and he had to let go of the hold he had on Silas. Silas leaned forward and pulled. Balor came tumbling forward. He landed on the ground in front of Silas. Silas picked up his foot and pressed it into Balor's chest.

"You have always been annoying," Silas grumbled as he pressed harder on Balor's chest.

"And you have always been an asshole," Balor grunted as Silas put more pressure on him.

Silas's eyes glowed as he pinned Balor down. Balor let out a small grunt. He wrapped his hand around Silas's ankle to push his foot up and off of him.

"You're in the way, too." Silas sighed. He shook his head and then let the darkness do what it was craving.

Balor winced as pain began to floor his body. He could feel it shattering and moving through his bones. His skin slowly turned ash colored.

"No!" Kere screamed as she got up and ran towards Silas.

Silas shifted his weight and turned towards Kere. He picked her up by the throat. He frowned and shook his head as he looked at her.

"Silas. Please. Don't!" Kere begged for him to stop hurting Balor.

"You should stay out of this. The next time you try to stop me I will forget you're my sister." He threw her back to the ground.

Kere hit the ground and slid past Ryan and into a tree . She was knocked into a daze as her head slammed into the trunk. Silas didn't even notice Ryan was standing there. He turned back to watch Balor. The darkness had reached his neck was slowly changing him.

"Augusyon, as soon as he is gone, I'm finishing you." Silas laughed.

Ryan walked slowly towards him. Part of her was in knots, terrified of what he was doing and what he had become. His entire face except the area around his left eye had turned to bone. The humanity in him was almost completely gone. She took another deep breath as she reached him to calm the heart that pounded in her chest.

"Silas. Stop." She reached out to touch him.

"I told you no one stops me!" He yelled. He snapped around and snatched Ryan by the throat.

He picked Ryan up and dangled her in the air. He wasn't seeing her. His blind rage blocked him from even realizing it was her. She reached her hand out slowly and cupped the side of his boney face.

"Silas, this needs to stop," she said calmly.

Silas's left eye blinked as if trying to make sure he was really seeing her. He slowly let her down though his hand still lingered on her throat.

"Ryan?" he whispered in disbelief. He stepped off Balor and turned completely to her.

"I'm here, Silas." She smiled and put her other hand over his hand on her throat.

"How?" Silas whispered. He moved his hand from her throat to the side of her face.

"I was just a little lost. I had a choice to make. Just like you do now." Ryan placed her hand on top of the boney hand on her cheek.

"Choice? What choice?" Silas asked, doubt pitted in his stomach, he still wasn't sure she was really here.

"You're real? This isn't some trick by some demon or god or duke of hell?" Silas eyes flickered over to Augusyon and his eyes glowed as the rage came boiling back.

"Silas, I am here. I am real. I'm with you." Ryan turned his face back to her.

"You're here." Silas murmured as his hand fell from her face and captured her waist. He pulled her body into him as he wrapped his arms around her.

"I am. I chose you," Ryan whispered to him as she embraced him.

"Now you need to choose. You need to let the darkness go," Ryan said gently.

He pulled back and rested his forehead against hers. His body shook as he tried to let go of the hate, rage, and pain that ripped through his body.

"I choose you." Silas let out a long breath, releasing all the pain.

His face slowly shifted back to flesh and the change traveled down the rest of his body. Augusyon instantly felt better and got to his feet. Anger rushed through him. He walked towards Silas. Silas pushed Ryan behind him and

stood protectively in front of him. In an instant Kere was by Silas's side ready to take on Augusyon and in the next breath Balor was on the other.

"You're still a fucking ass hole," Balor whispered to Silas with a small smirk.

Silas grunted at him but kept his eyes locked on Augusyon as he began threateningly walking towards them.

"There's been enough for today." Ryan said as she came out from behind the three of them.

"You." Augusyon said calmly when he saw her.

The vision he saw before flashed in front of his eyes once more. The woman in white standing with Death. The world is finally in order. The In-Between complete. Augusyon let out a sigh. He knew that if he did hurt Silas the In-Between would fall apart. He had seen the death of Ryan and Silas burning the In-Between to the ground; everything went spiraling out of control. There was nothing left. It didn't end well. He ran his hand across his forehead.

"I should banish you back to the forgotten place, but it seems you already know how to escape. I should rip you limb from limb and throw you to the underworld," Augusyon said bitterly.

"Augusyon," Ryan spoke softly as she tried to move towards him.

"Ryan, you are the key in all of this and the only reason why Silas will be just fine. You are meant to rule this realm together. You are the key to keeping him anchored and connected. If you hadn't come along he would have succumbed to darkness anyway," Augusyon said quietly.

"So…" Balor said. All of this had him confused.

"So there are still two things that need to be taken care of." Augusyon pinched the bridge of his nose in irritation.

"Nyx." Silas sighed. He knew where Augusyon was going with this.

"Nyx is gone. So one thing." Balor grinned brightly.

"Correct. Nyx is gone, that is the problem." Augusyon rolled his eyes.

"You need a Goddess of Darkness. She not only balanced good and evil but she brought the night. Her existence alone kept the world going." Kere whispered as she saw the huge problem.

"Ryan-" Balor started to say but Silas grumbled at her being suggested.

"It can't be Ryan, she is already the balance to Silas who is Death which is darkness." Augusyon sighed.

"Me," Kere offered quietly. She glanced at Balor.

"You?" Balor repeated. His stomach twisted in knots as the fear of what it meant for them ate at him.

"Yes, you are also a descendant of Nyx. You have shown great courage and responsibility. The ability to do what is right even if it means costing you everything. You have a fight in you. You were never meant to be just a demon." Augusyon smiled at her.

"So how do we do this?" Balor emphasized the we to let them know he was going with Kere.

"You. Yes, fortunately for you no one cares what you do with yourself. If she wants you to go with her you may." Augusyon was annoyed by Balor.

"What do we do?" Kere reached over and grabbed Balor's hand to let him know there was no way she was going without him.

"You must go to the darkest place on earth and see if the veil will let you pull it across the world. The universe needs to accept you. You have to try," Augusyon instructed.

"Ok." Kere said and looked at Silas.

"You've got this. You were never meant to roam here endlessly. You should have never became a demon. This is your chance. Go." Silas smiled at her as his hand reached back to take Ryan's.

"Night is due to be pulled across the sky soon," Augusyon hinted to her that it was time to go.

"Ok. Ok." Kere nodded. Her stomach in knots.

Kere stepped towards Ryan and Silas and squeezed them both. She took a deep breath as she stepped back. Balor came to her side and put his hand around her waist. She immediately felt better. She wrapped her arm around him and nodded to Silas.

"Ryan, take care of him," Kere said as they began to phase.

"I will," Ryn promised as she watched Kere disappear.

"What are we supposed to do?" Silas asked. He looked down at the top of Ryan's head.

"Same thing. You must make the In-Between whole," Augusyon answered quietly.

"How?" Silas asked as he grew annoyed.

"Come. I have an idea." Ryan smiled and squeezed Silas's hand.

"I'll leave you to it then." Augusyon smiled at Ryan as he began walking towards the underworld.

Chapter Thirty

Kere's toes touched down on he white sands of
Roque de los Muchachos Observatory. She watched the
waves hit the shore. The white foam they left behind on the
sands captivated her. Balor phased next to her and
grabbed her hand. The world seemed to pause. As the
return of the sun made the world shimmer in gold. Kere
looked around. She was unsure of what she was supposed
to do or how she was supposed to do it. She squeezed
Balor's hand in hopes it would take the nerves from her.

"Do you want me here?" Balor suddenly asked as if
the nerves she was sending him were his own fear.

"Of course. Why would you ask?" Kere asked and
looked at him.

"No one usually wants a chaos demon around."
Balor shrugged to cover his vulnerability.

"I have always loved chaos." Kere smirked as she
squeezed his hand.

Her first thought was to call him out and tease him
about being sensitive but when she saw the vulnerability in
his eyes she couldn't.

"So, any ideas?" Kere looked back to the sky.

"Umm…must try something. I don't know, see if you
reach out to the sky if something happens." Balor was not
really sure of his answer.

"That's what you got. Reach out and touch the sky.
Seriously?" Kere laughed.

"You have anything better?" Balor asked with a small laugh as he nudged her.

"Nope." Kere giggled. She dropped Balor's hand and walked to the shore.

The words "reach up and touch the sky" replayed in her head and made her laugh once more. She felt silly as she looked over to Balor and reached her hand up to touch the sky. She held her hand straight up in the air and stretched her finger tips for the sky. When nothing happened, she shook her head and looked back at Balor.

"See?" She suddenly she felt a pull as she started to bring her arm down.

She felt her hand being pulled upwards. Her eyes flashed to Balor's as she was yanked up into the sky. Balor rushed down the shoreline trying to grab her.

"Balor!" Kere yelled as she was pulled up into the sky, just out of reach.

"Kere! Hang on! Let me see if I can phase up there! I'm coming!" Balor shouted.

Balor closed his eyes and phased. In seconds, he was back on the shore in front of the ocean. He let out a growl and tried again. He phased and landed in the same spot.

"Kere!" Balor looked up to her.

Kere's head was tilted back and light wrapped around her. The sun stretched outward and wrapped her body in a gold light. It was like she was pulling all the light out of the world. The gold light that was wrapped around her was slowly changed to a deep indigo. The indigo color spread from Kere's outward into the sky. As the indigo color hit the sky it spread like a ripple effect. The sky

darkened and the color reached the sun at last. The sun's golden color disappeared and it turned solid white. The moon was now in its spot. Night now blanketed the sky and little twinkling stars slowly emerged. Kere floated back down to the shore. Her skin sparkled like the starlight and her hair glowed. Her feet touched the sand on the beach and the glow returned to the sky. Balor rushed to her and grabbed her hand.

"Are you ok?" Balor asked as he looked her over to make sure she wasn't hurt.

"Reach out and touch the sky, huh?" Kere laughed and put her hand over his.

"You just scared the shit out of me." Balor pulled her into his chest.

"Oh poor big scary demon." Kere wrapped her arms around him.

Balor grumbled as he looked down at her. Her eyes sparkled with mischief as she looked into his. His mouth moved towards her as he pulled her in for a kiss. Kere closed her eyes as their lips touched and enjoyed the feeling of his body against her. A small flash of light caught her eye and she pulled back.

"What?" Balor asked as he felt her pull away.

"Look." Kere pointed over his shoulder.

Balor turned and saw the small glowing light as well. He moved as if to protect Kere. Kere smiled at the gesture but she had power now. She could feel it running through her. She was now the goddess of night and did not need protection but she was going to let Balor protect her.

"What is it?" Balor asked quietly as he stood in front of her.

"I think that's where we go now," Kere said quietly as she patted his hand.

"Go?" Balor said.

"Yeah. Come on." Kere grabbed Balor's hand tightly and walked towards the light.

Balor followed cautiously behind. He was unsure of this and didn't know why Kere was being so trusting. They stopped right in front of the light.

"Kere, Goddess of Night it is so good to finally have you." The light glowed as a voice spoke from it.

"Thank you." Kere smiled. She felt a pull to the light and wondered what realm they would be entering.

"Come, come. Join us." The light grew brighter as the voice spoke again.

Kere smiled as she squeezed Balor's hand and began walking towards it.

"Only you can enter," the voice said firmly.

Kere stepped back immediately. The light dimmed as if it was angry with her.

"I'm not going anywhere without him," Kere said firmly.

"He cannot come. You must," the voice snapped.

"Then I will not," Kere said angrily.

"You cannot-" the light started to say.

"I am a goddess. I choose where I go and what I do," Kere fiercely cut the voice off.

"You and your brother are so entitled," the voice muttered as the light began to flicker angrily.

"You need a goddess of night. Without me there is no one else. Without night the world would turn to chaos

and things would die. Without the humans the gods would no longer exist," Kere said flatly.

There was silence from the light. Balor squeezed Kere's hand to let her know he was with her no matter what.

"Kere if you need to go then go. Don't worry about me," Balor said quietly.

"Fine!" the light snapped.

"It was always fine." Kere crossed her arms.

"You may remain on this island and this can be your home." It sounded as if it was rolling its eyes.

"I will be visiting the In-Between as well." Kere added to her demands.

"Fine," the light snapped.

"Thank you." Kere rolled her eyes back at the light.

The light seemed to huff and then disappeared. Kere shook her head and looked around at the island. She shrugged slightly. Balor stared at her.

"Can I help you?" Kere raised an eyebrow at him.

"You're fine with this? That was your summoning to be among the gods." Balor waved his arm towards where the light was.

"Come on, I'm sure there's a little beach hut somewhere around here. You can be my little pool boy but for the ocean." Kere smirked and winked at him.

"I'll be whatever you want but I promise it won't be little." Balor's said, his tone deepened as his eyes darkened.

Kere let out a squeak and took off running in the sand.

Silas looked at Ryan skeptically. How were they going to fix all of this? He watched her smirk as if she heard his thoughts. They walked together over his scorched footprints and as he passed over them the grass sprung back to life. He paused and looked down in confusion. Ryan's smirk turned into a smile and she led him towards the trees. She took the hand holding hers and brushed them along the blackened trees. As they touched each one together they came back to life.

"How?" Silas whispered as Ryan continued moving him forward.

They stopped at the spot where Silas had turned Acheron to ash. Silas made a face of disgust as he looked at Ryan.

"We don't really need to fix this part of it do we?" Silas asked. He still strongly disliked Acheron.

"Silas," Ryan said in a disapproving tone as she frowned at him.

"Fine." Sulas grumbled as he kneeled with Ryan.

Ryan took both their hands and ran them across the ground where Acheron once stood. She stood up and Silas stood with her. They stepped back and waited.

"Ryan, I don't know if what I did to him could be undone," Silas said as nothing happened.

"Wait," Ryan said quietly as the ground began to move.

The grass gathered all the pieces of ash and brought them to the last spot Acheron stood. They meshed together and in a flash of light Acheron appeared.

"Silas! You bastard!" Acheron screamed as he became whole.

"How dare you do that to me! I am a God!" Acheron screamed. He stepped towards Silas.

"Watch yourself," Silas said calmly and stepped protectively in front of Ryan.

"You're going to watch yourself become nothing," Acheron growled.

"Acheron!" Augusyon's voice came out of nowhere.

"Augusyon. You're here! Good. You can help me get rid of this… this-" Acheron began spitting out.

"Acheron, enough!" Augusyon snapped.

"But he-" Acheron stammered.

"I see and I know and everything is now equal," Augusyon announced.

"Equal? How?" Acheron asked.

"He was banished to the forgotten place because of you and he turned you to ash. He also brought you back. It would have been equal even to leave you as ash. So I would consider yourself lucky," Augusyon summarized.

"I…I…no." Acheron was not happy with Augusyon's decision.

"No?" Augusyon repeated angrily.

"Acheron, why don't we go fix the river." Ryan's voice broke over the top of theirs.

*My river?" Acheron asked quietly.

"Yes." Ryan smiled at him.

"You can?" Acheron asked in disbelief.

"I believe Silas and I can." Ryan nodded to him.

"If you can, I will let all this go," Acheron said as if he wasn't just ordered to.

Augusyon went to snap and say something but Ryan shook her head and winked at him.

"Lead the way." Ryan motioned for Acheron to go ahead.

Acheron looked at them almost suspiciously but started walking.

"I guess I will leave you both to it." Augusyon said with a nod to Silas and a small wink to Ryan. He then turned and walked away.

"I don't know how you did that," Silas whispered to her.

"It's called people skills. I guess being Death you have none." Ryan tried to keep a straight face but couldn't help laughing at her own joke.

"Funny." Silas shook his head as she laughed louder.

Acheron stopped at the river. The current was rapid and the ferry was nowhere to be seen. The waves were too chaotic for anyone to manage. The souls inside of it were being whipped around. Parts of the river formed small whirlpools.

"There's no fixing this," Acheron whispered.

Ryan tugged on Silas and began walking to the dock. Silas looked confused; he was unsure what they were going to be able to do to fix this.

"I didn't cause this," Silas whispered. Nyx had caused the river's chaos.

"You may not have caused this but you added to it. By protecting me you missed all these lost souls Nyx was feeding into the river," Ryan explained.

"We have to save them," Ryan whispered as she saw a soul's tormented face pass by.

"Ok," Silas agreed.

Ryan kneeled at the dock and patted it. Silas looked at her with a small shake of his head but kneeled too. Ryan took his hand in hers and placed them in the water. The water began to swirl around their hands and a light began radiating from them. The light began to swirl outwards into the river and as it went through and touched the souls, each one was set free. The water turned calm. The world around them glowed gently as the darkness slowly began to peel away. The scorched ground and dead blackened trees came back to life. The storm faded and was replaced by a light clear sky. The poison he had placed in the In-Between was being reversed.

"Thank you," Acheron said quietly behind them as he walked up to the edge of the dock.

"You're welcome." Ryan smiled as she watched Acerhon suddenly step off the dock and into the water. The current took him and guided him down the river.

"Well that was slightly dramatic." Silas rolled his eyes as he stood up.

He offered his hand to Ryan. She took it and stood. She leaned into his chest and sighed.

"Well you did it. You saved the In-Between, saved me and-" Silas said but stopped short when he saw Ryan's face.

"There's one more thing," Ryan whispered as she looked at the end of the dock. The banshees were there waiting.

"What do they want?" Silas growled as he stared them down.

"To be free." Ryan let go of his hand and walked towards them.

"Free!? Ryan!" Silas chased after her.

"Banshees are just women's souls that have been trapped. Doomed to roam the world mourning and foretelling death. No one needs to do that. You're already Death and the world knows all about it. Their souls need to be laid to rest," Ryan said with sadness in her voice.

Silas didn't say anything; part of him still did not trust them. He watched their every move as Ryan walked up to them. They all grasped each other's hand and the one in front held her hand out to Ryan. Silas flinched when Ryan reached out and took the banshee's outstretched hand. He was ready to kill them all if they tried to do anything to her. A light from Ryan went down her hand and into the hand of the banshee. The light floated from one to the other and when it reached the last one they all faded.

"Thank you." Their voices floated around her in unisom as they disappeared.

Silas let out a small breath of relief and walked over to Ryan. He slipped his arm around her.

"Done now?" Silas asked hopefully.

"For now." Ryan chuckled and leaned into him.

"Well, it's about damn time I got back here."
Charon's voice came from the dock.

"What took you so long, you missed all the
action." Silas smirked. He turned to Charon, still holding
on to Ryan.

"Well, you somehow did it. You got the girl."
Charon chuckled happily at the sight of them together.

"It was more that she saved me." Silas looked at
her face and watched the small blush run across her
cheeks.

"Death was always seen with a woman by his
side," Charon repeated the prophecy.

Ryan snuggled closer to Silas as she looked
around at her new home. Their home. She was meant to
be here with Silas. To help souls pass onto the next life.
She could feel it with everything in her.

<h1 style="text-align:center">S.E Dymek's Other works:</h1>

The Alpha's War Series:
Between the Alpha's War
Breaking the Alpha Council
The Beta's Betrayal

The Star Saga:
The Morning Star
The Evening Star
The North Star

Coming Soon:
The Renounced Alpha:

Two powerful Alphas struggling against fate in a world full of chaos and unknown threats. One Alpha in complete denial, trying to protect his pack. The other is willing to do anything to save his pack. Will they give in to each other?

"If you want my help you will need to renounce your title as Alpha and swear your loyalty to me and my pack," Alpha Rhett said. His stare was cold and icy as he looked at Alpha Aldric.

Alpha Aldric gritted his teeth. He wouldn't let his pack suffer anymore; he couldn't keep them safe. Their numbers had shrunk to almost nothing.

"It's the only way I can help protect your pack moving forward. It is too complicated with two Alphas

running around here. Take the offer or leave it," Rhett said through gritted teeth.

Aldric took a deep breath, part of him hated himself for letting it come to this; hated that he felt like he wasn't strong enough to keep going. He hung his head and dropped to his knees. He heard his pack members gasp behind him.

"I, Alpha Aldric of the Cold River Pack, renounce my title of Alpha and swear my loyalty to Alpha Rhett of the Dark Moon pack," Aldric said as pain ripped through him and caused him to fall forward onto his forearm.

He felt the bonds from his pack rip away like pieces of him were being stripped apart one by one. His pack behind him fell to their knees in pain as the bonds broke, sadness shaking the room.

"Now submit," Alpha Rhett said with a smirk across his lips as he sent out his Alpha aura onto Aldric.

Keeping You:

Jo finds herself stuck as she runs from her past and her ex boyfriend, Evan. Her old run down car is out of gas and she is out of money. She is running out of time. She drove as far as she could and now she needs to hide. He is coming for her. He wouldn't let her leave him. He would never stop. She changes her hair and her name and begins working at a bar. That's where she bumps into Malcom. He comes in one night for a drink and is captivated by Jo. After a few drinks and a long conversation he tells her his name. He slipped up and now he must kill her. She has no clue what the power of

knowing his name means and how she could control him with it. Can Jo change Malcolm's mind? Did she just trade one horrible situation for another? Will Evan catch up to her?